I0612622

LETHAL CATCH

CROSSING THE LINE

A SAM TRAVIS ADVENTURE

GK JURRENS
TOM KASPRZAK

UpLife
Press

Copyright © 2025 GK Jurrens
All rights reserved.

GKJurrens.com

eBook ISBN: 978-1-952165-40-5
Print ISBN: 978-1-952165-42-9
Audiobook ISBN: 978-1-952165-xx-x
v.250518
r.250720_2121

1

An evil brew muddied the Upper Normandy sky, even before the sun surrendered to the cityscape's shadows off to their west. Locals claimed this was a cursed ship. Sailors were a superstitious lot. Hooglie Maisé didn't buy into any of that nonsense. Not really.

In the bustling port of LeHavre, the water reeked of long-dead fish floating on its oily surface. The seven mooring lines of his beloved ship—each as big around as his forearms—creaked and strained.

Hooglie planned to take a monumental risk on this voyage—to be his fourth aboard the *Grand Francaise*. He knew his way around. Le Capitaine paid well—too well for their enterprise to be entirely legal. Besides, scuttlebutt held that they'd carry more special cargo than ever this trip.

As for earlier voyages, this special cargo had made its way to LeHavre from the Gostan Valley in

Afghanistan. Word had spread within a tight circle. Only one cargo from that region was worth the expense and secrecy. Now it was *his* turn. Hooglie was among le capitaine's most trusted. He'd leverage that trust after he helped load those crates. He even knew about their false bottoms. Yes, it *was* his turn. If he survived.

The stout breeze stunk like wet death. *Appropriate*, Capitaine Jacques Laurent mused. He'd likely lose one or two of his crew before reaching Halifax, 3,000 miles to their west across a violent North Atlantic. *Perhaps we'll lose one crew member in particular as soon as we clear port. The price of doing business, yes?* He often paid a high price in human lives, the highest in the fleet. He shrugged. His vessel required a 22-man crew, but they'd get by with fewer than 20.

The captain contemplated yet another routine crossing. Each had become a dreary affair. Lost in thought, the pudgy man with pock-marked cheeks listened to the clanging, grinding, and whining of heavy cargo-handling equipment between the wharf and this old tub. His men worked like dogs alongside the wharf rats. Soon they'd finish loading and securing cargo for this trip, except for the last of it—the trio of crates destined for his refrigerated hold halfway toward the bow—the front of the ship.

The huge hatches to his forward cargo holds nearest the bow still lay rolled open—maws that swallowed three large crates, his *specials* for this trip. He displayed his typical intense expression as a single crane hoisted them up, over, and down into his possession. *Great rewards demand ever greater risks, yes?*

Midnight approached. He peered toward the soon-to-be-deserted wharf 20-odd feet below his bridge wing. His sausage fingers clutched the rust-flaked railing. Forklifts and loadmasters scurried for the safety of their lairs—like cockroaches to their hides—now that they'd finished loading his precious cargo.

His 30-foot-square hatches clanked as they slid shut under the force of deck motors the size of small automobiles. That clanking prompted him to task his mechanical crew with lubricating those motors and tracks, likely encrusted with salt crystals from sea spray. *How many more voyages will this old rust bucket endure before costing Sur-Rapide more to maintain than she's worth?*

Commandant Javier LeCompteau, second-in-command aboard the *Grand Francaise,* stood tall and attentive to the little man's right on the starboard bridge wing. Addressing LeCompteau, Capitaine Laurent barked, "Watch that loader down there, Numéro Deux. His nose grows ever more itchy, yes?"

"Sir, Hooglie is one of our most trusted crew members. This will be his fourth crossing with us. But I've noticed, too. Should he disappear?"

"Take on a couple extra hands as insurance. We'll decide later whether the sea claims another of her own. Visit our friend at the Cork 'n Bottle. There's still time before our departure. He's a talented recruiter, and a fair hand at keeping rats off our ships."

"Oui, Capitaine. And I will ensure any new recruits remain sober once they're aboard. Sir."

"For as long as they survive, anyway. Correct, Numéro Deux?"

2

The newly minted Sergeant Sam Travis was first up and out of the house, with Kate in the shower and Brian loading up his backpack for school. "Don't forget your lunch in the fridge, Bri'!"

Sam's almost-fourteen-year-old son from his first wife hated school-provided lunches and made it a point to bring his own. *Besides, he loves my sandwiches.* After his first wife died from breast cancer three years earlier, learning to cook was a matter of survival. Turned out he enjoyed preparing a fine meal ever since.

A day like this, cloudy with winds out of the southwest, often meant warm temps were about to turn chilly. Winds threatened to shift—to come from the northwest. And *that* predicted a visit from Canada's coldest air of the season.

Sam jumped into his official cruiser and headed to the cleaners in the village to pick up his uniforms. He enjoyed the short drive out of the Berkshire Hills down to Tyringham in the Hop Brook Valley. Needed to retrieve his entire collection of uniform shirts, both of his dress uniforms, as well as his four BDUs. He smiled at the old Marine term *Battle Dress Uniforms* for daily use. Every one of them needed his new sergeant stripes sewn on.

He also received his new gold badge from Lt. Paul O'Neill, his immediate supervisor, with congratulations and a firm handshake. That was it. No ceremony. The department did send a memo announcing his promotion to sergeant. LT informed Sam that in his occasional absence, Sam would supervise Paul's entire region, too. He had not considered this added responsibility. He'd take it seriously enough, though.

Sam had surrendered his silver badge with a bit of reluctance and sadness. Badges were personal. His boss said, "As a new sergeant, you'll still be in charge of your district. That means several towns and their surrounding countryside are still under your watch as a Western Massachusetts State Environmental Police Officer." Everyone called them EPOs. "Plus, when an officer of an adjacent district is on leave or sick, you'll still also be responsible for both your and the absent EPO's districts, Sam."

Other officers pitched in whenever it got hectic, which was most of the time. Lieutenants managed even more territory—six or seven districts. This meant covering a huge chunk of real estate within the Commonwealth. And *that* came with managing more people, civilian complaints, cases to be worked... a shit-load more work. *And we are forever under-staffed. But this is the gig, eh, soldier?*

That's how he still thought of himself—a soldier who pushed through the pain—physical, emotional, whatever. Somehow, he slogged through any fresh dung heap threatened to suffocate him. But he did love his job. *What else am I even qualified for, except another law enforcement job I'd care less about?*

Sam enjoyed spending time in the kitchen, listening to Chris Isaak rockabilly tunes, working on new recipes. But outside of his home, he didn't talk about his penchant for the culinary arts. He didn't want his officers to picture him wearing an apron. He fancied himself a pretty damn good cook, unlike most cops, he figured. *I guess I'm not entirely predictable!*

Sam hated living in the past, especially his own. His mother was an alcoholic, and dear old dad was a state trooper who was never around. *Like me?* But he'd also not deny what got him here. Three recent cases had fast-tracked his promotion to sergeant.

First, he and his team closed down and prosecuted twenty-nine wildlife slaughterers in a multi-state and international bear-poaching operation. That case splashed all over the national news, Time, Newsweek, a bunch of other publications, and became the subject of a National Geographic feature documentary.

Second, working with the FBI, Sam had arrested two monsters who murdered and raped four women in three states along the Appalachian Trail.

And third, working with the FBI again, Sam's efforts helped to thwart a major domestic terrorism attack in Boston Harbor.

He almost died in each of those cases. One of them got his son kidnapped and his new wife—then girlfriend—beaten to a pulp. After all that, his high score on the sergeant's exam finally cinched his trio of stripes and a gold shield. *So, was it worth what it cost ya, Sam? Even after work invaded my home?*

Awards from the FBI adorned his home office wall, too. As two of the principles on the Appalachian case, both he and Captain Larry Jamison, his boss's boss who nearly died alongside him, received the FBI Star. That was a big deal, they said. *Whatever.*

In a private ceremony at FBI Headquarters, they also awarded Behavioral Analyst Agent Letty Mather the Medal of Meritorious Service and the Medal of Valor. *She'd helped Sam* on the Appalachian case. But God forbid the *feebs* should ever include *everyone* involved that contributed to *that* award, not that Sam gave a shit about awards. But he stood on principle, and that's the way the feebs ran their show. Another reason for the distrust of feds by local and state law enforcement. Not that he was a Boy Scout, especially when fraying ethical boundaries on an undercover gig.

Despite the rough miles already behind him, Sam was proud as he walked out of the cleaners with his plastic bag of updated uniforms now slung over his left shoulder. Some local folks in the know even showed their appreciation and acknowledged his bravery and sacrifice with a nod or a faux salute. Small town. The local papers had displayed pictures of the award ceremony. *So much for undercover work—around here, anyway.*

He brought his uniforms home, slid into one of the short-sleeved shirts, and buttoned it. Stared at the stripes in the mirror and pinned on the gold badge with unabashed pride. But not without a pang of guilt, knowing the price he and his family had already paid. But he had work to do. *Enough of this self-indulgent BS.*

His new bride Kate, a newspaper reporter, sometimes an investigative journalist, stood in the doorway. Without uttering a word, Sam sensed her watching him with her own obvious pride. Her dazzling smile, capable of melting glaciers, was on full display. *Has she forgiven me yet for almost getting all of us killed last year?*

Kate swelled with pride. She said, "Well, well, a brand-new sergeant." The stripes wouldn't change the man she loved. At least, that was her fervent hope; although she couldn't guarantee she would ever be her same old self. Still, she posted up a genuine smile of pride. "Well deserved, and now we look forward to the next promotion, right, *Sarge*?"

Sam looked a little embarrassed, but he smiled too, turned, closed the distance between them, and hugged her. Both quivered... in... what? Recovery? "Thanks, hon. But that's a long way off. I gotta run and you do too!"

A little love pat landed on her solid tush. She *whooped*. After a brief kiss, they both hustled their separate ways. Just as if all was right with the world.

3

The *special cargo* aboard the French freighter *Grand Francaise* had arrived by truck from a faraway land, various private agencies having bribed the usual border patrol agents through multiple countries.

Three-inch black letters stenciled three rough-hewn wooden crates, each the size of a large commercial refrigerator, identifying their contents as *BAIT*. More specifically, they had labeled one crate *SQUID*, one *SARDINES*, and one *HERRING*. No one asked questions. Each box featured a false bottom. That's what made them *special*.

Only six trusted souls, including veteran loader Hooglie Maisé, had off-loaded the truck and navigated those special crates into one of the refrigerated holds aboard the *Francaise*. Red signs and a high-security lock warned people to stay out:

RESTRICTED AREA
NO ENTRY BEYOND THIS POINT

On this special hold's steel door that stood nine feet tall, only the captain and the commandant knew the five-number combination of its lock. Or so they thought. They'd both felt this was overkill, and said so, even with the extraordinary value of this portion of their cargo. But knowing the severe consequences of losing or exposing their *product*, this notion of overkill flew by as a fleeting notion.

They kept the other sixteen crew members quarantined on the wharf until *the trusted* had secured this trio of large crates. They'd completed the final loading in darkness at 0300 hours. Only the harsh mercury-vapor lights on the wharf cut through the night. Looked like pools of hope to be left behind—abandoned.

4

Massachusetts EPOs needed to be jacks of all trades *and* masters of every one. Great satisfaction came with those high expectations. That also meant practice. Sam planned to meet another EPO for an off-the-books training exercise. He met John Comeaux, who had earned his excellent record. He was also one of Sam's trusted friends who ran an adjoining district.

Sam created this *shot chasing* exercise to hone their skills. They'd often receive complaints about gunshots in remote areas with little or no additional information. That made it difficult to determine where the shots originated. Especially with only the sketchiest location and direction information from untrained civilians, or law enforcement, for that matter.

For example, when an EPO on foot patrol in a wooded area heard a shot, it was always tough to track. Considering echoes in a mountainous area, it was damn near impossible to pinpoint a single shot. But multiple shots significantly improved the odds of locating the shooter.

That's why smart wildlife poachers didn't like to shoot more than once. Many resorted to using bows and arrows, and crossbows. In their illicit business, silence was golden. The range and accuracy of these deadly weapons using the latest bow-and-arrow technology had improved by orders of magnitude in recent years.

If a poacher wounded an animal, they'd be reluctant to fire again unless they had no choice. They'd rather track a wounded deer or bear and finish the job with a knife. Another common but nasty technique? They'd shove the barrel of their gun deep into the ear of a downed animal and fire a round into the brain to finish it. The animal's skull acts like a silencer. Yeah, stealth is a poacher's best friend. *And information is an EPO's best friend.*

Sam positioned himself midway up a ridge with EPO Comeaux about a half-mile distant on the opposite side of a valley. Comeaux was to fire a single .308 caliber round into the ground. For this shot-chasing exercise, Sam needed to determine where that shot came from by using not only auditory skills to locate Comeaux, but also his tracking acumen. *Practice.*

Both officers carried portable radios. The exercise began. Comeaux fired a round. Sam heard it. Did it originate from the other side of the valley? He thought so. He started hiking in that direction.

Comeaux picked up his brass, like an experienced poacher. Ballistic evidence was rock solid. No one with any poaching brains left a spent round on the ground. Comeaux walked a hundred yards from where he'd fired his shot. Found a suitable dead log on which to plant his hungry ass where he wolfed down a sandwich and a bottle of water he retrieved from his backpack. An hour drifted away.

As Sam walked, he took in the lay of the land. Aided by his binoculars, he identified a logical place to narrow down his search area. He climbed up the mountain slope. After another half hour, with no luck, he admitted defeat.

Sam radioed Comeaux and asked for his location. A quarter mile off. *Shit! But this is why we practice.* Round two. Comeaux changed location, as did Sam, and they repeated the exercise. Shot fired, and the search was on.

This time, Sam was deep in concentration when Comeaux fired the shot. He followed his ears and his instincts. The goal was for that to be second nature to both men. 45 minutes later, Sam resorted to leveraging his tracking skills. He spotted heel marks and leaf scuffs by getting his eyes right down on the ground. He determined Comeaux's stride and his vector. This was exacting work.

Sam returned to the last known confirmed track, where he re-evaluated Comeaux's heading. *Track, backtrack, re-evaluate every assumption and earlier observations.* At last, he found where Comeaux had slipped on some wet leaves, scraped 'em off his boot on a large boulder. Got him. He found his friend and colleague leaning up against a tree.

Now, Sam's objective was surprise. No, he wanted to scare the shit out of his quarry. As silent as a ghost, he walked up behind Comeaux to within ten feet and shouted, "Freeze!" It became rather self-evident that Comeaux damn-near soiled his britches. But he recovered and said too casually to be credible, "Took you long enough, Sarge."

This was the first time anyone other than Kate had called him that, and he didn't know how to react. He smiled and said, "Okay, your turn."

As the day passed, both men grew weary, but also more confident in locating shots fired. They both admitted to feeling pleased about improving a seldom-used and seldom-practiced skill set.

5

Harried hands and machines on the expansive wharf had hustled non-stop for the last nine hours. This bee-hive of activity to load the *Grande Francaise* with 50,000 tons of iron ore destined this cargo for the Port of Halifax, Nova Scotia. She also conveyed washers, dryers, refrigerators, and hundreds of crates listed as "miscellaneous supplies" on her manifest.

Dozens of port employees had slaved for non-union wages to load the *Francaise* and the other two ships like her on this mammoth wharf. Stevedores had driven lift trucks or wrestled smaller crates into place for transfer to the ship with nets and cranes. Operators had manipulated the massive cranes overhead, and port trucks fed their payloads to conveyors below.

Now, however, the constant din on the wharf had subsided. With their tasks for the day complete, most headed for one of several all-night watering holes nearby. These rowdy rat traps catered to thirsty second- and third-shift longshoremen—the *wharf rats* who worked hard and played hard. They called themselves *wharfies.* The cheap booze offered little more than short-term oblivion.

Of course, the port manager had met with le capitaine of the *Francaise.* He'd received a generous *gift.* In return, the port boss not only looked the other way, he'd manage the expectations of fussy customs inspectors within his domain. This had cleared the way for a certain trio of large crates containing commercial bait to make their way into the cavernous interior of the *Francaise's* select refrigerated hold without more than a cursory inspection. It was understood. This entire operation hummed along like a well-oiled machine. No, it was more like the well-practiced performance of a larcenous ballet.

With a 65-foot beam and over 400 feet long—half the length of a small aircraft carrier—the *Francaise* needed at least 22 feet of water when she was empty, more when loaded. That width, length, and her voluminous cargo-carrying capacity defined her as a queen of mid-sized cargo ships.

The load master ensured the vessel's balance—an even keel—to prevent later problems in severe weather, or especially when heavily loaded and at top speed. If some cargo were to shift during a violent North Atlantic storm, she'd remain stable. Probably.

Her top speed was a respectable 15 knots, more with favorable wind and sea conditions. Not only was she big and capable, she was fast, despite her age and deteriorating condition.

Capitaine Laurent, a 22-year veteran of the open sea, had made a hundred or more Atlantic crossings. He'd lost count. That's what log books were for, which were little more than necessary evils. The crew rarely spotted him anywhere except at the helm station on his huge bridge. They'd sometimes see him on deck. They'd greet him as *Capitaine* or *Sir*. No pleasantries. He neither expected nor sought any.

Maritime law mandated that while at sea, the captain was judge and jury. No one questioned his reasons for throwing anyone into the brig for any violation without recourse. Or when he denied rations, perhaps nothing but bread and water. With this captain, those whom he deemed a danger to his operation often met their end. Perhaps by a rogue wave or they'd consumed too much rum with an accidental slip over the side. Or so the official reports reflected.

Of course they'd report such unfortunate tragedies to *Les Garde-cotes Francais*—the French Coast Guard. The crew would offer a moment of silence on deck upon hearing a monotone announcement of such *accidents* over the tinny ship-wide speakers. They'd shed no tears, nor make any inquiries. Then it was back to work 20 seconds later. Or else. A lucrative salary made their hazardous existence tolerable.

Two hours later, at 0500, an ill wind and an ebbing tide tugged at the *Grand Francaise's* rust-encrusted hull. The huge mooring lines twisted and creaked as they stretched and sighed to remind anyone listening they performed their job, too. The long fore-and-aft spring lines protested the loudest as the tidal surge of the Seine's estuary teased them. Even Mother Nature seemed to draw this ship, her crew, and her special cargo, closer to an ignominious fate.

Some along the wharf whispered the *Francaise* carried a curse as part of her freight, or maybe they just carried cargos that demanded a steep price to be paid in lives throughout the years. Sailors were a superstitious lot. The captain had heard such tawdry scuttlebutt in the waterfront watering holes he frequented. Some said too frequently. He thought, *Anyone who utters such gibberish aboard **my** ship will deal with lungs full of water, and perhaps a bullet or two for good measure.*

6

A hiker on the Appalachian Trail—the A.T.—where it passed through Western Massachusetts, relayed a "shot fired" complaint. This was just a day after EPOs Travis and Comeaux practiced shot chasing. The EPO communications center in Boston relayed the message. Coincidence? The complainant reported he'd heard the shot in Beartown State Forest. He was wrong.

The hiker received a cell call from Sergeant Travis, who asked him several questions to clarify his location when the shot rang out. The hiker did his best, but it wasn't much to go on. He reported a single shot—no doubt a poacher's shot.

After quizzing the caller on what landmarks he'd seen, Sam started out near Round Mountain. He checked the area on foot. From there, he looked for signs of vehicles, human tracks, or any evidence of recent human activity. The rather small mountain, especially compared to the surrounding Berkshire Hills, was so named because of the mile-long circular trail around it.

Logging roads crisscrossed Round Mountain, which was covered in red oaks, white birches, and swamp maples with a sizable track of swampland near its base. Part way up one slope, beavers dammed up the stream that fed a small swampy area. That allowed water to remain in that wetland up here year-round. Moose fed in this area because they favored underwater plants and vegetation.

Sam froze as he spotted a large cow, a female moose, wading thigh-deep in the rich weeds. He kneeled behind a blackberry thicket. The cow's ears flinched. *Has she heard me?* She scanned her world with sharp eyes and a sensitive nose. Satisfied there was no immediate danger, she continued to munch away.

Time passed as Sam indulged in simply watching her. By far and away, he loved this part of his job the most—the peaceful communing with Mother Nature. *And* catching the bad guys that violated her. The magnificent cow finished eating and sloshed onto dry land. She shook off the chilled water and scanned her surroundings again, just in case. *A cautious one, alright.*

A light breeze fanned the vast white birch tree overhead. The fragrant leaves whispered to Sam. The round mountain's dimness had hovered over him, but now yielded to the rising sun's warmth and light. Sam smiled. He wondered, *Just how many shades of green are possible?*

At about 8:40 am, another shot rang out. The shot came from a rifle. And it was close. Leveraging yesterday's shot-chasing exercise with John Comeaux, Sam hiked to the top of the mountain, a thirty-minute climb, for a better perspective. This time of year, hunting regulations banned rifles for certain animals.

Sam was familiar with every logging road off Round Mountain, and there were only a couple of places where a poacher might stash his vehicle from prying eyes in the general direction of that second shot. A quick-time hustle to each of those places revealed a mid-sized green pickup at the third one off to the side of an old logging header—little more than a trail—with camouflaged netting over the truck. The owner did *not* want his truck discovered. Sam's poacher's truck, for sure. He concealed himself 75 feet away.

With his trusty old Pentax 8x35 binoculars, he spotted and called in the plate on his portable radio in a hushed tone. He listened over the earpiece so only he'd hear the radio's squawk. *Is the poacher nearby?* The comm center reported the plate came back to a local man named Richard Cellini, who lived on Field Street in Lee.

Sam figured he had some time, so he jogged back to retrieve his cruiser, a quarter-mile away. Kicked his ride into four-wheel-drive-low—he needed it—to block this poacher's truck and to prevent his escape. This guy was a local Sam had seen around. He ran Cellini's name through various law enforcement data-bases. This guy popped for previous trouble with New York's EnCon—their Environmental Conservation Police—and with other EPOs here in Mass, but not with Sam. He was good, lucky, or both.

Sam then approached the trail that surrounded the mountain uphill from the vehicles. A severe incline provided a perfect blind side to anyone approaching. Mr. Poacher would soon find out. Now, beginning his quick but silent descent back down to the most likely trail that led back to the trucks, he chose his steps with care. The percussive crack of a dry twig snapping carried a long way, especially with no wind to mask it. Sam chose his spot, then stood, and waited in a concealed position between where he figured the poacher would descend the trail and his pickup.

On his way back to his truck, Dick Cellini squinted his eyes. He peered down the trail and spotted the dark green four-wheel-drive SUV with a state seal on its doors. *Shit!* And they'd parked it on a forty-five-degree angle to the trail. Blocked his only exit.

With few options, Cellini continued towards his truck. *Yup, this is gonna cost me!*

7

Game time. Sam slipped out from behind a large oak to the middle of the trail behind the poacher like a ghost. It was obvious the perp had killed an animal. He'd have taken the best parts and made a beeline back to his truck. Like he was doing right now. A light breeze now fanned the forest and foretold of an inevitable confrontation. The sun dappled the uneven ground under the surrounding oaks and hemlocks as it peeked in and out of cotton candy clouds.

Experienced poachers knew the loins and hindquarters of their prey were the choice parts. They'd leave the rest to the bears and coyotes, or to rot. They called the loins *backstraps*. And they'd be in this guy's huge backpack.

Sam's right hand rested on the butt of his trusty Smith and Wesson .357 revolver. Many found his right-side holster peculiar, given that he was left-handed and left-eye dominant. He shot well with either hand, like one percent of the entire planet's population. This was part of his training, which he'd found helpful in countless situations. He practiced this skill with regularity. Strapping his piece on his right side kept that mindset front and center—at the bullseye of his consciousness. *Not that I'm obsessive-compulsive or anything. Yeah, keep telling yourself that, soldier.*

Dick Cellini had slung his rifle—a Remington Model 700—over his right shoulder. This *thirty-ought-six* was his favorite rifle. He owned many. Dick wore head-to-toe green camouflaged clothing, no hat. *Hats are for sissies.* Carried a large backpack over his left shoulder that contained a couple of large backstraps from the moose he'd killed less than two hours earlier. It had taken a second shot after almost an hour of tracking her.

Cellini was a large man with broad shoulders. He felt he was in good shape for 40, the graying hair sprouting at his temples notwithstanding. He hiked with ease, even carrying a few extra pounds of his own, plus the moose meat in his pack. The choice hindquarters of *his* large moose, however, were too large and heavy to portage out. He'd return at twilight with a meat saw to haul them out one at a time. And that's when an unexpected sound behind him scared the bajeezus out of him.

It was obvious to Sam the guy's pack was heavy. A baseball sized red stain in the bottom right corner looked like blood. As he stood in the middle of the trail, now fifteen paces behind this big-boned poacher, he cleared his throat. Cellini stopped, jerked in surprise. He wheeled a one-eighty, froze, and stared at Sam in full uniform, minus a hat. Sam hated hats.

He growled a command to this poacher. It was not a request. "Mr. Cellini, slowly remove your rifle from your shoulder and place it on the ground." Sam didn't like what he saw in this guy's eyes. With his right hand resting atop his unsnapped holster, Sam said, "Don't even think about it. You'd be signing your death warrant."

After the initial shock and Sam's warning, Cellini's eyes still darted around as his brain weighed his options, calculating cause and effect. Sam continued, louder now, "You have only one smart choice here." His hand shifted from resting on the butt of his revolver to gripping it. But he stopped short of drawing it. For the moment.

A deep exhale from Cellini signaled he now resigned himself to his fate. He laid his rifle down on the bed of leaves at his feet. "Now turn around and get on your knees, ankles crossed. Right now." He complied while issuing grunts of disgust. Sam approached with caution, knowing from hard-earned experience this was the sweet spot for fight or flight.

Still three healthy paces back, Sam unsnapped his cuffs from his equipment belt. Most don't realize that cuffs carry a certain heft. They're a decent fallback weapon if you grip one cuff and sling the dangler with force toward the side of a perp's head. Like a cop's martial arts nun-chucks. Looked like this one was complying, though. Not as stupid as he looks.

"Sir, remove your backpack and place it to your right. Then put your hands behind your back. Do nothing other than what you are told. You are under arrest for several hunting violations which I will explain to you in a moment."

Sam cuffed him. Recited the Miranda notification. Then, nudged his boot in the center of this poacher's back where his butt rested on his haunches. Now confident he was in control, Sam recovered the back-pack. Opened the zipper. As he suspected, he spotted the tops of two bloody moose loins. Backstraps.

He slung the hefty pack over his own left shoulder. He'd take samples from each of the loins and send them to the State Lab for testing to ensure they were, in fact, moose meat. Some EPOs assumed their testi-mony was evidence enough. He'd not make that mistake. Even with a moose carcass a short distance from where they stood, minus its loins, he'd need DNA testing to match those loins to that carcass. A good EPO left nothing to chance between arrest and conviction. Protocol existed for a reason.

Sam hoisted his big prisoner to his feet with little effort. At 37, he was in his prime. Besides, it was important to show physical superiority, even to a cuffed offender. Less chance of a surprise head butt or leg sweep from a detainee. This was an attitude instilled by his training in the military as well as at the EPO and State Police academies. "Sir, you are under arrest for the illegal possession of moose meat, closed season, firearms violations, and more."

Cellini remained silent. A fifth amendment exercise. No problem. No need for conversation right then and there, anyway. They completed the walk back to the vehicles in silence. Cellini chuffed several times, sounding pissed at himself. Sam guessed not from guilt, but from getting caught.

He opened the rear door of his cruiser and pushed Cellini's head down as he dropped into the caged rear seat. With his prisoner secure, he retrieved his camera and retraced Cellini's footsteps back up the trail. Within ten minutes, he came upon the dead female moose. The carcass lay near the expanse of a large six-foot-deep swamp surrounded by higher ground. Probably spring-fed this high up. An experienced knife had indeed removed its loins. This guy had done so many times. Sam took copious photos and notes.

. . .

He returned to his cruiser. Slipped into the driver's seat to call it in now that he had a solid case... with evidence—photographic *and* eyewitness. "Unit 21 with one in custody. Call Harris's tow company to retrieve a pickup truck belonging to one Richard Cellini." He reported the plate number and location as precisely as possible.

"Also, please *ten-three* John Leahey." That was code for *make a phone call* to the president of the local rod and gun club who'd retrieve the carcass with help from club members. They'd process the cow and deliver the meat to a local food bank—minus a steak or two. "Have John call me if he's unable to locate the female moose carcass, please."

Roxie, the new dispatcher, replied with her angelic voice, "Roger that, Sergeant. " Sam wondered what she looked like. He walked back to scour the crime scene one more time to search for spent cartridges. Looked like two shots had indeed taken down the moose. Two spent cartridges would tie Cellini's gun to the moose. He did not find them. Cellini had done this before. *No rookie, this one.* He'd either tossed them or tucked them into one of his pockets. Sam bet on the latter. Cellini also looked like the type who re-loaded his own ammo. Need the cartridges for that.

They departed the scene without a single word between officer and offender.

8

Sur-Rapide Exports owned the French freighter *Grand Francaise*, a member of their small fleet of trans-Atlantic ships. They cared about ore and appliances, but the "miscellaneous supplies" such as shipments of *commercial bait*, grew vital to their profitability, especially from this voyage. Margins had been diminishing, and these bait shipments meant producing financials that avoided awkward discussions with their ruthless investors who were... demanding. That called for risky rapid expansion into marginal markets.

And of late, Capitaine Laurent's specific financials had been shrinking. He claimed adverse weather events took their toll. So, Sur-Rapide's watchdogs had kept him under scrutiny, and he did not appreciate that one bit.

Of dubious reputation in its own right, Sur-Rapide, whose name translated to "safe and fast" in English, possessed expertise in concealing illicit profits in numerous foreign accounts. Each advance in surveillance technology, however, along with increased cooperation among international law enforcement agencies, threatened to expose their less-public ventures. Their board of directors now re-evaluated their entire business model. That analysis focused less on profit versus loss, and more on risk versus reward.

Pivotal decisions loomed on their horizon.

Capitaine Laurent's first mate aboard the *Francaise*, his second in command, Javier LeCompteau, oversaw the day-to-day operation of the ship. Everyone called him Commandant, or just Javier. The crew viewed him as approachable even though he was also Capitaine Laurent's enforcer while underway. *They need not be entirely aware of how profoundly I affect their lives on behalf of le capitaine. If they had any idea....*

For example, Javier levied unequivocal wrath on any crew member caught in the restricted area of the hold. Everyone knew that. Nobody uttered a word if an offender disappeared. Nobody dared ask questions. The understanding? Keep your eyes, ears and mouth shut. The commandant often said, "God gave you two ears and one mouth. Listen more, talk less." Any issues? You took them to Javier, *not* to the captain.

GK JURRENS & TOM KASPRZAK

Everyone said you did not bother le capitaine with menial shit. Or with anything, for that matter.

However, neither did Commandant LeCompteau suffer fools. He was a capable man who'd once put down three men—with ease—the stuff of *Francaise* shipboard legend. He was not a large man at five-foot-ten and 190 pounds, but he was solid and muscular and clever like a demon. In short sleeves and shorts, crewcut hair, with dark penetrating eyes, the commandant fostered well-deserved respect and fear. He carried himself like a military man. The crew heard rumors he was a former French Legionnaire. No one to fuck with. Kill you as easily as look at you. The reason didn't matter. Was he 35 or 55? No one dared or cared to ask.

9

When they searched moose poacher Richard Cellini at the Mass State Police barracks, they discovered two spent shells in his right front pocket. He hadn't figured on getting caught. No one ever does. They placed him in a cell without a word where he'd await the Clerk Magistrate for bail. Sam double-checked he'd had Cellini remove his shoelaces. Protocol.

Then, "What do you have to say for yourself, Mr. Cellini?"

Cellini responded, "Phone call. Lawyer."

Sam said, "Sure thing, as soon as I button up a few things."

Trooper Ronnie Jackson worked the desk and commented to Sam, "Got a quiet one this time, huh?"

Sam said, "Better than a combative screamer or a spitter, Ronnie."

Cellini had been through the system before. Sam

then tagged and photographed the rifle and placed the guy's belongings in an evidence bag. The loins needed refrigeration. Sam had his own refrigerator/freezer in the garage at the barracks. He'd found it at a tag sale for 50 bucks.

Yeah, Sam had done this before, too. Trooper Jackson asked him if he wanted to run Cellini for wants, warrants, NCIC—the *National Crime Information Center*—and other databases. Sam said, "Yes, please. I had our dispatcher run him, but check PACER, too." That was the database called *Public Access to Court Electronic Records* database. Sam chuckled to himself. *I wonder who names these databases? Somebody dug deep for that one.*

Turns out Cellini had accumulated a decent jacket with law enforcement in neighboring New York state for fish and wildlife violations, and now in Massachusetts, too. Nothing heavy, but an obvious asshole. His priors included neighborhood disputes, traffic violations, possession of stolen goods, and disorderly conduct. Plus, several game violations rounded out his dance card. *Yup, an asshole.* Sam left him there at the barracks after securing the evidence against this moose poacher.

To Ronnie, he said, "Hey, you're bored and looking to get on the log for activity besides pet cats in a tree, Ronnie. I get it." Yeah, ever the wise-ass. But he and the troopers with whom he worked shared a shit-ton of mutual respect. Same with the local PDs.

He was the brunt of razzing, too. He'd retaliated last week with a road-killed skunk planted behind one of the state cruisers down for repairs. It took 'em two days to find it. And so, the playfulness continued. The barracks commander, Lt. Bobby Silverman, approached Sam and asked for *a word*.

Sam thought, *Uh oh! The skunk is gonna be an issue*. Its stench still hung in the air. "Have a seat, Sergeant, and congratulations on the well-deserved promotion."

"Thank you, sir." Sam always respected the rank, but not necessarily the person.

The lieutenant sat down behind his desk. Formal, not friendly-like. "It appears our mutual playfulness has reached a point where we need to put the brakes on it for a while. The captain visited yesterday. We used the excuse that a trooper ran over a skunk and its sac burst open, sprayed the undercarriage. It's parked outside to be de-fumigated, and pressure washed."

Sam never admitted to doing the deed, but everyone got it. Almost brought a smile to his face, but he dared not let the lieutenant see *that*. He added, "I am declaring a temporary truce to the fun and games. You good with that, Sergeant?"

"Yessir, I am. Sure stinks in here, even with your windows open."

The lieutenant smiled a little and said, "Dismissed." They shook hands, and Sam smiled all the way out once he'd turned his back.

. . .

After leaving the barracks, about ten minutes down the road, he noticed a terrible odor that got worse by the minute. *What the hell?* 30 minutes later, he stopped. No choice. It was that bad. He pulled over, shut off his cruiser's engine and popped the hood, and hopped out. As he rounded the grill guarded by his brush guard, it was impossible to miss the two-foot-long catfish, half-cooked, on the almost-red-hot exhaust manifold. He smiled and said to himself, *Revenge is a dish best served cold, unlike this catfish.*

No one at the barracks said a word about grilled catfish on his two subsequent visits. Neither did he. This transcended words. On his way out after that second visit, he spotted State Police cruiser #774 at the gas pump. Sam knew who drove 774 whenever possible, not that it mattered, but this was Karma at its best. His unofficial investigation revealed Trooper Rackner had planted that fish under Sam's hood. And now, a golden opportunity. But cameras monitored that pump. He knew if the lieutenant found out what he was about to perpetrate, he'd be in for a seriously healthy ass-chewing, especially after agreeing to a ceasefire, half-cooked catfish or not.

Naturally, Sam planted just a small spike-horn buck's antler under the Billy Rackner's driver's seat so it protruded upward through that seat three inches right where Billy would plop his butt. Sam knew how to avoid cameras, even though it would require getting his BDU laundered. So worth it. He skedaddled, but didn't go far.

Sam turned off a side street where he surveilled 774. Trooper Rackner came out, still talking with someone as he dropped into the cruiser's driver seat. He howled and leaped back out, massaging his right butt cheek. Then, he bent over into the cruiser head-first and ripped the antler out of the driver's seat by accessing its underside from the rear door. He flung it aside in frustration. Scanned his surroundings for the guilty party. He knew who'd done it, and was lookin' for blood. *Mischief managed.* Score 4-3 in Sam's favor.

He took the short drive up Pixley Mountain to his home office. Wrote up the case report for the assistant district attorney and his direct boss, Lt. O'Neill. They'd set a court date for Richard Cellini's arraignment, then a pre-trial conference, followed by a plea or continuance for a trial date. He felt comfortable they'd find Cellini guilty and hit him with a hefty fine. Sam requested the man's Remington 700 be remanded to the Commonwealth for disposition.

10

At 14 knots, they'd steam for nine days to complete their 3,000-mile voyage from LeHavre, France to Halifax, Nova Scotia—barring weather catastrophes, of course. Add another twelve hours to complete their covert ship-to-ship rendezvous somewhat out of their way.

Many excuses could adequately obscure the time required for this detour from the authorities if anyone inquired, which was unlikely. They'd declare bad weather, mechanical issues, electronic malfunction, fuel contamination, time to reposition the load for improved balance of the ship after bad weather.... The list was suitably endless.

Capitaine Laurent planned to update the Canadian DFO—their Department of Fisheries and Oceans—as prescribed by admiralty law. But unknown to them, he'd plotted his route to an off-book rendezvous 75 miles southwest of the Flemish Cap.

The long-range forecast projected a large low-pressure system likely to intercept them near those coordinates. He was not concerned about his ship, but the smaller vessel they'd meet might suffer a rough ride to get there and to remain on station. *Captain Matos' problem, not mine,* he thought.

With the plot of his voyage complete on the charts, both electronic and on paper as a backup, he set the ship's radar detection range to 20 miles. He'd switch to the instrument's 50-mile range after they entered international waters. With his vessel now loaded, cargo secure, and a full crew onboard, he gave the order from the starboard bridge wing to single-up mooring lines. After less than five minutes, his second-in-command reported in. "All lines singled-up."

His squeaky voice shouted, "Cast off!" He then turned to his Number Two and delivered an order in a rather bored tone. "Commandant LeCompteau, please liaison with the harbor pilot to see us underway and clear of the terminal control area. Then, get him off of my ship."

Schedules were strict, as were official and legal protocols. Worse for them if heavy seas were to delay the covert cargo transfer of bait to the swordfish boat. There were people to whom Capitaine Laurent must answer. He'd notify the DFO well before his arrival in Canadian waters and advise them of his ports of call.

To hide the location of their intended rendezvous, however, he'd disable his AIS, or Automatic Identification System, a *lo-jack* for commercial ships, so nobody would be the wiser. If questioned, he'd blame this on electrical systems damage from the storm. He'd also ensure radio silence to prevent triangulation of their position by radio direction finder.

During the day, they kept the crew busy sanding and painting the endless appearance of rust or replacing damaged parts. He paid them to work, not sit on their derrières. Capitaine Laurent and Commandant LeCompteau had vetted each permanent crew member before hiring him. They needed trustworthy men. In return, they paid each of them well to keep their mouths shut. The captain awarded bonuses to the six most trusted men at the end of each trip—his unilateral decision. The other sixteen received their deckhand wages, which were generous by cargo ship standards. But for each voyage, they'd see fresh faces because of retirements, injuries, or those who weren't a good fit for the *Grand Francaise*.

Capitaine Laurent scratched his stubbled jowls.

Those who had served with him recognized his default expression was not a sneer, but a smug smile of secret satisfaction. *This will be my most profitable voyage yet. I will retire in two weeks **if** this trip goes well.*

11

Le capitaine and le commandant trusted Hooglie Maisé. The short but strong crew member planned to leverage that trust to get a taste of the good life for himself. They'd not miss a half-kilo of their special cargo. He'd discovered the lock's combination on the refrigerated hold. Easy. In and out in ten minutes. Max.

Hooglie made his way to the forward hold via the passageway four levels below the weather deck of the *Grand Francaise*. While underway, everyone grabbed their sleep between 0100 and 0500 hours. His only concern? The solitary watch-stander. But he was six decks up and a 30 meters farther aft on the bridge with his eyes trained on the horizon—if he was even awake.

Despite Hooglie's confidence, his stomach lurched as he approached the huge red and white warning sign painted on the locked door that now towered over him. He wasn't a big man. Slender, though muscular, and not much taller than five feet. Only after an enormous meal, *maybe* he'd weigh in at a buck-forty. Some suggested he missed his calling as a professional jockey. But he and horses didn't get along.

The stout little man did cling to big dreams, though. He wanted to own a winery in the Burgundy region of France. They said their soil there was the best in the world for vineyards. That took money. He'd been saving. Now, he needed just enough to realize his dream at last—half a key of purest product.

But now, Hooglie had been second-guessing himself for a full ten minutes. He stood in front of that door with that bright red and white warning sign glaring down at him. At last, he grunted and entered the combo lock's five digits he'd seen the commandant enter when they started loading the specials for this voyage earlier in the day. And that's when he heard, "You of all people, Hooglie?" He wheeled around to spot the commandant towering over him. "I cannot begin to tell you how disappointed I am."

It wasn't like little Hooglie didn't see the huge back hand coming. Still, it surprised him. He figured he regained consciousness 15 minutes later. That's the time Javier needed to carry him up to the weather deck slung over his shoulder like a sack of trash to be jettisoned at sea.

Next thing? He found himself in the frigid water of

the North Atlantic, watching the freighter's towering hull slide past at speed, along with his modest dreams still aboard. As he struggled to keep the surface despite the turbulence churned up by the freighter's hull and propeller wash, he inhaled more than one breath of frigid sea water—not on purpose. His ship left him behind. He thought, *I deserve this. I got greedy. It is so dark... so cold... so....*

12

Sergeant Sam Travis checked local ponds for fishing activity as a routine matter. A key part of his job was to catch poachers—those who violated wildlife protection laws. He spotted three men fishing on Long Pond, near the burg of Hartsville. The pond wasn't long, just narrow... skinny, the locals said. Sam guessed *Long Pond* sounded better than *Skinny Pond*. Each man displayed their fishing licenses on their outer garments. That was required by law.

Sam pulled into one of his hides to surveil the causeway and the suspicious trio. Dug out his thirty-year-old Pentax binocs. The unit featured quality Japanese optics. He had dropped, mistreated, and subjected those binoculars to foul weather and tons of brutal wear-and-tear. That brand of tender loving care would have killed any normal pair of binoculars long ago.

He watched the three guys catch a few small fish and attach them to a stringer they dangled in the water. After an hour, Sam made his move. He approached the men. greeted them, and asked for their required licenses. A Massachusetts fishing license comprises three equal parts. This year, they featured black print on a field of blue.

The first man displayed the proper face part of the license on his vest. The second wore the middle part. And the third gentleman wore the third part *of the same license* inside a clear plastic sleeve on his chest. The fidgety men clearly hoped this EPO wouldn't catch the obvious—three fishermen, one license. They had torn it at the folds into three parts. They presumed anyone, especially an EPO using binoculars from a distance was only likely to detect three blue licenses inside clear plastic holders attached to each of their pricey vests.

Sam asked each of the men for their names. He then challenged the first man. "Take off your pants Mr. Breyman."

Dumbfounded, the man said, "Say what?"

"I speak the same language as you. Drop your trousers, please."

"You're crazy!"

"Well, this license says your name is Madeleine, that you're five-seven, and weigh 140 pounds. You're more like six-two and about 220. I need to be sure. You understand."

"Oh, sorry, Officer, I must have grabbed my wife's license by mistake."

"Yeah, I figured it must be something like that. And then each of you tore Madeleine's license into three pieces. Straight up here, guys, I'm guessing not one of you has a valid license. Let's have a peek at that stringer."

"Oh, that's not ours, Officer. That must belong to someone else."

"Nope it's yours. I've been watching you for over an hour. Each of you put one or more fish on it. So, lose the bullshit, okay?"

Silence.

Sam reached down, pulled up the stringer himself. He eyeballed five undersized fish. Those Eastern Chain Pickerel were under a foot long. Legal minimum size? 15 inches. None were even close. *Not enough meat here to fill a tooth cavity.*

Sam asked them to turn around and raise their arms. He patted each down for weapons. Only a couple of small pocketknives. He asked them to step three full paces forward—away from him. He laid each fish on the ground with care and measured them before releasing them back into Long Pond. Used his portable to run the trio of offenders for warrants. Nothing of significance. At least he got to hear Roxie's silky tones in EPO Dispatch.

Sam booked all three for using the license of another, fishing without a license, and illegal possession of five undersized Eastern Chain Pickerel. He cited them for an appearance in court and seized their gear.

The court date came up fast and Sam testified to the facts of the case. The presiding judge didn't know Sam as he was in town substituting for another judge recovering from surgery. It was apparent this judge didn't see many fish and game violations in his part of the state. So, he wasn't shy about asking Sergeant Travis to approach the bench. "Are these important game fish, Sergeant?"

Sam replied, "Your Honor, these fish are on the State Fish and Game seal. Very important." Sam stretched it a bit. A *long* bit.

The uncertain judge asked, "What do you think is an appropriate disposition in this case, Sergeant? I've reviewed the statute and the penalties are quite severe."

"Your Honor, I suggest maximum fines for using the license of another, along with the intentional and conscious decision to tear the license apart. So, maximum fines on fishing without a license, and minimum fines of fifty dollars for each fish. Plus, I'd recommend the statutory loss of license for one year from the date of conviction. Sir."

"Thank you, Sergeant. Please step back."

"Of course, Your Honor."

After finding the three anglers guilty on all counts, the judge assessed fines totaling $525. Police officers in the gallery for other cases and from other jurisdictions struggled to contain their laughter. One local cop whispered, "Don't know how you do it, Sergeant Travis, but damn, you wired their asses up good. And the judge asking what *you* wanted for a disposition? Priceless!"

Sam smirked and said, "Just doing my job, partner." He followed that with a wink and left the courtroom rather pleased with himself.

13

Later that evening, after returning from dinner out at the East Side Cafe, Kate, Brian, and Sam lounged in their family room. Kate and Sam had grown drowsy from too much pizza. The beer contributed, too. It was late. Brian, though, chirped after downing four glasses of Coke, "Boy, Dad, you and Kate sure wolfed down a lot of pizza." His voice cracked, but none of them took notice.

"Yeah, I guess we had a hole to fill."

"Huh?"

Kate murmured as she leaned her head on Sam's left shoulder. "What's next on your agenda?" Her curiosity got the better of her. A reporter's curse. But she also sounded serious.

"I'm hoping things settle down, hon, but my gut says they never will. Hey, let's take some of the money we've saved and spend a weekend away on a mini-vacation."

Brian whooped, startling them, and said, "Yeah! Where we gonna go? Someplace exciting. Maybe climb a mountain, catch some big fish, eat junk food—"

Sam interrupted, "You know, that sounds like a terrific idea. But Kate, do you have something else in mind?"

She lit up, too. "Yes, actually! Shopping for one thing. I need some new outfits for this win—"

Brian and Sam both let out groans like they'd each taken a slug in the gut. They all laughed and surrendered to a group hug.

"Kate, why don't you look up a hotel in Conway, New Hampshire where all of us can find something we like and can do together? Fall is around the corner and if we head up soon we'll beat the big tourist leaf-peeper crush. What say we start the ball rolling?"

Ever the realist, Kate said, "Sure! I'll make some calls tomorrow. Homework done, Brian?"

"Uh, almost."

Sam smiled. Whispered like he was sharing a secret with his son. "Go on up and finish. Yell when you're done. Then we'll catch an episode of Nat Geo?"

"Sure, Dad. Sounds awesome."

As they watched their teenager clump off toward the stairs, Kate snuggled up closer to Sam and let out a mighty sigh. "I love you, Sam Travis." She dove deep into Sam's brownish-green eyes.

"Love you too, and I'm so happy right now I could just rush you up to bed and—"

She placed two fingers against his lips as her eyes widened. "Hold that thought until Brian is asleep, okay?"

"Deal!"

For the first time in a long time, both he and Kate felt at peace. Sam couldn't help but worry how fast that would change.

14

Sam received an unexpected phone call the next day while he carved his way through a mountain of paperwork at their EPO regional office in Granville. Besides being Sam's friend, Captain Larry Jamison served as the commandant and hand-to-hand combat instructor at the EPO Academy in Framingham, Massachusetts. Sam heard, "Morning, Sergeant. Getting used to that title yet?"

"Not yet, Captain, but I'm liking it, along with the extra money. I'm afraid to ask this question because it most often means trouble is on its way. What's up?"

"Yeah, well, we're working on something that I'd like you to take point on. But it's not in the Berkshires. It's on the coast."

Sam resisted asking more, but his curiosity got the best of him, as it often did. "The coast? Take point?"

"Commissioner Verdi has tasked us to help a

couple of coastal officers nab a handful of divers who have been raiding lobster gear near Rockport. Our EPOs' faces and cruisers are so well-known over there they can't get near these guys. Small town. I propose you go undercover to put a stop to this.

"These offenders have every detail planned out from when they return to shore after molesting lobster pots to transporting them without providing us probable cause to stop them. I have an unmarked van here for you. Lodging and expenses during the assignment won't be a problem."

"Whew, Captain, that's a lot to consider. I gotta leave Kate and Brian alone? Again? For how long? They're different courts and local PDs over there... everything I'll need to stop these guys. And how many divers are we talking? What about back-up?"

"We just want your usual best effort, Sam. I'm sure once you see the layout you'll create a plan. The coastal guys will be at your disposal for whatever support you need. If you're on an op they won't be more than a block away. Hidden, of course. I want you to meet with Lt. Mark Gerraine, the regional supervisor over there, along with his two men, and we'll go over everything. As far as time goes, how fast can you catch these assholes? My guess is after your usual due diligence you'd wrap this up in less than a month. Of course I'll keep Lt. O'Neill in the loop."

· · ·

The captain had to sense from Sam's silence on the phone. He obviously worried about this ask. "Hey, you go home on your days off. I'll authorize whatever over-time, and no red tape or shit from anyone. Everything will go through me, and you trust me."

Sam did trust his boss and friend. Still, he worried about Kate and Brian. But the case sounded damn interesting. "When do you need my answer, Larry?"

"Today is Wednesday and I'd like this op to begin this weekend. These poachers must have jobs during the week. They strike on weekends."

"Geezus, Larry, I was gonna take a little time off to take Kate and Brian up north for a couple days. We need a break."

Now Captain Jamison fell silent. Finally, "Look, Sam, you deserve a break. How about you take, say, a long four-day weekend and we start this party the following weekend? I'll arrange for Lt. Gerraine and his two EPOs to meet us here in Framingham to go over details on Wednesday the thirteenth at 0900. You'll start the following Friday the fifteenth. Then, you'll spend some time with the two district EPOs, get familiar with their layout, discuss reconnaissance, and answer questions, or address any issues. The three of you plan your op, map out equipment requirements, and implement. Any issues? Consider me your personal plow to clear the road."

"You're a plow alright, Larry. More like a D-9 bull-dozer. Look, I'm in, as long as my new wife doesn't

GK JURRENS & TOM KASPRZAK

divorce me. And my kid doesn't start shopping for a different dad."

"Okay, we're good, Sam. You'll enjoy putting these poachers on their asses. But if memory serves, in the last three big cases you've wound up on *your* ass. That's because you needed more training and assistance to get you through them."

They both chuckled, knowing what Larry said rang true to the bone. More as a friend than his big boss and combat training instructor, Larry had spent a lot of time with Sam. He helped hone his skills in Brazilian Jiu Jitsu, Muay Thai, and Judo. He now said, "I'm going to schedule a training session with you, Sam. See you on Wednesday, and enjoy your time off. Say hi to Kate and Brian for me."

"Roger that, boss." Sam left his office and headed out for the half-hour drive home. His head spun so fast he feared it'd spin right off his neck. Now a hundred questions gushed through his head. Yet another potentially tricky undercover op. Gonna be a hard sell.

Newly minted teenagers wreak havoc on themselves *and* their entire families. Sam remembered his own adolescent years. Sometimes it was fun, but it was always confusing and chaotic as hormones ravaged his emotional stability. Not to mention those darn girls confusing the heck out of him!

Sam's mother was a druggie and his deceased father a state trooper. From his own experience, Sam's gut told him Brian needed him at home more to get through his early teen years, the kind of help he missed as a teen. He wondered, *How do people with three or four kids do it? One step at a time, I guess. But when do I hit 'em with this new UC gig?* Probably the last night of their time away together so as not to ruin the entire trip? *Yeah.*

Poaching—stealing—lobster is a felony in many coastal states, but not in Massachusetts. Here, it was a misdemeanor, but with heavy penalties *and* jail time. Okay, a change of work scenery might be good for him. He recalled his earlier days on the coast with trepidation and satisfaction. He remained conflicted about that time. More people died from boredom in the Berkshires than murders or suicides. Coastal life presented a different... reality.

15

The Travis family enjoyed making plans for their weekend mini-vacation. Once on their way to Conway, New Hampshire, they laughed, and talked, and laughed some more. But beneath all of that, Sam struggled to drag his mind away from thoughts of the new job on the coast.

The town of Conway looked like a postcard. In an idyllic village surrounded by mountains and ski resorts, they grinned at the sight of so many restaurants, shops, hiking trails, and manicured parks—everywhere. The crowds were manageable now, but it'd get crazy in another three weeks. Warm temps graced them during the day and it grew cool at night. Conway was a shop-til-you-drop kind of place if there ever was one. The town and its surrounding area offered a bounty of beauty and recreation.

As they walked through town, Kate wanted to stop

at a shop to check out winter jackets. Sam knew of three that already hung in their big closet at home, but no matter. It was her vacation, too. And if she wanted a new jacket.... Sam and Brian felt adrift in that store, but both remained patient.

An attractive teenage girl carried a large canvas bag across one shoulder, along with two other clothing store bags. She browsed through a variety of small purses. Sam noticed her eyes darting around. His cop instincts alerted him, but he hoped he'd misread the situation.

Brian whispered, "Dad? What's wrong?

"Ah, nothing son. Just people watching."

"Dad, I know better. You've got that look. You spotted something, didn't ya?"

"Not yet." The young girl wore baggy clothes. Sam watched her drop the new purse she was looking at into her canvas bag. She continued her stroll through the store before heading toward the exit. Sam followed and hoped she'd stop at the register. She didn't. He told Brian to hang back. "I need to speak with that girl," and nodded toward Miss Baggy.

Brian surprised his dad. "She stole that purse, didn't she, Dad?"

"Yes, son, good eye. Looks like she did. But I have to wait for something called *asportation*. Means I need to wait until she leaves the store without paying. Once she's out that door I'll approach her. But we're in another state. Here in New Hampshire, I'm a civilian, not a cop. I gotta be careful. You wait here, okay?" He didn't need to wait for Brian to answer.

Sam moved through the shop toward the exit. As he passed the register, he spotted the manager's name tag. "Ms. Sullivan, please call security." Now outside the store, the shoplifter walked down the street at a quick pace. Sam closed the distance. "Miss? Miss!" The girl looked over her shoulder. Her body language made it clear she was deciding whether to run. She stopped as Sam approached her. He said, "Please return to the store and take back what you've stolen, or at least tell them you forgot to pay for it."

The girl looked at Sam, her eyes squinted half shut. "Are you a cop or security, mister? Because if you aren't, I'm not hanging around."

Sam reached into his back pocket and did a quick flash of his ID and badge, too quick for her to read. A badge is a badge and her widened eyes said she spotted the word *Police* on it. He did not identify himself as a police officer. He said, "Let's go. I'd hate to embarrass you in front of all these people."

She sighed and walked back to the store with him. The manager, Ms. Sullivan, focused on them approaching. Brian waited at the register. Sam said, "Ms. Sullivan, my name is Sam Travis and I am a police officer from Massachusetts. This young lady forgot to pay for an item from this store. She is here to either pay for it or to return it."

Quick to realize what was happening, Ms. Sullivan addressed the young girl. "What's your name, miss?"

"Tanya Colbert."

"Tanya, you look like a decent girl. A criminal record of petty theft will follow you for the rest of your life. Do you intend to pay for that purse or return it?" Tanya appeared angry but resigned.

As she handed the small purse to Ms. Sullivan, the girl asked, "Am I under arrest?"

The manager replied as she nodded down at the purse the girl had handed her. "Please do not come into this store again."

Tanya hung her head and muttered, "Sorry."

"What? I didn't hear you, Tanya."

In a louder voice Tanya said, "I'm sorry, ma'am."

"Now please leave this store and learn a lesson from this."

Tanya walked out the door, beaten and embarrassed. Ms. Sullivan looked at Sam and smiled at Brian with a still-wrinkled brow. She said, "Thank you, sir. We appreciate your diligence and the effort to make this incident a teaching moment for that girl."

Now, unbeknownst to Sam, Kate stood behind Brian with her hands on the boy's shoulders. Sam didn't know how long she'd been there. He muttered, "You're welcome, Ms. Sullivan, I'm sure my son here learned a valuable lesson, too. Allow me to introduce my wife Kate and our son Brian."

"Hello, Kate, Brian. It's nice to meet you both. May

I offer you our family discount on that jacket you've picked out, Kate?"

"Thank you, but my husband and son did the right thing, not me. I appreciate the offer. A pleasure meeting you, Ms. Sullivan."

Sam paid for the jacket. Full price.

The Travis family walked out of that store with a lightness in their step. No words, just smiles.

16

Sam dropped his bomb after a satisfying meal at Burberry's Steak House in Conway on the last night of their family getaway. He sat across the U-shaped booth from Kate with Brian between them. "Uh, I have something to tell you guys about work."

Both Kate and Brian looked puzzled, but their body language told him they sensed what was coming. Another undercover assignment. Kate responded first, in what sounded like an accusative tone. "Where are you going and what are you getting yourself into, this time, Sam?" Brian remained silent, watching this new drama play out. He'd hoisted a small frown and left it there with a forkful of lemon meringue pie frozen halfway to his mouth.

"They assigned me to work a job on the coast. I'm helping a couple of EPOs with a case. Some divers are stealing lobsters from licensed fishermen. They're

GK JURRENS & TOM KASPRZAK

sneaky and our guys can't get near them. A new face, civilian clothes, an unmarked car, and help less than a block away. That's about it."

"How many of these heroes are we talking about? How long of an assignment? Can't they get someone else? You've done your share and then some, Sam." Kate drew in a deep breath before continuing. "C'mon, cut us some slack, here." She'd been patient with his three previous cases in rapid succession, each of which almost got him killed. One got her beat up, and Brian kidnapped by a team of violent criminals. He sure didn't want to break the camel's back with this particular straw.

Brian was a smart kid. He kept silent with his head down, but his eyes followed each exchange of words. He'd even stopped eating his pie, now. But a worried frown on his face deepened. Bad memories resurfaced. He had convinced himself that kidnapping thing last year was behind him. Dad worried every new job away would be rough on him, but he didn't want to appear weak. Dad's important job helped people. He admired that. But he also knew Kate—Mom—had a point. *Why can't they get somebody else for once?*

Brian thought about how much fun they were having together at that moment. *Why can't we do more of **this**?*

Kate watched Sam recite his next excuse with more conviction than he obviously felt. "This is not like the other assignments, guys. It's like a buy-bust case. Crack a couple of these guys, get them before a judge, and they're stopped. That's it."

She looked away, frustrated. *He's going to do what he's going to do.* "What if something comes up and we need you at home?"

"Then I'll come home and take care of it. I'll even be home on my days off."

Brian asked, "Is this dangerous stuff, Dad?"

"No, Brian. It's not like those other cases, but I promise I'll be super careful, anyway. These are illegal divers, not murderers or kidnappers. Kinda routine, actually. And I'll have plenty of back-up watching, so my butt won't get into trouble. They need a face nobody'll recognize over there. The element of surprise."

Kate's face was now 100% solemn. She seemed resigned to this next brick in the wall. "Larry assigned you to this, didn't he?"

"Yeah."

"Nobody else to do this?"

"Hon, I have a knack for this stuff. I've worked on the coast before. I'll be fine and I'll be done with this thing pretty quick." Sounded to her like he didn't even believe his own words.

Brian finally flat-toned in. "Can we go back to the hotel now?" He pushed his plate away leaving half of his pie.

Kate stood up and grabbed Brian's hand, almost dragging him. Sam figured the conversation was over. *Nope. Not yet.* She asked, "When does this start?"

"Wednesday to Friday for area familiarization, recon and scouting. Then a couple weeks depending on the weather. No need to worry." He slid out of the booth behind them and left cash with a generous tip. He half-assed smiled at their server, shrugged at her sympathetic return smile, and slumped out behind his disappointed family.

As soon as they got back to their room, they packed up, checked out, and headed for the car. It was a quiet and tense ride home. Each person wallowed in their own thoughts.

They arrived home two-and-a-half-hours later. Brian slumped up the stairs to bed soon after he slipped through the front door with his little suitcase. *I just want to get invisible.* He'd said shopping had worn him out, but thanked his dad for the new fishing lures. Though only nine-thirty, he muttered the day's excitement, along with the tiring drive had done him in. He didn't want to think about Dad leaving again.

Mom came upstairs, too. Brian heard her say to Dad who still stood by the front door, "Goodnight, hon. I love you." She caught Brian before he dragged his suitcase into his bedroom and kissed him on the cheek. He hugged her hard, not wanting to cry. He thought, *After all, thirteen-year-olds don't cry.* He said, "I'm worried, Mom."

"Sweetie, Dad'll be fine. Sorry about earlier."

"That's okay. We gotta worry together, just in case, right?" He smiled at his little joke, trying to be strong for her. *Like a man.*

A half-hour later, Dad came up. It was getting late, and he told him he'd make one of his famous Italian grinders for his school lunch tomorrow. "Thanks, Dad. I love you too. I'm just scared."

"I know, son, but I'll be fine. I promise. And you know I always keep my promises. Right?"

"Yeah, you do."

"Okay, then. Night, son."

Geez, I hate it when he makes promises like that. Means he's really scared, too.

17

Kate wrestled with herself. She'd lived with Sam before they married. But this was a lot. *Am I the wife? Or the mistress? Does it even matter?* She never dreamed that old cliché was the real deal. Now, though, she got it. *Second place is still winning, right?* As long as he loved her above all other women, she'd sometimes have to take second place to the job. She stayed upstairs in bed with only a reading light on the book she'd started weeks ago, even though she was a fast reader.

Sam trudged to the refrigerator to retrieve the makings of the sandwich he promised Brian. Built the damn thing, even though his stomach churned like a cement mixer. He put the completed work of culinary art in the fridge and formed the semblance of a heart on the foil he'd wrapped it in. Looked more like a squashed bug on a windshield.

Kate came downstairs to the kitchen, retrieved a glass of water, gave him a kiss on the cheek, and without a word, padded back upstairs to their bedroom. Sam retreated to his recliner. Poured himself a stiff tumbler of vodka from the table beside him. Topped it off with seltzer and two lime wedges he'd retrieved from the fridge, with just enough room below the rim for a single cube.

The old anger re-surfaced. Again. The savagery inside him was not to be denied indefinitely. Like when he brutally beat that corrupt Special Agent Mason for trying to kill him after murdering his partner, good old Frank Murdock. If two large Boston police officers hadn't intervened, Sam would have murdered Mason.

He'd tried like hell to suppress the beast in him that night. And that wasn't the only time. He sat there in the dark with his drink. Alone. Only a solitary candle lit his dark mood. No lights. No TV. Nobody else. Even the flickering shadows pissed him off right now, for no sane reason.

The utter silence thundered inside his head. Like the splattering buzz and ringing right after a shoot in a closed space. He panted like he'd just run down a perp half his age. Or like he'd already sucked all the air out of the room and there wasn't any left. He felt buried alive.

Sam drifted off into a tortured reverie. Other long-buried memories piled on. He recalled basic training and time served after that, like it had been a prison sentence. Marines didn't fool around. Advanced combat tactics and life in the jungle taught him how to survive and how to kill.

He remembered the dope smokers he knew who were sent on a patrol in the Viet Nam bush loaded to the teeth, and not only with weapons. Because that's what *they* did to survive. And the heavy drinkers *thought* they were survivors, but then many weren't. Sam kept to himself. He saw things, did the things they trained him to do. Hell of a thing to kill a man.

Chaos, stinky mud, choking fires, oppressive jungle heat, humidity thick enough to chew, blinding sweat, dehydration, and countless moments of sheer terror led to hours of numbing boredom. All that shit had burned into his soul forever. He did his job, and they recognized him for it. A hell of a thing to take lives and to be congratulated for it with a stupid ribbon.

Sam got no satisfaction from the ribbons and insignias they pinned over the holes already drilled through his heart. The few, the proud, the mentally scarred for life. Flashbacks. Shots fired, blood every-where. A limb here. Blinded by a pink mist from a friend's head exploding inches away from his. Screams of agony and the stench, but the worst? *The silence—loudest of all and hardest to bury.*

Silver-haired geniuses who never dirtied their

hands start wars. They send the young, the strong, and the principled for somebody else's greater good. They convince us our families' freedoms hinge on fighting justifiable wars. *Some of those youth now live without limbs, or are burned beyond recognition. Their lives will never to be the same.*

It was all a lie. The politicians who chase votes, or defense contractors who build swords *and* shields, love it all and profit from death and destruction. Political friends today are enemies tomorrow. And for what? But there *is* evil in this world. Sometimes wicked and cruel deeds done to humanity demand justice. *I still believe that.*

A skinny little staff sergeant at the ripe-old age of twenty-two toward the end of his second tour in Viet Nam told Sam like he had so many others. "You know by now, don't ya? Don't get close to anybody. Ever. What if you need to pick up his body parts four hours from now? Save what's left of your sanity for when you get back to the world."

Like a lot of combat veterans, Sam did not speak of his horrific experiences. To anyone. Except to himself during nightmares or drunken stupors, like tonight. He was sure Kate and Brian would most certainly ask him someday. *How will I respond, if at all?*

Ten minutes later, he hoisted himself out of his recliner. Hid the rest of the bottle, and scrubbed his glass as if destroying evidence of the past hour before going to bed. Kate was in bed and appeared to be asleep, but his instincts told him otherwise. He'd talk to her tomorrow, to reassure her. Somehow. He leaned over and kissed her on the cheek. Neither said a word.

After a restless night, he awoke to the sounds of Brian leaving. Kate was in the shower. He crawled out of their neutral zone and went downstairs to brew a pot of coffee. Heard her hair dryer on high, then medium, then low. The bedroom door remained closed. Pictured her getting ready for work. She came downstairs and said, "Good morning, Sam. Did you sleep well?"

"Morning, hon. No, not really. I was thinking about you and us and the job."

"Well, did you solve anything?"

"No, I really didn't."

"Well, you'll have some time on this new assignment to think about that." The sarcasm in her voice wasn't ice-hard, but she drove home her point. NO, she didn't like this one bit.

"I love you, Kate." Didn't mean to sound like he was pleading. He failed.

"I love you too, and that won't stop. It's... I worry about you. I know you attract the worst kinds of assignments. You're a shit magnet, Sam. I gotta go. I'm late. See you tonight."

18

Sam put on his uniform, still finding the new stripes strange. He wondered if this was to be a slow day since he'd finished his paperwork. Nothing else scheduled but a routine patrol. No sooner had he left the house in his new cruiser, though, than dispatch notified him of an urgent call. It was from the operations manager at the famous Tanglewood venue, summer home of the Boston Symphony Orchestra.

Tanglewood drew eight to ten thousand visitors to listen to the orchestra under the stars with magnificent mountain views. On warm evenings, well-behaved crowds picnicked on blankets in the grass, sipped wine, and snacked on brie with crackers while listening to symphonic splendor.

"21, you have a call from a Mr. John Riley."

"This is 21. Put him through, please."

"Sam?"

"John, ole buddy. What's up?"

"We have a situation. A squirrel bit a distinguished guest on the neck."

He thought, *Huh. Another weird call. Oh, well. Shouldn't be too dangerous, at least.*

"Sam, this happened at a reserved home in the heart of the resort. The guest was standing on the deck when a squirrel jumped off the roof, landed on his shoulder, and bit him on the neck before he swatted him off. And Sam, the critter looked pretty sick. Didn't even scurry off. It might be rabid. We gave the guy First Aid. First responders are here, now. The guest doesn't think this is a big deal and is staying put. Typical VIP. Pete, one of our maintenance guys, shot the squirrel, but avoided the head. What should we do with the animal?"

The brain was what the state lab in Jamaica Plain near Boston would need to test the animal for rabies. "Okay, John. I remember Pete took my class a couple of years ago. Glad he remembered what he learned."

"Yeah, that's what he said. He placed the squirrel in a small cooler with ice. What now? Any words of wisdom, here, my friend?"

Sam had already hit the lights, but not the siren, en route to Tanglewood ten minutes away. "Okay, here's what we do. I'm on my way. I'll retrieve Pete's cooler with the animal's remains and run it over to Jamaica Plain to be tested. Meet me at the resort office?"

· · ·

After arriving, Sam spotted John running toward him with a small red and white cooler. Out of breath, he handed it over. Sam opened it to examine the ratty squirrel. Adjusted the ice to ensure it covered its head. "Thanks, John. You saved me some time. You'll know something when I do. Okay?"

"You bet, Sam. Thanks."

This warranted great urgency. That meant a high-speed 130-mile drive to the testing lab. With the cooler in hand, Sam ran toward his cruiser's still-open door. He visualized the run to Boston from the Berkshires. *So much for a routine day. At least I have enough gas.* Sam flew *Code 3*—lights and siren—through Lenox, Lee, and on toward the Mass Turnpike. En route, he called the Westfield State Police barracks and spoke with Lt. Kowalski. Requested an escort. Sam and the lieutenant had known each other for a couple of years. The LT said, "497 is hell on wheels. You'll have all you can do to keep up with her."

Kowalski arranged State Police escorts right into Boston. The first escort, Cruiser 497, picked him up at the barracks location in the eastbound lane at Montgomery. She spotted Sam's emergency lights heading down toward him off Blandford Mountain on the *pike*, as they called the Massachusetts Turnpike. 497 lit up, broke into the passing lane, and watched in his rear-view mirror as the EPO cruiser descended the steep grade toward her.

The medium-density traffic would get heavier as they neared Boston. Traffic in the city was never not a nightmare. Sirens had little effect at high speed. People don't hear them. Sam had studied and practiced high speed runs at the State Police Driving School and at FLETC, the Federal Law Enforcement Training Center, in Glynco, Georgia. Sam had graduated from both.

There, they'd practiced controlled skids, recovering from slides, powering out of turns, aggressively slowing down to approach a turn... all under pressure of the clock. And, of course, caution was an absolute necessity going through construction sites. Focused workers there operated noisy equipment and most wore serious ear protection. He remembered all this training, now a matter of well-practiced routine.

Sam hit the Westfield River bridge and switched to channel five on his radio. He hailed MSP cruiser 497. Lt. Kowalski had warned him its driver, Trooper Channing, was hell on wheels. Sam followed close behind her. *The LT was not kidding about Channing!* Cars moved aside for the two cruisers humming along at triple digits all the way to the intersection of Route 290. Sam thanked Channing. Another cruiser already waited for him in the left lane. They merged and off they blasted, still *Code 3*. Their destination was to be 305 South Street in Jamaica Plain.

More white-knuckle driving. In no time, they met a third cruiser. 394 merged in smoothly and took over as his escort. At the intersection of Route 95 and the pike, Sam called the rabies testing lab on his cell to advise them of his ETA. The security officer said he'd meet Sam at the door. The lab was already gearing up for the test. Determining if a small animal had the virus only took a few hours. Sam said he'd wait for the results. Without treatment, rabies was always deadly.

All proceeded as planned—seamless, professional, and fast. The security officer asked Sam if he'd like to wait in the lounge with vending machines and couches. He added, "Feel free to stretch out." Maybe the observant officer smelled last night's vodka. But Sam was too wired, although sitting in a quiet room helped bring his heart rate down. At five pm, three hours downrange from his arrival at the lab, Sam grew fidgety. He wondered.

As that thought came and went, a middle-age nurse rushed into the lounge. She wore blue scrubs. She carried herself with an air of competence and authority. Sam said, "Hi. Results?"

"Yes, the animal tested positive for rabies. You'll need to get the person who was bitten to a hospital as soon as possible to begin the four-shot regimen over 14 days to kill the virus. Where was he or she bitten?"

"On the neck."

"Okay, yes, since the bite was so close to the brain, I would strongly suggest getting that patient to a hospital ASAP."

"I'm on it, and thanks to everyone. Very professional."

All business. Sam said his goodbyes and jumped on the phone. The nurse nodded and rushed off. He told John Riley the squirrel was positive and to get his guest rushed to a hospital for the vaccine regimen, and to waste no time, or he'd die. "I'm grateful, Sam. Stop by when you get the chance."

Sam then called Kate and told her he'd be late getting in. On his drive home, he swung by the Framingham Environmental State Police Barracks where he'd graduated basic EPO training. Topped off the cruiser with fuel. Hailed his lieutenant to give him a quick briefing of the case, and headed back to the Mass Pike for remainder of the trip home. He then radioed the Westfield State Police Barracks and brought them up to speed on the case. Sam thanked Lt. Kowalski for the escort and support.

"Always glad to help a brother officer. Call us anytime, Sam."

Sometimes this job could make you feel really good. This was one of those times. But... late getting home again? Not so much. Kate and Brian would understand once he explained the emergency.

He'd helped save a life.

19

Wednesday came fast. After a tough goodbye to Kate and Brian, Sam was en route to his new gig. A picturesque village on the coast northeast of Boston on Cape Ann, Rockport appeared postcard perfect. Gloucester (pronounced 'Glou'ster') lay south along the coast, another legendary Massachusetts town. This is where the storied Andrea Gail had moored. She was lost at sea in 1991 during what came to be known as *The Perfect Storm*.

Sam wanted his first impressions of his target area to be his own. He drove along the cape's coastline, heading south to Gloucester, then northwest to Annisquam. Couldn't help but admire the idyllic scenery before him toward the north at Ipswich Bay. He then returned to a diner in Rockport called Sea Biscuits, where he was to meet the two EPOs he didn't really know, but he'd seen at meetings. Phil Armstrong and Manny Pizzelli arrived an hour after Sam had ordered his first black coffee.

He spotted their official green cruiser pull into the parking lot through the diner's windows. Sam favored a window booth—best for situational awareness. He sauntered out to meet them in the lot. After hand-shakes and shoulder slaps, the three EPOs headed back in together.

The place transported its customers back to the fifties. It featured authentic wear 'n tear on booths of chrome and red vinyl. Generations of owners had patched more than a few cracks in the seating with color-coordinated duct tape. Mostly.

The smells, sights, and sounds of an era long gone engulfed them. Waitresses dressed alike in white dresses with white aprons and mostly still-white shoes. Their uniforms almost made them look like nurses with tiara-style white hats, too. They treated their customers like they had indeed traveled back in time. Things were simpler back then without all the computerized shit permeating everything. They exuded common courtesy and superior service.

A smattering of customers momentarily stared at the trio of newcomers—two fish cops and a civilian. Sam had chosen a booth farthest away from everyone. His waitress had topped off his coffee in his absence. Its steam swirled toward the Studebaker-green hammered-steel ceiling. *Class act, this place. Too bad it wasn't truly a simpler time back in the fifties. It just seemed that way. But that's another kettle of fish.*

Pizzelli, the shorter of the two, was built like a fire hydrant at five-nine and 200 pounds, but no fat. Armstrong was tall and slender - six-two with corded muscle in his forearms, at maybe a buck-eighty. Sam liked their appearance: clean and pressed uniforms adorned with shiny gear all polished and sharp. That reflected pride in the uniform. From that, he surmised they were likely good at their jobs, too.

It was obvious these guys were in awe of Sergeant Sam Travis. They said they'd heard the stories and watched the news reports. Sam supposed not all EPOs caught as many shit cases as him. He wondered about that again.

Armstrong said, "Nice to be in the company of greatness. Even the feebs talk kindly about you, Sarge, and that's saying something. We got the skinny from the NMFS." He pronounced it *Nimfies*, a short handle for National Marine Fisheries Service agents.

Sam chuckled at the complimentary remarks, slightly embarrassed, and muttered, "I've been lucky."

Pizzelli snorted. "Yeah, like Ted Williams was a marginal hitter. Glad to have you aboard, Sam."

Sam didn't blush. He just said, "Hey, guys, I understand the reason I'm here is you need a new face not known to be law enforcement. So, do I need to worry about you already blowing my cover, here? Aren't we targeting *local* divers?" He worried about the EPO cruiser outside, their uniforms inside, and his proximity to them in the same booth in this diner.

Pizzelli said, "Not a chance. Look around. This place attracts boomers who grew up in the fifties. These divers are young bucks who favor fast food and artisan cappuccinos. And we know most of these regulars. Besides, our surveillance for the past month hasn't shown them anywhere near this joint. And they hit lobbie pots down the coast on the cape. We're good, Sarge."

Sam nodded. They ordered the Sea Biscuits legendary sausage biscuits 'n gravy. Pizzelli continued. "Here's our situation. Everybody knows our faces and probably our routines, too. Small towns out here. These lobster poachers have been raiding both commercial and recreational lobbie pots the entire summer. And there's been no let-up going into fall, likely because the weather and water conditions are still summer-like.

"We've tried every trick to catch these bozos, but once one of us is within a quarter mile of the water, the word gets out. The worst bunch runs a pickup and usually a team of four or five divers with a lookout posted ashore by his truck. The bastards take shorts, eggers, everything. They even leave the doors open on the pots they hit, the arrogant pricks."

Sam held his palms up in front of him. "Hold on. So I'm fresh on the terms, *shorts* are lobsters that are shorter than the legal length and eggers are female egg-bearing lobsters which are *really* off-limits, right?"

Pizzelli did most of the talking for this dynamic duo. "Yup, you got it. They go in the water off the seawall on Newport Street on the other side of Rockport. We'll take a quick drive-by after we're done here. The lookout by the pickup will hold up a beer can if everything is kosher. The first diver out of the water looks up at him from about 50 yards away. Three divers up front usually carry all their tanks, masks and fins. And two guys in the rear haul the netted bags of lobsters. Any sign of trouble, the rear two divers toss the evidence back in the water. The first two or three then provide cover so you can't see, but we know what they're doing.

"They'll open the zippered bag and out the lobsters go before we get anywhere near 'em. These boys are young, strong, and full of piss 'n vinegar. You *will* get challenged. You'll be alone with these young bucks for 30 seconds or so till we get there. But as you're aware, Sam, a lot can happen in half a minute.

"If the coast is clear, they rush to the truck, and toss their gear into the truck bed. The lobsters go into several large coolers in the back of the truck packed with ice and wet newspapers, and off they go. They don't even get out of their wetsuits. Time elapsed about one minute from clearing the water until they're underway on the road. They sometimes use a second truck with an extra lookout, maybe if one of the divers is hung over. A wild card. They've got this routine nailed."

Sam said nothing while his wheels turned. Timing would be everything. Then, "I assume you've run the plates and have addresses."

Pizzelli handed a manila folder to Sam. "It's all in here, Sarge. Everything we've surveilled and done and attempted. We follow 'em, but with a marked cruiser they're impossible to tail. Once we get spotted, they're gone."

"You don't have access to an unmarked?"

Armstrong replied, "Yeah, but you know what our unmarked cars look like? You might as well have a neon sign that says, 'we're not EPOs.' We could just flash that in red, white and blue. Or green. Small towns. What will you use for a vehicle?"

"I've got one of Captain Jamison's POVs." Sam had driven Larry's privately owned vehicle—an old blue '86 Chevy van. "I figure these guys might just have a connection to a local PD who'd run plates for 'em. Even a rental could spook these guys if they're as clever as you say. The plate will come back to Jamison's ex. He never changed it after their divorce."

Unlike the movies, unmarked vehicles for undercover ops didn't just magically appear from somewhere. Budget considerations, equipment access issues, and crooks with access to law enforcement databases often complicated matters.

Armstrong raised his eyebrows, glanced over at Pizzelli. "Impressive, Sarge. Good thinking."

Sam nodded. Their orders arrived. He said, "Let's eat and take a ride."

20

They left Sam's POV at the diner. Wouldn't do to have that vehicle seen in the company of a marked EPO cruiser, just in case. Pizzelli took them along the same road as Sam's recon 90 minutes earlier. A picturesque route ran alongside a seawall about four feet high that divided beach from land. The narrow road that followed the seawall, windswept with wisps of sand, had parking on the beach side only with two-hour meters. Good thing Sam had brought plenty of quarters.

Pizzelli said, "This is where they usually park. Then they enter the water around sunrise, sometimes later, but this crew always beats feet out of the area long before 1000 hours."

"You've got their addresses. Have you staked out their houses?"

"Of course. They show up without their gear or

lobsters, in street clothes, and strut right into their houses. If we had probable cause we'd stop them as soon as they leave the beach. But without that PC we're screwed. Plus, you'd think the judge here would be tough on illegal lobstering, but he's not. Or these guys got a hook into local law enforcement. Or we got some talkative officers. Small towns.

"Either way, we're on our own. We have a tough time with Presiding Justice Sean Fielding. We do better with Associate Justice Janice Weller, but we usually get Fielding. Fair warning." Pizzelli fell quiet.

Sam sensed Pizzelli didn't want to lay on more bad news. He rubbed his chin. After a five-second pause, Sam chuffed, rolled his eyes, landed his left hand on the table with a solid thwack next to his almost-still-steaming coffee mug, recently topped off for about the fifth time. He said, "Guys, lay it out for me. I gotta know it all."

Armstrong picked it up, now in a hurried tone. "Yeah, a course, Sarge. This isn't the only crew playin' this game. There are others. But this bunch is the most clever. Their op is smooth, efficient 'n almost professional. That's why we need your help, here."

Sam smirked. These guys took turns laying it all out. They were a tight unit. Armstrong continued. "Let's go to the state park 'n borrow the supervisor's office. We need to stare at some maps. Halibut Point State Park is prime real estate, an' you just gotta see the layout."

. . .

When they got there a few minutes later, the place looked super squared away for a state park. Neat, clean, not a single piece of paper or can on the ground. Pizzelli said, "I've got a key to the supervisor's office. If Jack Cavender isn't here, we let ourselves in. The walls are covered with road maps and nautical charts."

Cavender wasn't in. They entered a room with a view of the bay. Sure enough, nautical charts meticulously noting shoals, rocks, and other maritime hazards covered the walls, not plaques and administrative nonsense. This supervisor knew the waters around here as well as Pizzelli and Armstrong. Maybe better. Helluva resource.

Sam asked, "Have you tried nailing these guys by using unmarked boats?"

Armstrong's turn. "Yeah. We thought of putting a couple guys in civvies with fishing rods in small skiffs, but still wouldn't get near enough before they dump the lobbies."

Sam examined the most detailed chart of the target area. "Okay, put me on the seawall in a bathing suit, here," he pointed to a spot on Beach Road next to a large cove, "in a flowery Jimmy Buffet shirt with a few days growth. Prop me with a cooler full of beer cans filled with water, a sandwich, and one of our portables so you get to me fast when I holler. I'll hang out. The trick is gonna be to get close, but not too close to frighten 'em off."

Pizzelli replied, "I'm good with that, but when they come out of the water, how soon do you make your move?"

"Shortly before they reach their truck. Ten yards maybe, their farthest point from the water. I catch 'em in a 40-yard dash from the seawall."

Armstrong's turn again. "You think you're gonna catch them before they get back to the water 'n toss the bags?"

The tough and cut 37-year-old Sam replied, "You bet your ass. I go straight at the last two with the lobbies and take 'em down. You two need to be there in seconds because I'll do okay with two, but not more than that. Not quick enough, anyway. Even we three against five or six aren't great odds, depending on their size and fitness, but it's what we got. Are you two good enough with hand-to-hand to help me out? And in time?"

"We have to be. Not gonna leave your ass dangling' in the wind, Sarge. We want these guys. We'll find a spot close by, but not until they park their truck. So, we'll move in after you give us the word the op is on. If for whatever reason you scrub the op, we move away, and no one is the wiser. We begin again the next day or next weekend. A lotta times these guys show up even if the weather is crappy. We've plotted out which days they've worked for the last month.

That's in the file for your review. They keep no set schedule except early in and early out."

The trio hopped back into their cruiser with Sam in the back seat. Armstrong turned with alarming abruptness to face Pizzelli in the passenger's seat. "Manny, did you just fart?"

"Uh, yeah, a little one."

"Dammit, somethin' crawl up your ass and croak two years ago? Sorry Sarge."

Sam grinned. He'd already rolled down his window. He said, "That one had some serious hate to it, Manny."

21

The weekend forecast predicted half lousy and half decent weather. Cool drizzle with wind out of the northeast blew in on Saturday. A front moved through. But Sunday was to be partly cloudy with temps near eighty and a light breeze out of the southwest. The small cove offered a spacious sandy beach with baby breakers. Water temps were still in the sixties, even this late in the year. The three EPOs met for coffee Saturday morning to go over the final preparations.

An hour later, now flyin' solo, Sam found a vacant meter for his van on Beach Road. He was on station at 0800. Pizzelli and Armstrong parked close by on a blind side street. The weather sucked. So, instead of dressing like a parrot-head—a Jimmy Buffett fan—Sam wore a light slicker, shorts, and casual boat shoes. He learned from experience those shoes served him well in a foot chase only when laced up tight. The waiting game began.

Nothing at 0900. As agreed, nothing to report comprised two clicks on the portable radio in his pocket. Acknowledgement? The same. They weren't taking any chances. Lobster boats crawled across the bay about a mile out. Few recreational boats braved the crappy weather this morning, only some brave anglers who took their fishing seriously. 1000 hours? The same. Nothing to report.

Eleven o'clock? Nothing to report. Same at noon. Today wasn't the day. Sam took his Motorola MT1000 out of his slicker pocket and brought it to his mouth, but obscured it with the front of his slicker. Just in case. Sam called the op for the day. They'd start again tomorrow.

Sam returned to his motel. He flopped onto his room's queen bed, a decent mattress in a motel that catered to fussy coastal tourists. He got on the phone with Kate and Brian to set their minds at ease. He then called Captain Jamison. The same. The case folder he spread open on the bed captured a half-dozen two-hole-punched pages with twin metal prongs at the top on each side. He pored over the case report again to see if he'd missed anything.

Watched some news on TV. It didn't take long to grow mind-numbingly bored. Sam went for a run by the seawall. Like a local. Nothing new. Feeling hollow, he walked down to a nearby diner recommended by Pizzelli and Armstrong. They claimed the place offered a decent captain's plate for dinner. They weren't wrong. He sauntered back to the motel to hit the rack early. Sam was beat after the long day. Even though nothing happened, UCs—undercover operatives—accumulated emotional stress just as if something did.

Sunday dawned sunny with a cool start, but the forecast predicted a nice warm-up. The three officers met at 0700 hours for breakfast at the fifties diner north of town—all in plain clothes and in their POVs, just in case—and scoured the plan again, looking for soft spots. Like the day before, they were on station by 0800.

Once more, Sam parked next to the seawall. Got his little fanny cushion out because that damn concrete wall hadn't done his butt any favors yesterday. He wore sunglasses, a baseball cap with a large red *B*, like a Red Sox fan, and a raggedy t-shirt with Jimmy Buffett on the back. Yesterday's boat shoes were once again laced up tight. He hid his trusty .357 revolver on his right hip in a slim-line holster. Ensured his shirt was blousy enough to keep his piece well-hidden, but not so big a stiff breeze blew it upward. A savvy operative paid attention to such details.

Sam also carried a belt clip badge-holder, and two sets of Smith and Wesson handcuffs between his belt and his undershorts, but he was used to it. He also packed his waterproof wallet with ID cards plus a speed loader stuffed with law enforcement +P Winchester 158-grain hollow-point ammo.

Years of UC experience taught him how to keep that collection of essential hardware invisible to the civilian eye. Another cop might spot his normally trim waistline was a little paunchy, but otherwise, he was just another less-than-trim beach-going Sox fan who also enjoyed tropical boat music.

The cooler's contents included the Italian grinder from the diner for lunch, ice, a few beer cans filled with water, and some sunscreen. He placed it next to him on the seawall, along with a couple of energy bars and his portable radio inside on top of his sandwich. He'd found John D. MacDonald's paperback novel entitled *Pale Gray for Guilt* in his room and brought it along. The book was both a prop and entertainment while he also remained hyper-vigilant.

Sam plopped down onto his butt pad on the wall and made himself as comfortable as possible. At 0900 there was nothing to report. He performed a radio check by reaching into the cooler for the double-click thing with Pizzelli and Armstrong. They echoed back in like kind. He gazed at the ruffled waters of the cove. *Due diligence does not prevent enjoying a little beach time, eh, sport?*

22

At 0925, two pickups pulled into nearby parking spaces twenty paces from Sam's perch on the seawall —one black-on-black, and one bright red with lots of chrome. Three young men piled out of each truck. Scuba gear half-filled the beds of both pickups. These had to be their bozos—in their twenties, young, strong, and mischievous. Energy fizzed off these boys.

Sam sized them up. Not monsters, but feisty, fit 'n trim punks popping beers before ten am. Four of them were already in wet suits. They geared up the rest of the way. Sam alerted Pizzelli and Armstrong with three clicks on the transmit button from inside his cooler. He heard them respond in kind. *The op is on.*

The six men scrutinized the area. *Yup, these are our boys.* Two gave Sam the eyeball and dismissed him as a non-threat. Just an older guy with an open beer, sitting, reading, and soaking up some rays. Sam offered his best 'nothing to see here' impression as they finished gearing up. Sea gulls and terns screamed for attention as they tussled over scraps that had washed up during the night.

Two didn't suit up—the trucks' drivers. They were obviously the lookouts. They'd done this before. Each diver performed a safety check on his buddy. Each strapped an ankle knife. The drivers stayed with the trucks while the four divers worked their way down toward the water in their black quarter-inch-thick "foam rubber" wet suits. Those thick neoprene skins would keep them relatively warm in the cool water— any temp colder than their body temps was chilly.

Each diver wore a buoyancy control device (vest), or BCD, already rigged with a regulator (mouth piece) and octopus (a spare emergency mouthpiece). Divers almost always rigged such a spare regulator for emergencies. Each also carried a single compressed air tank on his back and wore a weight belt to counteract the natural buoyancy of the wet suit. In a spare hand, each slung a pair of fins with heel straps they'd wear over their neoprene booties once they entered the water.

On a forty-foot dive, the tanks they used provided about 45 minutes of air, though exertion at depth shortened that time. They were weightless in the water, but on the beach, their seventy-five pounds of gear slowed them down. Each diver helped his buddy strap on their fins, also clumsy until in deeper water, but essential once submerged. They knew what they were doing.

Sam checked the time as they entered the water. He noticed that each diver also carried a pliers-like device about 48 inches long. They'd use that to pry a lobster from a hiding place under one of the many medium and large boulders on the bottom of the cove. Probably for cover since they weren't planning any legitimate lobbie hunting at all. Not only were they experienced divers, they were careful with their cover.

Two packed a mesh bag for stowing poached lobsters. Each gave the other three a thumbs-up and turned to the truck with the two lookouts. Gave them a thumbs up, too. The lookouts were both medium-size men wearing sunglasses, shorts, and tank tops. Sam estimated he was bigger than either of them.

The EPO plan? When Sam called Pizzelli and Armstrong to the scene, their first move would be to grab the keys for the two pickups. That'd disable their getaway vehicles. The lookouts were complicit and, as the law states, equally culpable for the crime.

The minutes ticked by. Seemed an eternity. Sam let the circumstances dictate how he'd approach his perps as the scene unfolded. The case report said the two trailing divers exiting the water always toted the bags full of lobsters. In the past, the two or three leading divers, the first out of the water, protected them.

• • •

40 minutes had passed. Sam tensed more and more as the seconds burned away. Showtime had to be getting close. And then, he watched the first two emerge from the baby surf. They peered up towards the two lookouts near the seawall. After they scanned the area, the divers got the high sign—both lookouts grabbed a beer and held it high. So far, so good.

23

The two lead divers slogged out of the water and up the beach toward the trucks some 50 yards away. They carried their cumbersome fins. Sam thought, *Okay, it's showtime.* He triple-clicked his radio in the cooler for Pizzelli and Armstrong to move in on the lookouts.

The remaining two divers emerged from the water with two large yellow meshed bags bulging with lobsters. They moved as fast as possible, but their gear made it slow slogging. They, too, carried their fins, but still wore the rest of their heavy and cumbersome gear.

Sam focused on the lobsters—the evidence. The lead pair of divers, the guards, were now within 15 yards of the truck. The two divers with the lobbies trailed them by 10 yards, now farther than that from the water. Perfect.

Sam launched himself off the seawall and started running at full speed toward the lead divers. He shouted, "EPO, EPO! Throw nothing into the water!"

One of the two lead divers shouted back at his confederates, "Dump 'em, dump 'em!" The pair with the mesh bags hesitated, as Sam suspected. He now ran flat out like a halfback, with an open field between him and the goal post. One of the lead divers moved toward Sam with fists clenched, thinking Sam was coming for him. He wasn't.

Sam didn't even slow down. The guy dropped his guard a little. Sam ran right past him, but stuck out his right arm as he pivoted enough to get him within striking distance. He clotheslined the wide-eyed poacher at the neck with his extended arm—right at the elbow. The man hit the sand fast, like someone had grabbed his ankles and ripped 'em out from under him.

Sam heard yelling behind him. He knew EPOs Pizzelli and Armstrong were right on time. So, he continued his beeline for the divers who were retreating to the water. The one farthest from the water stepped into Sam's path to slow him down. Sam lowered his right shoulder at full speed and knocked him on his wet-suited ass. The man dropped his bag of lobsters on the beach.

The second diver with the other bag almost made it back to the water. He attempted a half-hearted toss in panic. The bag arced toward the water as if in slow motion. Sam ignored the diver, waded at a full run into the shallow water, and retrieved the bag. The diver looked confused, but ran and stumbled. Sam laid the lobsters on the beach and overtook that closest diver in a matter of seconds. Knocked him down, too. Cuffed him in the wet sand near the water's edge. He still wore his tank.

Diver number one had dropped his bag and ran toward the truck. As he was struggling over the seawall, Pizzelli ducked under a sweeping right hook from one lookout. Manny feinted right, wound up and unleashed a home-run left hook to the dude's liver. Then he delivered an overhand looping right cross. Dropped him like a stone.

Meanwhile, Armstrong dealt with the other lookout and diver number one. The one that Sam had elbow-slammed his throat still writhed on the sandy beach, flat on his back, struggling to breathe.

Armstrong then faced the other two divers, still standing and still looking feisty despite their losing battle. He spoke in a loud voice that was both firm and steady. "Easy way or hard way, boys? We're ready for either. You all are under arrest. Get on your knees. Now!" The two divers looked at each other. There was no running or fighting wearing all that gear. They kneeled. Armstrong finished strong. "Interlock your fingers behind your head and cross your ankles. Do not resist." They complied. Cuffed and stuffed.

Meanwhile, Sam dragged both cuffed divers—the lobster mules—from the beach and over the seawall. One clutched his side and moaned. *Probably a couple of cracked ribs. Maybe broken. Seriously painful. Tough shit, chew harder.*

The EPOs then bunched the six men in the bed of the red pickup after stripping the four divers of their heavy tanks. They all sat cross-legged, looking real stupid. In their presence, Sam took each lobster out of the mesh bags, measured it with his official lobster gauge, and checked for female egg-bearing lobsters. The total? Fifty-two lobsters. A pretty fair haul for one dive. They took Polaroids of each lobbie, both on top and their undercarriage. The bottoms revealed forbidden *eggers*. Sam then re-bagged the lobsters, hiked back down to the shore, and released them all.

Fifteen short lobbies and four eggers, along with thirty-three legals. Sam checked their tanks. The last four digits of their lobster license number was supposed to be stenciled on each tank according to state law. Nope. None and done.

They each mirandized two men. Then, while they sat cuffed in the bed of their red truck, Sam asked, "Do *any* of you birds have a legal lobster license? Do you assholes even have a lobster gauge? No? Didn't think so." He dug through their belongings and asked Armstrong to run their driver's licenses through dispatch for records, wants, and warrants.

"Okay, then. Each of you will be charged with

lobstering without a license, possession of fifteen short lobsters, and four egg-bearing females. That carries double the fine. You'll also be charged with not displaying the required numbers on your tanks. That's for starters."

They transported the entire crew to the local lock-up since no court sat on Sunday. A clerk magistrate would come to the police department to arrange for bail and to calendar a future court appearance, probably on Monday. Sam and the boys seized all the gear and stowed it in the two EPO cruisers. They found no outstanding warrants, although each had traffic infractions on their records. One had an assault adjudication, a DUI for another, but no outstanding warrants on the other four.

The six poachers left the Rockport PD after filling out a bunch of forms and the magistrate released them on bail. None requested medical attention, although the two men that Sam and Pizzelli tagged would move like chilled molasses for a while. Because their trucks were towed, they called for transportation.

The PD had collected all pertinent information on their domiciles, places of employment, and marital status. If they failed to appear in court, a *capias warrant* would follow—they'd be located and apprehended. Still, EPO Armstrong warned them in no uncertain terms that if they didn't show, they'd be arrested and thrown in jail until the next appearance got on the docket. That was how it was supposed to work, anyway.

The three EPOs then drove over to the State Park in two cruisers to secure the confiscated gear. They grouped it together, attached an inventory sheet and chain of custody forms to accompany each set of gear. By then, it was three pm and the EPOs were famished. Sam's clothes had dried by now except for his boat shoes, which still squeaked from saltwater saturation. Armstrong said, "Sounds like you won't be sneakin' up on anyone in those babies any time soon."

Sam smiled and thought, *God help me, I **do** love this shit!* He said, "Good catch today, guys. And nobody died, not even any lobsters." Ten minutes later, they pulled into their now-favorite diner and wolfed down three huge captain's plates and about a gallon of black coffee in less than 20 minutes. Sam told the boys, "I'm headed home. You handle the arraignment tomorrow, or holler if there's a continuance for a pre-trial conference. Call me when you get that date and I'll be here."

Armstrong said, "Sure thing, Sarge. You were everything we expected, and more. Outstanding plan and execution." They shook hands. Pizzelli winced and grunted, "Sheesh, nice grip, Sarge. By the way, where did you play football?"

"What makes you think I played football?"

"Well, you clotheslined that first guy pretty good. And that second doofus went totally airborne when you nailed him full tilt. That's serious linebacker shit right there."

"Nah, I played basketball. One was a pick and roll with more pick than roll and the other like blocking a foul on a pick." They laughed together, although it was clear neither Pizzelli nor Armstrong knew what picking and rolling meant. Didn't matter.

24

During the long ride home across most of the state of Massachusetts, Sam replayed the op in his head a couple of times, wondering what they might have done differently. Didn't come up with much except maybe he could have nailed that one diver's throat less energetically. *Now we need the court to slam these poachers.*

He greeted Kate and Brian at the door and, of course, the first words out of their mouths in unison were, "Did ya get 'em?"

"Yep. We did. I'll have to go back for court, but that won't be for a week. I missed you guys.

Kate said, "I fixed one of your favorites. Flounder Piccata for dinner."

Sam still burped up the meal he'd wolfed down two hours earlier, but said, "Great, hon! With that risotto rice and broccoli?"

"Yep. You got it." During dinner, they wanted to hear every detail about the op. Sam thought, *These guys are as close to law enforcement as our dispatcher, for cryin' out loud. Closer, even.*

Less than an hour after dinner, they all crashed, especially Sam. Yeah, partly from the stress and exertion of the case, but more from two full meals in three hours. He'd check for stretch marks in the morning.

25

The next day, Sam received another call from Captain Larry Jamison. "Well, Sam, since you were so successful on that lobster op, Commissioner Verdi requested you continue for another two weekends. If the poaching quiets down, I still want you to hang around and maybe catch what the resident EPOs can't or aren't able to see.

Yep, no good deed goes unpunished. "Are you serious, Larry?" Sam had grown bone-weary of these extraordinary disruptions in his life, more so than any other EPO he knew. "So, you want me to sacrifice my marriage, too?" But as soon as he said that, he shook his head, dropped his gaze. "Aw, I'm sorry, boss. That was a low blow."

"Look, Sam, you're my best. I need your best. And need I remind you that even with your recent promotion, I still outrank you?"

GK JURRENS & TOM KASPRZAK

So much for friendship. Fuck!

"The short of it? Sergeant Travis, get your ass in gear and get it done."

In their longstanding work relationship and friendship spanning more than a decade, they were truly angry with each other for the first time.

Jamison understood he was burning out one of his best, if not *the* best officer under his command, but he had orders, too. He reminded himself to smooth things over before Sam headed out for the coast again. Sam would once again have to tell Kate and Brian. The last time that'd gone over about as well as a grenade in church.

The court date for the four poaching divers arrived. Sam, along with EPOs Armstrong and Pizzelli, waited in the courtroom to testify as standby witnesses if needed. The local EPOs had warned Sam. Presiding Justice Sean Fielding rarely treated marine fisheries violations as serious offenses. Still, Sam said, "I *gotta* believe he'll convict *these* offenders and levy heavy fines."

Armstrong and Pizzelli both rolled their eyes to signal they knew Fielding would only deliver the *same old, same old.* But Pizzelli said, "We'll see. You're pretty persuasive, Sarge." The unmistakable skepticism in his voice didn't sit well with Sam.

While he still mulled over Pizzelli's doubts—and now his own—he heard the prosecutor say, "We call Sergeant Sam Travis to the stand." The bailiff repeated the call in his loud and official bailiff voice. Sam straightened his tie and tugged his snappy uniform pant legs as he stood. *Don't fuck this up!*

His footsteps echoed on the hardwood floor as he marched forward through the fancy little swinging gate and to the elevated chair to the right of the judge's bench. Cleared his throat twice en route. Before he mounted the stand, the monotone bailiff swore him in. He pivoted, took two crisp steps up to the witness stand, pivoted again, and sat down. Kept his back board-straight. All business. He wanted to remain clear and professional.

Sam answered more than a dozen specific questions from the prosecutor, with only three cursory objections by the divers' defense attorney. After ten long minutes of laying out what Sam had witnessed, Judge Fielding said, "Your witness," to the defense attorney.

"I have no questions for the officer, Your Honor."

The judge said, "You may step down, Sergeant."

So, Sam returned to his seat next to Pizzelli and Armstrong in the front row of the gallery on the DA's side of the courtroom. Before he even sat down, the judge continued, "The Court finds sufficient evidence to warrant a finding of guilty. But since this is their first offense for marine fisheries violations, I will continue this case without a finding for six months. Further, I will assess court costs of $50 to each defendant."

What the fuck! But Sam retained a mask of granite. Never a good idea to let the court see a negative reaction. Judges talk like little old ladies at church socials. And if word got out that your testimony was dubious or untrue, or that you did not respect a judgment, you were pretty much done with more than one justice.

One judge told Sam something early in his career when he reacted by jerking his head around to look at the judge who let a defendant off. The judge noticed it and said, "Officer, your job is to get 'em here before the Court. My job is to decide what to do with them, not yours."

None of the trio of EPOs had other cases that day. So, they stood, and in unison, marched out of the courtroom. The six divers and their attorney stood at the bottom of the courthouse steps. *Fuckers are laughing?* Pizzelli and Armstrong headed right for them like a couple of bulls who saw nothing but blood-red. Sam grabbed their arms with both of his own. He *ordered* them in no uncertain terms to follow him. More specifically, he physically hauled their asses in the opposite direction.

Sam half-whispered with one of them on either

side of him, "Any words exchanged now are worse than useless, *Officers*." Pizzelli and Armstrong obeyed, but fumed at not getting their licks in. Sam continued as they hustled, "This isn't the schoolyard, kids. We did our damn jobs. The court did theirs. We don't have to like it. Now, let's get the fuck outta here, okay, fellas?"

They took Armstrong's cruiser to *their* diner. For the longest time, nobody said a word. Then Sam spoke up. "Well, boys, you warned me. This ain't natural. But nothing we can do about a lousy judge except bring forward cases and evidence and testimony. Every violation, every time. We book 'em. That's it. We drive him nuts seeing our green uniforms with more boating, fishing, and lobstering violations."

"We been doin' that, Sarge. But nothin' changes."

Sam scratched his chin, then his neck. "Hey, send me a copy of your entire file with this guy for the past year? No rush. I only wanna see a charge and a result for each case. That's it. Okay, guys?"

Both officers nodded, but Pizzelli spoke up first. "What good'll that do?"

"Not sure yet, but I need information before coming up with a plan to change his perspective."

This puzzled both EPOs, but then their expressions transformed from that of confusion to hope to... conspiratorial? All in a matter of seconds. They both grinned big. Sam rewarded them with a smirk of his own... and a wink.

26

Two more weeks slipped away. Travis, Pizzelli, and Armstrong staged a full court press on any violations they found, and to get them in front of Fielding. They booked over twenty cases and twenty times Fielding delivered shitty dispositions. Sam realized the guy was *not* getting the message. The three EPOs sat in the diner over mugs of the strong black stuff. Pizzelli said, "Okay, we tried it your way, Sarge. Now what?"

With frustration oozing from within, Sam said, "There's gotta be a way. Tell me, does the judge hold a non-commercial ten-pot license to take lobster?"

Armstrong puckered and frowned. "Yeah, he does. And he puts in around the same general area as that first team of divers we busted."

"Alright, then. I need to do some research. Gonna extend my stay here if you two don't mind. I won't bother you too much, but this cannot stand. I gotta figure out how to persuade this turkey to treat these violations seriously, to realize how negatively his shitty behavior affects the environment and the fishery we're supposed to protect. Give me a couple days. Then we'll patrol that area by boat. We need to check out who's *legally* catching lobsters, both commercially and recreationally." They agreed to go along with Sam... again.

Sam called Captain Jamison to ask about an appointment. Another holiday was coming up. After that, most lobster pots would get pulled out of the water. He wanted another shot at Fielding. The next morning, Sam drove inland to the Environmental Police Academy in Framingham. Larry's secretary was not at her desk at 0900, so he knocked.

"Enter."

Captain Jamison stood and offered his hand. A subtle peace offering. Sam noticed. He muttered, "Sorry to tie you up longer, Sam, but that place needs some ass-kicking."

"It's okay, Larry. I agree. But the problem is not with the officers. There's a judge who doesn't discourage these violations."

"What do you have in mind?"

"I need leverage with this guy. I need him to see

our point of view. A face-to-face meeting with him won't do it. I feel that in my bones."

Silence. Then, "EPO Pizzelli told me this Judge Fielding has a recreational lobster license."

"Go on, Sam. Spit it out."

"Well, I'm thinking we find out his buoy color pattern and the last four digits of his lobster license printed on each of his buoys. Then, we find out where he sets 'em. Surveil him from shore, or from an unmarked boat. We need intel."

"Okay, I'm with you. So, how will you use this... intel?"

Jamison knew Travis well enough to realize he was dreaming up some dubious mischief. For plausible deniability—he still liked his job and preferred to keep it—did he really want to know what was going on in that sneaky head of his? Something told him he didn't.

"Uh, haven't thought it through yet, but I do have an idea."

Larry had to ask. "Are you sharing this marvelous revelation with me?"

"Uh, not yet, Larry, but only because I'm not sure I have what I need to make this brain fart work."

"Sam, I say this for your own good. Tread carefully here. He's a judge and if I'm reading between the lines here, it might cost you your job. Neither of us want that."

"Understood."

"At least be discreet. And don't get caught." End of meeting.

Sam smiled and winked at Larry as he rose and left without uttering another syllable, like he was on a mission.

Captain Larry Jamison, Commandant of the EPO Academy and Sam's boss mused, *He's a great officer when he stays on the reservation. I sure hope I don't have to fire his ass.*

27

Sam arrived home at the end of his shift and signed off the air with a *10-7 at station* on his cruiser's radio. He walked into the house and expected Kate and Brian to be there. "Hell-o! Anyone home?"

After a pause, he headed toward a muffled response. "Up here, hon." Sam trundled up the stairs with fatigue slowing each step. Kate sat beside Brian on his bed, holding an ice-pack to his left eye. Another bruise on his lower right cheek looked equally fresh.

Sam's eyes widened. His fists flexed. Then he smiled. Just enough. "Hey, bud, pick on the wrong girl?" But two serious stares told him joking was not called for. Kate lowered the ice pack. Sam stared at a purple, gold, and yellow bruise under Brian's swollen eye. *Geez, the kid took a couple of pretty solid shots.*

Now all business, Sam said, "Talk to me son. Tell me what happened." Brian didn't want to. He stopped short of crying. Thirteen-year-old men don't cry, he'd say. If he only knew how many more tears life was going to throw at him. They had told him life was hard, and he'd had a taste of that already. Sam asked again.

Brian took a deep breath. "Um, just a stupid fight with two older kids."

"Why? Who started it?'

"You started it Dad, but not on purpose." He barely understood Brian's mumbled words. They came out pinched and strained. But they lit a fire not to be quenched. *Oh, dear God, no. Not again.*

"Say what, now? How did I do that, son?"

"You arrested the father of these two kids last week." He pointed to his own injured cheek. "Cellini's their last name. They came at me while I was waiting for the bus. I tried to fight back, Dad." He held up his right fist to show off his bruised knuckles. Sam's almost-fourteen-year-old man-child's voice broke. A silent whimper. "But they were too big and strong, Dad. I swung and hit one on his cheek after they hit me, but it didn't stop 'em."

Sam's blood rose from a bitter simmer to a rolling boil. "Are you hurt anywhere else, son?"

"My side hurts where I got kicked." Lifting his flannel shirt, he exposed a bruise that looked like a smiley-face the size of a softball.

Kate's pleading expression broke his heart for the second time in the last 60 seconds. Sam clenched and unclenched his fists—in his mind. He appeared calm and confident, but inside.... "Are you up for a little ride, Brian?"

"I, I guess so. Where we goin'?"

"To pay a visit to someone who needs some serious advice."

Kate and Brian looked at each other, both puzzled by Sam's reaction. Then Kate's eyes grew wide. She sensed what was about to happen. "Please don't make it worse for him, Sam."

"I won't. Let's go Brian. Grab a jacket. It's getting cool out." Both remained silent as Sam took his POV, his personal pickup, down to 15 Field Street in Lee. The Cellini house. He remembered the address.

They pulled over 20 minutes later. Brian asked, "Who lives here, Dad?"

"The boys who did this to you live here. I need to make it clear to them that their behavior will not be tolerated."

"Geez, Dad, that'll just make it worse!"

"Trust me, son. I won't make it worse. I'll make it end right here, right now. We *are* doing this."

28

Brian looked over at his dad behind the wheel. *Yep, that's totally an order. Not a request. He never drives this fast when I'm in the truck. Sometimes he stops people just by using his scary voice.*

They jumped out of the truck, and marched up the driveway. Dad knocked on the front door so hard it made the windows on both sides vibrate. Ten seconds later, he pounded on it again. An older guy, maybe Dad's age, swung open that door. He looked really, really mad. He hollered, "What the fuck do you want?"

Dad spoke softly through his teeth. "Watch your mouth. Look at my boy here, Cellini. Your two hoodlum sons did this."

Okay, so this is their dad?

The man said, "Bullshit." He smelled bad, and his t-shirt looked awfully dirty.

"Get them out here now, Cellini, or I'm coming

back with an arrest warrant and a few local police offi-cers in tow for both your sons. If my prayers are answered, you'll do something crazy that lets us arrest you, again. Please give me one... little... excuse."

Old man Cellini looked like he was deciding if Dad was bluffing. *I guess Dad **is** pretty scary when he feels it's necessary!* Old man Cellini yelled from the doorway, "Davy! Tommy! Get out here!"

Sam would have had a tough time getting an arrest warrant, so he was pleased to see his bluff was working. The two boys came to the door. Their eyes got big at the sight of Brian with a swollen cheek and a black eye.

"Did you two do this to this kid? And no fucking bullshit." They sheepishly looked at their dad and stared up at Sam, who towered over them all. Now, though, Sam wasn't hiding how pissed he was... at all.

The older boy, Davy, spoke first and said, "Yeah, we pushed him around because he," pointed to Sam, "arrested you last week. We did it for you, Pop." Cellini grunted an approval.

Sam hissed, "You two bigger, older, and stronger kids beat on, not pushed or shoved, *beat on and kicked*, one smaller boy who's two years younger than you. Is that what your dad taught you?"

Cellini said, "No, I didn't teach—".

Sam pointed and *shouted,* "***You***, shut up. Let them talk." Sam mustered every remaining shred of discipline to keep himself under control. He clenched and unclenched his fists.

Cellini's eyes darted between Sam's eyes and those flexing fists. A half-blind hunter couldn't miss Sam's jaw grinding in an effort to not unleash Holy Hell on the lot of 'em.

Yeah, it was all too obvious to Cellini that he was looking into the eyes of a father about to explode. He'd heard from others that this Travis asshole was damn good with his hands and feet. Small towns. A tinge of reconsideration and respect surfaced. Though Cellini was a *cazzuto*—a pretty tough Italian who took care of himself in a scuffle—*his* old man taught him *you don't respect what you don't fear.*

"Now what, Officer Travis?"

"I'll tell you what's going to happen if there's a next time. If either of your boys goes near my son again, they'll be arrested. They'll be suspended from school. They'll both have criminal records for assault and battery. Even though they're juveniles, don't rule out thirty days at the reform school in Pittsfield. Jailers there are my friends. It won't be an easy thirty days for either one of these bullies." He wagged his fingers toward the two boys, now hiding behind their father's bulk.

"Further, if you allow or encourage any type of retribution toward my son, or encourage others to do so, I will be back here. But I will be in uniform, with police, and handcuffs for every single one of you. Don't think so? *Please,* tempt me. If you want to make this personal between you and me, I'm happy to oblige you, Cellini. You'd regret it till the day they bury you. Ask around."

It was time to go, but first... "I want both of your boys to apologize to my son. *Now!*" Both boys looked down, ashamed. Each told Brian they were sorry. Didn't sound sincere, but Sam looked at Brian. "Okay, son?" Brian nodded in silence.

Sam then said, "You both understand what you did was wrong and uncalled for, right?" He waited for both to nod. "You also understand you are to stay away from my son. You see him coming, you go the other way. Understood?" Nothing. Sam roared at them so loud that Cellini backed away, bumping into his sons behind him. ***"Do you both understand?"***

Now, the boys snapped in unison, and with what sounded like genuine respect. Or abject fear. Sam didn't care which. "Yessir!"

Sam got his nose to within a few inches of Cellini's and delivered a prolonged icy stare atop a fierce grimace. He executed a smart about-face bumping Cellini hard with his shoulder as he wheeled around to leave. He draped his right arm protectively over Brian's shoulder as they marched back to the truck and peeled out, spitting gravel onto Cellini's shabby lawn.

Sam glanced repeatedly at Brian while he drove. His calm voice injected a surreal punctuation to his near-violent demeanor of 20 seconds earlier. "You okay, Brian?"

"Yes, Dad. Thanks for making it clear to leave me alone."

"I'm sorry that doing my job caused you to suffer. Any more problems, you let me know. That's my job as your dad. Okay?"

"Sure. And Dad?"

"Yeah, Brian?" He feared the boy's next words.

"That was... totally frickin' *awesome!*" Though his left eye had now swollen entirely shut, he grinned like Christmas morning."

Yeah, I'm raising one tough little man right here. Sam couldn't help but grin. He quickly said, "Now, Brian—"

"I know, violence is never a solution, and we probably should leave out some details when we talk to Kate, to Mom. We don't need to worry her... unless you want to because you don't keep secrets, and all that grown-up romantic stuff. Right, Dad?" The kid grinned again. *Damn, how did I get so lucky?*

"Let's go get some ice on that eye, kiddo."

Now Sam had to face Kate and go through the hard discussion all over again. But she *should* be angry and worried. Sam's job once again had come home. He'd promised to make that stop. But he knew in his heart of hearts this was not the last time. *Shit!*

After dinner, things calmed down. Deflated and depressed, he needed to go for a head-clearing walk. He said, "Be back in an hour. Gotta settle things down up here before tomorrow." He jammed a finger into his left temple so hard his head bumped to his right.

Kate winced at his gesture, but chirped, "Want some company?"

Geez, she really is trying so hard. "Nah... thanks, hon. I need a little quiet space."

"Understood, Sam. We'll be here when you come back."

He reminded her with another apologetic grin and a nod toward Brian, "Keep ice on that eye for 15 minutes and take it off for 10. Then, re-apply. Okay?"

"Sure."

Old logging roads crisscrossed the area. He found the woods calming. She understood. They hugged. He took off at a slow jog, grunting with each step—*instead of* screaming.

. . .

When he arrived home after an hour of kicking rocks and walking real fast to nowhere and back, the sun had set. Kate and Brian had already eaten. He hugged his tolerant love, longer than either of their moods might have otherwise allowed. *Yeah, I'm one lucky asshole.*

They all naturally drifted toward the tube, but Sam was so distracted by the coastal stuff, it was as if he was at home, but he really wasn't. And that whole business with Cellini? *Gifts that keep on giving.*

29

Early the next morning, Sam made a call to Marine Fisheries. It took more than one call. He asked for the buoy colors of a Sean Fielding, gave the address, and waited for the computer to do its work. Less than a minute later, he had his answers. White over orange over red, and 2452 were the last 4 of his lobster ticket. They'd be painted on his buoys, too.

He called Pizzelli. "Hey, I got some intel. We need more. Bring fishing rods and we'll cruise Gull Point tomorrow at first light in civvies."

"Sure thing, Sarge. Meet me at the public boat ramp in Gloucester, but not til 1000 hours. Um, what're we up to, here? Want Armstrong standing by on shore?"

He ignored Pizzelli's first question. "Yeah. Please. Ten o'clock it is. Thanks, Manny."

The ride to Gloucester early the next morning was long and circuitous. No easy way to get there. Sam remembered an old saying, *You can't get there from here. Ya gotta go someplace else, first.* The day brought some wind out of the northwest at 15 miles per hour on the coast, per the forecast. Not ideal small craft conditions on open water. A chop could present a challenge, depending on Pizzelli's boat.

Despite his early start from Tyringham, he arrived 15 minutes late. "Sorry, Pizzelli. Insert believable excuse, here."

Pizzelli waved it off. "No worries. We're just glad you're leading us down the yellow brick road. Hey, Sarge, are we gonna lose our paychecks over this little intel-gathering gambit? Will we be surveilling a circuit judge today?"

Pizzelli was fishing, or joking, or both, but Sam said nothing. He just jerked his head sideways without intending to do so. Looked more like an autonomic spasm. Pizzelli didn't push it.

They boarded a nineteen-foot center-console fish killer, as the civvies called a serious recreational fishing boat like this. She bobbed alongside the public boat ramp's floating dock. It sported a four-stroke 250-horsepower outboard. *A little seagoing monster!* Sam's appreciative appraisal of the boat was not lost on Pizzelli. He grinned, too. Sam thought, *Yeah, this baby will handle a two or three foot chop, no problem.*

Once underway, they looked like two weekend anglers chasing stripers. They arrived off Gull Point at 1130 hours, examined their chart, and then scanned for the white-over-orange-over-red buoys—their targets—the judge's buoys that would mark his personal lobster pots.

Let the games begin.

30

They scanned the horizon before approaching the area since what they planned wasn't 100% legal. More like 0%. No boats close enough to be problematic. An hour later, they spotted the judge's first pot.

Since they were screwing around with lobster gear, they displayed on their hull side the mandatory display of colors corresponding to *their* pots. That way, they'd *appear* to be inspecting their own gear. They marked the judge's first pot's location on their chart, and then, over the next four hours, did the same for his other nine pots as they found them.

In idle conversation, Pizzelli told Travis he overheard some women in the courthouse during past visits discussing the judge's big lobster party scheduled for the upcoming Columbus Day holiday weekend. He'd invited a lot of dignitaries: other judges, state legislators, and assorted VIPs. None of the women he overheard had been invited, and none sounded too happy about that, especially the judge's Clerk Magistrate. They called him *the stuffy old bastard.* Pizzelli said Fielding would need at least 50 lobsters and two bushels of clams to steam for that crowd.

Sam said, "That means he'll need a fish car to store them. We need to locate that, too." A fish car is a buoyed, rectangular holding cage about the same configuration as a pot, but a lot bigger. They stored lobsters in ocean water to keep them alive until ready for pickup by the owner.

It took Pizzelli and Travis another hour to find the judge's car much closer to shore, hidden in plain sight amongst hundreds of lobster pots. They hauled it up and dropped it onto their open deck behind the helm station. There were three dozen lobsters inside. A couple of them looked to be short.

A sharp EPO could spot a short lobster amongst other legals. The law required them to be at least 3-3/16" as measured with a lobster gauge from the rear of the lobbie's eye socket to the edge of its carapace. *Yup, the stuffy old bastard is keeping six illegal shorts.*

They pushed the car back over the side. Sam daydreamed. *Boy, what a case. Lock up a judge and then convict him?* But he knew that was never going to happen. They guy would be tending his traps daily now to make sure he'd score enough lobbies for his fancy soiree. Or he'd hire someone else to do it for him.

Either way, he was in for a helluva surprise, and really soon.

They headed back toward the boat ramp after advising Armstrong of their ETA by radio. Armstrong timed his arrival with the truck and trailer at the ramp as they approached. He backed the truck until the trailer descended far enough into the water on the ramp. Pizzelli eased the boat onto the trailer and raised the outboard. Armstrong stood on the trailer's tongue to hook the boat's bow pad-eye to the trailer's winch line snap hook. He winched the boat snug up onto the trailer with the winch's hand crank while the boat was still somewhat buoyant. Phil pulled the boat clear of the water. Manny and Sam hopped down onto the parking lot adjacent to the ramp.

They stowed their gear and took the marked-up charts with them for further study. Hosed the salt off the boat and motor at the public rinse station, flushed the engine, slung a winch strap over the boat just forward of the outboard to secure her to the trailer, and fueled her up with zero-ethanol gas at a station down the road.

Back at their office, Pizzelli asked Travis, "What's next?" Armstrong kept his mouth shut. Travis said,

"Look, my new friends, I got this. And the less you guys know here on out, the better."

Pizzelli smiled, knowing what Travis was going to do and grinned from ear-to-ear while shaking his head. Armstrong hung his head, wearing a neutral mask; that is until he hoisted up his own contemptuous smirk. He could no more hide what he thought any more than Pizzelli could keep his nasty flatulence to himself.

Later, they stopped at their usual diner and sat in a back booth along the windows for privacy. Hot black coffee, grilled sandwiches, burgers, fries, and onion rings damn-near filled the booth's tabletop... cop health food. That donut thing and cops was a stereotype... mostly. Besides, donuts were *not* diner food.

Pizzelli asked Sam. "When you gonna make your move, Sarge?" Armstrong chipped in, "Gonna have to be quick because the holiday weekend is only four days away."

Sam tailed off, thinking about his plan. "Gonna use a marked boat with all the bells and whistles because there'll be a lot of parties and people tending their pots. How about setting up that same nineteen-footer and leave it at your office? I'll pick it up early Thursday."

Armstrong: "No problem, hoss. Manny and I will —" He noticed his partner covertly inching one butt cheek off the booth's padded surface as he rolled his eyes toward the diner's ceiling. He hissed at Pizzelli,

"Don't you *dare* unleash that foul asshole in here, Manny. I will chuck your bony ass right out onto the street!"

Pizzelli righted himself and whispered in a sheepish tone, "If you gents'll excuse me for the briefest moment, there's a restroom right over there calling my asshole's name."

Sam stifled his laughter. They were a solid team. "After we're done eating, drop me off at the motel. Gonna pick up my gear, go home, take a day off. It's Tuesday, so I'll be back bright and early on Thursday. You guys go back to work and play dumb."

"Sarge, is there anything else you need from us on Thursday?"

"How about you keep your distance, but monitor your portables or the radio in your cruiser. I'll holler if I need back-up. And thanks for asking. I mean it, guys."

20 minutes later, they sauntered out of the diner to go their separate ways. After cramming his essentials back into his overnight bag at the motel, Travis headed west on the Mass Pike. His mind raced ahead of him. *Do I stop to check in with Jamison? Or just execute this brain fart on my own?*

Since he'd pass close by the academy, he'd stop in to brief the boss. He asked Roxie over their tactical channel to see if he was in. She purred, "21, wait one." After less than a minute she came back. "He's in, 21. I'm told he'll be waiting for you in the academy gym."

31

A flushed Captain Larry Jamison bloomed sweat and determination in his workout gear. Swiped his face, hands, and arms with a large white towel. Spotted his favorite EPO entering the gym door closest to the collapsible bleachers. "Hey, Sam. Ready to sharpen your skills? You need it. Got your ass kicked a few times on the last few cases. You just got lucky with that ass-hat Mason."

"I'll take a rain check. I'm beat."

"Best time to do it, Sam. And by the looks of ya, you need a physical distraction to relieve some stress." Larry was still breathing heavy as he walked toward Sam from near the center of a 20-foot-square mat at the edge of the basketball court. No doubt he'd just finished an intense jiu jitsu training regimen by the looks of his heavy white cotton uniform called a *Gi*.

"Geez, boss. Rain check, please?" He didn't mean to whine.

"Okay, let's walk over to my office."

They sat, each gulping down ice water. "Whatcha got for me? And by the way, I have something for you."

Sam laid out his plan. He skimmed past a little white lie here and there, and declared he intended monitoring the judge's pots and his fish car that had shorts in it. "We didn't hang around to avoid raising suspicion."

"I almost believe you. Flimsy plan, truth be told. You're better and sneakier than that. I know you won't tell me, so let me fill you in on a strange call *I* got from the Federal Drug Enforcement Administration's Special Agent in Charge out of Rockport."

Sam's ears perked up. He'd just driven over from Rockport. He didn't really want to hear it, but curiosity needled him despite the warning his stomach screamed at him as it lurched. Larry pushed forward when Sam leaned into his words. "DEA SAC Chuck Sawyer told me about a major case they're working. At least he was honest enough to share with me he had pulled your and my files going back to puberty."

"Why in what kinda hell would they do that?"

Larry's expression warned Sam he was about to

experience some of that famous Jamison sarcasm. "Maybe they got a covert personnel problem and they're scraping the bottom of the barrel for under-cover operatives."

"*What*? The DEA wants to use *us* for one of *their* UC cases? There even a precedent for that? Never mind. Where, when, how, length of op, how many people, and what kind of dope are we talkin'? EPOs workin' undercover for the DEA? Sounds like a bar joke."

"You done?"

Now flustered to the point of broadcasting a flushed face and fidgety body language, Sam was the one who now pressed on, failing to disguise the excitement in his voice. "Hell no, I got a ton more questions. Why us? Why not use MSP?"

"All in good time, my good sergeant. First thing, we put a wrap on this judge. Then we'll talk again when we meet with the DEA. For now, it's business as usual. When I know more, you will too."

———

Larry perceived a deeply conflicted man sitting before him. Sam was also a friend, and the best officer in the outfit. He swallowed and muttered, "Please listen to me. Nothing is happening right away, so complete the mission you're on. We'll see what the whole thing entails later, and we go from there. Okay, Sam?"

Sam inhaled a deep breath and let it out with slow and noisy deliberation as he murmured his reply. "Okay, Larry." After another long exhale, Sam *rose* from the chair and left the building without uttering another word.

32

Sam's mind rocketed around dire feelings of dread. A hundred questions spun in his head. He crawled into his cruiser. Like a reset robot, he started it, only because he'd been programmed to do so. Headed for home and some much-deserved rest. He also needed to review his plan for Thursday, even though he might not even *be* a sergeant on Friday. *Or* an EPO.

He arrived at his last and best refuge at six pm. Kate just said, "Hi." Then he heard what sounded like a small buffalo thundering down the stairs. Sam's heart pounded with gratitude to see Brian's joy that *Dad was home.* A lucky man, he was. He didn't deserve his son or his new wife. Brian was growing like a weed. And his every other word sounded like a man's voice before it broke back into a boy's. Was that fuzz on his face now a bit darker and... and a little thicker, too?

Travis remembered his own transition to manhood had been laced with profound confusion, awkwardness, and a lack of confidence. About anything. *Gonna have your hands full with this one.* He hugged Kate too hard and too long. She pulled away with a gentleness born of concern. She dove deep into his eyes with hers, as if troubled. He asked, "What do you see, my love?"

"I see an exhausted man, even a conflicted one, but the man I love. I'll take him any way I can get him." With a little mood-lightening chuckle, Kate muttered they had eaten, but she'd gladly warm up the leftovers.

He shook his head. "I'd rather pour a drink, a stiff one." She offered him a muted smile as she lowered her head and shuffled off. Sam sat down and talked in low tones with Brian about school, sports, grades. And... he'd stopped calling all girls icky. *Uh-oh.* Nobody mentioned anything about the Cellini boys, and Sam didn't ask.

"Wanna watch some TV, Dad?"

"Sure, but give me a few minutes to settle in, okay?"

"Okay, Dad. How does two minutes sound?"

Sam chuckled and grinned. "Make it 15. Give me a chance to catch up with Kate—with Mom—okay?"

Having fetched his drink, Kate sat beside him on

the couch. Even though they snuggled close, his thoughts transported him far away.

She said, "Whatcha got going on now, Sarge?"

"Got tomorrow off. I know you have to work, but any chance of you bailing early to walk together a bit of the A.T. before dinner?"

"I'll make it happen, hon."

"We'll bring Brian and go right after he comes home from school. Sound okay?"

"That sounds terrific. What do you have lined up for the end of the week?" Yeah, Kate probed like a concerned wife *and* like an investigative reporter.

"Working on a tough case that has some risk to it. Upon hearing the word *risk*, Kate bristled. Observing her visceral reaction, he added that it was a moral and ethical risk, not a physical one. He went on. "So, I'm struggling with whether the means justify ends."

"Are you going to do something not altogether according to the book?"

Sam took a deep swig from his drink while he thought about how to answer. Then, "The book, babe? There *is* no book for this one. I'm on my own. It's my choice and I consider it justified."

Kate did not respond, but she listened.

Sam said to her, "My armor's never felt so thin."

"Is there any alternative?"

Sam thought before speaking. "Not really. We've gone too far down this road to pull out now. I've committed to this. Gotta wiggle my ethical boundaries for this. When you're busy plotting and scheming on the fly, you don't spend a lot of time contemplating every ramification. Now that I'm here with you and Brian, away from the situation, I have that time to think. While I'm not crazy about what I'm going to do, there isn't another way. I gotta live with that."

Kate considered what to say next. "You know your judgement, while not always pure, is logical. Now it sounds like you've planted yourself between a rock and a hard place. Trust your instincts, Sam. They've served you well to this point, right? I'll be at your side no matter what."

Sam put his drink down and wrapped his arms around her before he whispered, "I love you."

———

Brian appeared out of nowhere and blurted, "You two kissy-faces at it again? 15 minutes are up, Dad. Crank that thang." Mimicking a southern accent, he waved in the general direction of the TV that was on with the sound muted. He slammed his almost-lanky form into his dad's recliner. It fit him pretty well these days. MASH was on. Brian loved that show, but he grew serious the next second with a squinted-up forehead. "Dad, was it like that during the war?"

"Parts of it are slightly realistic. But in general? No, son, this show is more of a comedy. War isn't funny. Now, let's watch." Sam knew this was a probe launched by his son, who'd always been curious about his father's combat experience. He'd found Brian staring at his old Marine dress uniform in the attic a while back. The ribbons and shiny medals that covered the jacket fueled his curiosity.

The topic was sure to come up again, but for now it was all about Hawkeye, Radar, and Hot Lips.

33

After a day off, Sam was wide awake at 0200 hours. He started planning his op as he considered sea state, tide, wind speed, and wind direction. He figured the judge kept the lobsters alive until the day before the big weekend party. No one wanted to eat dead lobsters. Sam planned to "inspect" the *stuffy old bastard's* lobster pots on Thursday—today—even though he was cutting it close.

After an hour of worrying that he called planning, Sam put on his uniform. That included a thirteen-pound equipment belt with holster, firearm (that he kept in a locked safe), expandable baton, and portable radio. He slipped into his Sam Brown belt—a leather belt with a supporting strap that passed over his right shoulder—and the rest of his gear.

Sam kissed Kate goodbye. Barely awake, she mumbled, "Luf you, mmm." He checked in on Brian—

out like a light. Gave him a quick peck on the cheek. He was too big now to kiss when he was conscious. *What happened to my little boy? Damn-near a man now.* He was going to be bigger than his dad. *Gotta train with him on some hand-to-hand stuff to give him confidence.*

He walked down the house's porch steps, across the yard, and fired up his official four-wheel-drive cruiser rigged with a full array of lights, radios, and decals. He quietly headed down the mountain and across the state for the boat ramp in Gloucester. He was ready.

During the ride, Sam bombarded himself with the same ethical questions about violating his oath and breaking the law while performing his duty—something Larry called *awful-izing.* He cycled through the "ends justify the means" argument, again. If caught, he'd likely lose his job, perhaps even get jail time, or more likely, a suspended sentence. The press'd crucify him. Wouldn't be able to go anywhere in public in his beloved Berkshires without a wise-crack or a look of scorn from someone, possibly everyone. He'd go from a decorated officer to a bum in a cell. Maybe. *Gotta do everything right and fast if this is gonna work.*

But the judge was bound by an oath, too. He was making a mockery of *his* oath. That scumbag ignored the law and deserved the penalties, too. Way too many violators had walked out of his courtroom with a grin. *That* must stop, and *that* spurred Sam on again. He'd completely convinced himself to act at last.

The pre-dawn twilight lent the waterfront scene a pinkish hue. He loaded his small duffel bag into the boat which was dripping with morning dew. It was marked *ENVIRONMENTAL POLICE*. He toweled off the seat so his butt wouldn't get soaked. Then, the same to the windshield and grip rails. Performed a safety check on the nineteen-foot center-console Mako with its powerful outboard. The sea was close to calm, with clear skies. A light fog drifted low above the water's surface. The wind was sure to pick up after the sun rose and blow that fog offshore.

A flight of gulls and other sea birds had already begun their active search for food, screeching as they transited overhead. They'd forecasted 10 to 15 knot winds out of the northwest—a sea breeze. He heard other boats already underway in the distance. The sky now gave way to gray and pink in the east, but still mostly dark to the west above the low hills. During his coastal days, he had witnessed many gorgeous sunrises. Sam preferred sunsets, but this was still nature at its finest.

· · ·

Pizzelli and Armstrong had informed Sam just before they left the diner on Tuesday, they were men of conviction, too, despite the risk. Armstrong had grunted, "No argument, Sarge. We're all in with you." That surprised Sam, but he gladly accepted the help he just might need.

After Sam joined Phil at the launch in what was now a very official EPO boat complete with lights and siren, they radioed Manny. "21 and M-26, over." Yup, Manny responded on the agreed-to tactical channel with his radio call sign. "M-25 here."

"21," his own EPO handle, "underway and en route. Please acknowledge."

Pizzelli said, "I see you." Armstrong said over the radio so Manny could hear, "I'll stay closer to the boat launch. On location in five."

Sam smiled. They were pros. "Channel four. Acknowledge?"

Both EPOs confirmed the change in frequency. Channel four was a private frequency that scanners were unable to receive. Potentially hundreds of scanners regularly tracked EPOs, not only from homes, boats, cars, and fishing vessels, but from police stations and news reporter's desks, as well.

Sam still kept it cryptic. "Gentlemen, it's time."

34

Pizzelli had arrived at his designated spot before sunrise. He hid his cruiser in the pucker brush a quarter-mile away. Dressed in full camo, he walked the tree line to his OP—his observation post. His mission? To provide an overwatch of Sam's operation with a 100-power adjustable spotting scope. Binoculars didn't provide sufficient magnification. Pizzelli expressed some pride in this piece of personal gear. "With this baby, I'm able to ID the sexual orientation of a tick on an alligator's ass from 300 yards."

Armstrong and Travis looked at each other in the boat before Phil headed to his station in a nearby mall parking lot to stand by. Sam said, "So, Phil, what's the likelihood of a tick of any sex being on an alligator's ass? Or spotting an alligator in Massachusetts?" Sam had kept the push-to-talk button on the boat's radio depressed while they conversed.

They laughed some more, especially when Manny spouted off in return. "Hysterical, guys. This here's quality optics!" *Click-click.* They knuckle-bumped and rolled their eyes. Armstrong stepped ashore and took off.

Sam approached his designated starting point 20 minutes later, a mile offshore northeast of Cape Ann, according to his GPS. He scanned the area, noting a half-dozen lobstermen hauling their gear. He passed one close enough for him to wave. Yup, it was routine to see a uniformed EPO in a patrol boat randomly checking compliance for lobster licenses and catches, or violations. He'd be sure to check a few to legitimize his patrol.

Then Pizzelli squawked, "M-25. All clear, Sarge." Sam knew he had work to do. As he patrolled at less than five knots, he scanned for the white, orange, and red buoys owned by the judge. Checked his marked-up chart versus his GPS location and corrected his course. Thoughts crashed in like a freight train off its rails. What if this? What if that? Not too late to cancel. *How would I explain this? Calm down. Get your head straight and complete the mission. You've done much worse.* The jungle invaded his mental barrage. He'd taken greater risks than this before, too, and not for the last time.

He came up on the first buoy. The rest were scattered over a half-mile run now marked on his chart, according to their earlier recon. Hauling the pots was easier these days. Wire pots replaced many of the old heavy wooden pots, like slatted crates. Wire was lighter, but more expensive. Sam muttered to himself, *The judge surely has the latest and best. He's got money.* Besides, as he'd heard from the courthouse ladies, he was a *stuffy **old** bastard.* He'd want to make lobstering in his old age easy-cheesy.

The first pot contained a couple of crabs, two short lobsters, and one lobbie of legal size. He threw them overboard. Threw the pot back over, too, with its door hanging open. That made it obvious that someone had molested the trap. He watched it re-submerge with a few bubbles. Moved on down the line and repeated the process with the remainder of the judge's entire ten-pot spread. He checked with Pizzelli every so often for any concerns. "Negative, Sarge. All good."

Sam hauled other owners' pots as well, just in case, and just to inspect. Then he came to the judge's lobster car. Hauled up the big rectangular cage. The sun shone higher in the sky now, and the weather had warmed up. Sweat dribbled from Sam's brow. Saw about thirty-five lobsters inside that the judge had obviously transferred to the car since Sam's last visit a few days earlier. Both illegal shorts and legals, plus a couple of forbidden eggers. *So, he's knowingly breaking the frickin' law.*

He grunted with a mighty effort and turned the large device upside down over the side. The lobsters spilled out into the water, their crustaceous shells clattering on their way to freedom. He left that door open, too. There could be no doubt. Someone had molested the judge's pots and car, wrecking his big holiday plans to serve his ill-gotten gains to his VIP guests. Sam hauled and inspected a few more pots of other colors. Ceased his endless scanning, and to check in with Pizzelli now and then. Manny said, "All good, Sarge. Nice work."

Sam felt completely drained, his mind heavy with fatigue. So, he pressed the throttle forward to its stops. The boat surged forward, rapidly accelerating to 35 knots, and stayed there. Spray enveloped the aft two-thirds of his sleek hull as it flew just atop the smooth sea. He always found speed over water exhilarating.

As he rounded the cape with the heavy boat skimming on plane—on top of the water's surface—to clear his head, he found himself about five miles farther east than planned. With a tinge of reluctance, he spun the wheel to reverse his course, to head back to the ramp in Gloucester. After tying up, he unloaded the boat, secured his gear, and got on the radio. "M-25, M-26, this is 21. Rendezvous for chow?"

Click-click.

Click-click.

Sam smiled. Mischief managed.

35

Over captain's platters and black coffee at the Sea Biscuit, Sam answered all of Manny's and Phil's questions. "Yes, I *inspected* ten pots and a suspicious fish car again, along with a bunch of others. It appears *somebody* set free about fifty lobsters, most of them legal, but also more than a few illegals, including some of each in a suspicious fish car."

Armstrong boomed, *"Suh-WEET!"* A few patrons turned their heads at the sudden ruckus in the quiet diner.

Pizzelli nodded and grinned like a mad hatter. "Let's see what happens in our next court case. Or better yet, what say we drop by the courthouse after Monday's holiday? Can't wait to discover if there's any change in *judicial behavior*.

The weekend came. Sam spent quality time with Kate and Brian. Because of Sam's silence about the previous Thursday's op, Kate's curiosity finally got the best of her. "*Well*, sailor, how'd it go this last week? And why no briefing for the home team?"

After he explained *the mission*, and Kate dismissed his rogue behavior, he concluded with a semi-guilty smirk, "The net of it? Worked as planned. I'm headed to court over there on Monday. I'll be eager for any reaction from the judge. My guess is that he'll be in a sour mood."

Brian was curious about the op, too. Sam had remained vague on purpose with him. He did not want his son to know. That felt weird.

Sam arrived at the courthouse in full uniform. He exchanged pleasantries with the staff and the Clerk Magistrate. The judge, the "honorable" Sean Fielding, caught Sam's eye and approached him. "May I have a word with you in chambers, Sergeant Travis?"

Sam looked at his wristwatch because he wanted the judge to know he had a schedule, too. "Certainly, Your Honor. I have some time." They entered the judge's chambers. The office was expansive, with two large windows behind Fielding's extravagant desk. Law books lined one entire wall from floor to ceiling, even replete with an old-fashion library ladder on wheels, top and bottom.

Diplomas and pictures portraying the judge posing with recognizable dignitaries lined the walls where books or windows didn't. On the other side of the office, two large solid-wood file cabinets perched behind another smaller desk with a reading lamp that illuminated a comfy-looking leather recliner. A reading nook. Orderly.

Fielding invited Sam to sit in one of the two guest chairs in front of his rather massive judicial desk with almost nothing on its glassy surface. He asked, "Coffee, Sergeant?"

"No, thank you. What's on your mind, Your Honor?"

"I'd like to discuss an issue with you and ask for your input."

"Sure, fire away."

"Someone raided my lobster traps and fish car this weekend. Left me with nothing. To salvage my annual holiday party, I had to buy 50 lobsters to replace the ones that were stolen. Cost me $700, and that's with my discount."

Sam feigned shock and offered a sideways head shake of disappointment. "Sorry to hear that, Judge. Any witnesses? Or something for us to help discover who did this? I've a couple of complaints from other folks, too." Sam fibbed about that. "We can request more boat patrols in the area to apprehend the perpetrators. We just need some more info."

The judge rubbed his chin. After a prolonged troubled silence, Sam said, "Judge, permission to speak freely?"

"Of course."

"We have been bringing a host of marine fisheries and boating violations before you. Your decisions about penalties, well, lack teeth. There is no deterrent. I expect these violations will continue, or even worsen unless we punish these bad actors. Set some examples. Kick some asses... hard. Pardon my French, sir."

"I see what you're getting at. You think I'm too soft, Sergeant Travis?"

"Sir, since I'm speaking freely here, with *all* due respect, you've been softer than a marshmallow."

The judge's eyes widened. He leaned back in his fancy executive chair. It creaked. He had fallen silent. *Oh, shit, did I just go too far?* After an awkward pause, the judge chose his words, as if each brought him pain. He half-whispered, "So, you believe a tougher stance would deter this behavior?"

Sam responded, but *he* did *not* whisper. "Absolutely, Your Honor. For us to be successful we need to set firm precedents. That won't end it, but it will worry the borderline guys. I've seen it happen in other courts and jurisdictions."

"Well, I suppose we need to help them realize actions have consequences."

"Your Honor, that will be most helpful. The EPOs that work the commercial and non-commercial lobstering operations in your jurisdiction are good men and women. They bring good cases with solid evidence. To be blunt, the perpetrators walk down the steps of your court with smiles on their faces. Some even laugh. I suggest we hit them square in the wallet, *and* perhaps a week, or maybe even a month in the House of Correction for the more serious cases. *That*, along with some press coverage, will get their attention. That'll wipe those smiles off their smug faces." Sam delivered this pronunciation with potent conviction.

The judge remained silent for a few beats, just watching Sam. Then, "I get the message, Sergeant. I'll see what I can do to slow down these thieves."

"Thank you, sir. And we'll do our best to stop trap molesting, yours included. The jail time per the statutes is high for such violations, and the fines, too. With your help, we'll make these criminals feel the impact from your gavel." Sam smiled inside. His outward demeanor, however, broadcast nothing but the business of justice.

"Sergeant, I appreciate your efforts and those of your men and women."

Sam rose from his chair when the judge arose. End of meeting. They did not shake hands. "Thank you, Your Honor. We look forward to earning your support." EPO Travis left the courthouse, happy with the choices he'd made on his circuitous path to justice.

He agreed to meet Manny Pizzelli and Phil Armstrong over coffee and a burger at the diner. While walking up to its front door together, Pizzelli farted. It wasn't subtle, according to at least two of their five senses. Phil said, "You're unbelievable, Manny. I've seen cats hiss and run up trees, birds fly off their roosts, and dogs whimper, tail between their legs, all because of your nasty ass, man."

Sam grinned and shook his head. 30 seconds later, they plopped down into *their* booth. He relayed his conversation with the judge. The two men grinned from ear to ear. Sam reminded them to keep their means and methods confidential.

Pizzelli said, "No problem there, Sarge. And we'll keep you posted to see if he keeps his word." Armstrong nodded his agreement.

Sam still stared at them both to reinforce the absolute gravitas of his warning. "He will. But it wouldn't hurt to remind him from time to time that his pots are not invulnerable to poachers, even with you two on the job." They shook hands and shared conspiratorial smirks.

"Roger that, Sarge."

After chowing down, handshakes, and shoulder slaps, Sam left for the Berkshires. He stopped and briefed Captain Jamison.

Later, he wished he hadn't.

36

DEA Agent Jim Estes conducted surveillance on his target sword boat at Commercial Pier Seven in Gloucester Harbor. She'd leave the following day, or the day after that at the latest. He bet with himself they'd hightail it at night. If his suspicions were correct, they'd return eight or nine days later with another boatload of swordfish, *and* another shipment of heroin—H. It seemed there wasn't a damn thing anyone could do about it.

The following morning, he'd report to his boss, Special Agent in Charge Chuck Sawyer in their Rockport DEA substation. They'd chosen to locate in Rockport. Just too many eyes in Gloucester: too near the action, and too near the docks where the suspected smugglers moored. That was typical of Sawyer—careful and demanding.

Estes thought, *I better have something to report.* So, he took a chance.

Chuck Sawyer was a twenty-year veteran of the US Federal Drug Enforcement Administration. His superiors assigned him and his team the task of apprehending several drug-smuggling commercial fishing boat captains and their crews. Chuck was out of shape, some said *portly*, with graying hair at his temples and age lines radiating from... everywhere.

But SAC Sawyer's eyes burned with undeniable intensity. His team envied his knowledge and the unquestionable confidence he projected with his impressive command presence. Because of him, his unit worked with precision. They were effective. They were also careful. And they produced results.

North Coast Fisheries appeared far too lucrative for a legitimate commercial swordfish boat. Chuck's every instinct told him they were smuggling drugs. But from where? And how? He had access to satellite imagery with the aid of the DFO — the Canadian Department of Fisheries and Oceans. They monitored ships fishing in the US Northeastern Exclusive Economic Zone, or EEZ, via aircraft and satellite surveillance.

Strict rules applied to commercial captains. And Canada enforced the most stringent commercial fishing regulations of any country in the world. Customs officials required entry requests twenty-four hours prior to arrival in Canadian waters. Vessels were to have no fishing gear deployed at that time. Also, they must likewise notify the DFO prior to their departure.

Such vessels also needed an EEZ Port Access License. Rules governing this vast maritime coastal zone was the only way Canadian officials enforced their nation's strict fisheries laws. They were also the only country that required ICCAT certification. This defined the International Commission for the Conservation of Atlantic Tuna. That legislation included rigorous fishing rules regarding swordfish, marlin, shark, and other highly migratory species, as well as tuna. The DFO employed over 600 field officers, plus staff, various types of vessels, aircraft, and satellite imagery.

Sawyer said, "Coffee, Agent Estes?"

'Nah, I'm good. This is the one we're looking for." He pointed to a satellite photo he'd requested from their surveillance gig. He'd pissed off a few folks over there just so he'd have this for his boss today.

"Explain."

Imagery showed the sword boat *Miss Guided One* engaged in an unreported offshore rendezvous with a large cargo ship. "We've seen this before, boss. Always at night with minimal lighting and with their AIS disabled so they can't be tracked electronically. They meet in international waters to take on bait and ice. Yeah, right. The sword boat then returns to the EEZ." It was not uncommon for a boat to resupply for bait at sea. But it must be ordered beforehand at a specific time and at reported coordinates for such a rendezvous. This was not that.

"Their pattern is clear. They fish for a week and return to Gloucester to sell their cored swords." A cored swordfish was one whose head, gills, entrails, fins were excised, then iced down, and placed in the boat's holds for sale at auction in port.

Sawyer asked, "Name of the mother ship?"

"Unremarkable and unreadable, but the DFO and we think she is of French Registry. She's a decent-sized freighter around 400 feet in length. The satellite imagery isn't great, but it does put the two vessels meeting briefly and then going their separate ways. We're going to try a couple of things. I wanted to run this by you, first."

"Let's hear it." Sawyer was a man of few words.

"Boss, we've thought about dropping a helicopter in when they meet up, but they'd need two refuels to get that far offshore. We wouldn't make it out there, conduct a boarding, and return. Besides, our helos are not refuel-capable and there's no place onboard to land a boarding party.

"Options?"

"It'd be nice to stick a guy posing as a fisheries monitor on board the *Miss G,* someone with undercover training and experience. No place for a rookie, that's for sure."

"We got any of our UCs available?"

"None that have the skills to fit in on an ocean boat like this, not even the college dinks who have a pretty solid marine background. Those sword boats? Rough trade, sir."

"How about a National Marine Fisheries agent?"

"Already pinged 'em. Nobody available with hard-core UC skills. And undercover ops just aren't their style. So where does that leave us, boss? I'm out of ideas, here."

DEA Sawyer grinned as he scratched his balding head and grinned out of one corner of his rather large mouth, like he had an ace up his sleeve. He grabbed a thick file from the towering stacks of paper and photos on his desk. The manila folder featured bright red lettering—*CONFIDENTIAL.* He tossed it over the top of the piles on his desk. Estes picked it up, slapped it open on his lap. A personnel file, a thick one. He scanned the first page. As his eyes widened, he lifted them to meet Sawyer's.

His voice rose a half-octave as he spoke. "Are you kidding, boss? Look at this jacket. Former decorated combat Marine, exemplary record, and awards up the ass... including the FBI Star? This guy has come up against some heavy hitters, even capital offenses, and threw 'em in prison. Two others got the needle."

"He's *just* a state officer, and *only* a sergeant, no less, but with coastal and marine law enforcement experience. I spoke to his boss on the phone for an hour this afternoon. Captain Jamison is an FBI Star recipient himself. This EPO Sergeant Sam Travis is also a graduate of the Federal Law Enforcement Training Center's Undercover Ops program. He's also graduated from both the regular and advanced FLETC boat operator's courses. I know, for a fact, both of those courses are ball busters. He's had years of UC experience, *and* he's still around."

Estes could read this for himself, given time, but Sawyer continued to summarize, as if time were of the essence. "I also called the Boston FBI SAC. He confirmed and recommended this Sergeant Travis. But I'm sure his captain will demand he be in the loop, too.

"Is he available, sir? Sounds too good to be true."

"Well, Jamison told me he's working a UC case on the coast south of here right now, but he normally operates out of the Berkshires. He said Travis has been rode hard and put away wet, lately. But Jamison also said this sergeant is quite the hard-nose. We won't know until we brief them both. Then we'll have a better idea. He'd be a perfect fit as he also knows the fisheries side of things. Plant him onboard our target sword boat with his cover as a National Marine Fisheries Service monitor—a fish counter. He'd be an official but non-threatening presence, and he'd have the access of a crew member. Most any of our DEA agents would be rather clueless, sorry to say."

"Boy, boss, you're all over this."

"That's why they pay me the big bucks, son. Let me work on a case outline with exactly what we'd want this guy to do. This Travis has even held a Special Federal Police Officer's slot for the FBI on a previous case, so we do the same. He'd have the same authority as a Nimfy agent."

Estes still browsed through the file of Sergeant Sam Travis. "I'd like to keep this file and go through it."

"No problem, as long as it doesn't leave this office."

After a pause, the weathered agent said, "You don't spray a lot of trust around, do you?"

"Policy, procedures, and OpSec, Jim." He referred to operational security, critical to any undercover op, even within law enforcement ranks. "Follow them and you keep your ass off the hot seat. You don't take this shit dead serious and field agents get dead. You know that all too well, don't you, son?"

"Yeah, you're right, boss." *And what we'll be asking this guy to do? He's gonna need serious OpSec to stay not dead!*

37

Only two days had passed since Sam's discussion with Judge Fielding. He'd traveled the path between his home outside Tyringham on Pixley Mountain and the EPO academy in Framingham so many times, his cruiser knew the route without his brain getting in the way.

Travis remembered his time here as a cadet. Not much had changed over the years, partly because this campus was built on longstanding traditions that repelled change. Like the painted brick buildings and manicured campus. A sense of excitement and anticipation never eluded him each time he visited. A gilded sign of gold, black, and green, with white letters on the lawn near the facility's entrance gate and guardhouse announced this remained a military-style installation:

ENVIRONMENTAL POLICE ACADEMY

FRAMINGHAM, MASSACHUSETTS

Some of the old-fashioned buildings on the campus looked even more old-fashioned, because of pillars and ornamental porches. Between the hours that followed morning chow and lowering colors at sunset, small groups of cadets marched with drill instructors counting cadence.

After parking his cruiser in the lot across the street from the main administration building, Sam approached an ordinary door in a narrow hallway on the main floor. The familiar sign on the frosted glass door read:

Captain L. Jamison,
Academy Commandant

Sam knocked and entered the outer office. His smile hid his sense of dread over what his boss's boss was likely to "ask" him to do now. He smiled and turned on the charm with Jamison's long-time secretary, gatekeeper, and executive assistant. "Ellie, we *must* stop meeting like this. You look lovely as ever."

Ellie blushed. Though well past her prime, she remained a beauty and a force of nature. "Sam, so nice to see you, too. And I hear congratulations are in order, *Sergeant.*"

"News travels fast." He grinned.

Sam entered Captain Larry Jamison's office.

Straight from a workout, Larry still wore sweatpants and a tank top. Sam marveled at the older man's physical shape for the topside of 50. He no longer sported six-pack abs, but still trimmed out pretty damn tight. Since his divorce a year earlier, he'd spent a lot more time in the gym. It showed. *The divorce diet?*

38

Larry Jamison had been pondering how to persuade Sam and Kate, his friends, to accept this DEA case without harming their relationship with each other and with him. He truly believed brutal honesty served best. Not that he'd lie to Sam, but neither would he gloss over the potential risks. He'd vow no undercover assignments for a minimum of six months after this one, and he'd keep his word.

His new sergeant would take the assignment, albeit reluctantly. Larry might have to call to Kate to plead his case and hopefully earn *her* support, too. It was the right thing to do.

Sam arrived on time, as usual. "Good morning, Sergeant Travis. Coffee? Donut?"

"Sure, I'll have a coffee but no thanks to the sugar bomb. Gotta maintain my girlish figure."

"Let's get to it then. The DEA SAC out of Rockport

was straight up with me. He and I will be your only contacts and we will be available to you twenty-four/seven."

"That sounds good, Larry, but how in this particular hell do I reach either of you? No cell service offshore. And sat phones are as scarce as cocktail lounges in Tehran. Any ideas there, boss?"

"Reasonable point, Sam. Let me check with MSP. See if I can get a loaner. Or it's possible the DEA has one available. After all, it's their op. As feds, they usually have access to the latest toys. The target boat's name is *Miss Guided One,* a 72-foot commercial sword-fishing boat that hails out of Gloucester. You'd be an NMFS monitor."

"A Nimfy?"

"Yep. That's your cover. But in reality, you're a UC for the DEA, a Special Federal Officer. Again."

"I'll be a temporary feeb again. Oh, boy."

"Satellite photos from Canada's Department of Fisheries and Oceans surveilled the same two vessels rendezvous offshore three times in the last two months. They meet up for a short time south of the Flemish Cap and then split. The DEA is certain the cargo ship and the *Miss G* are engaged in an ongoing smuggling operation.

"The DEA has avoided boarding her because they don't want any red flags to alter their op. Your job will be to find out what they're smuggling and where their drop is ashore. Find out if they meet another US boat for a transfer, or if they make straight for Gloucester."

Larry scrutinized Sam's body language. He still appeared receptive, so he pressed on. "They have to accept a monitor, or NMFS freezes them in port."

"And I'd be your Nimfy monitor aboard this suspected smuggling vessel, a sword boat."

"I've been demanding a lot from you, Sam. Brentwood was my first choice for this assignment, but he fractured an ankle. He'll be in a cast for six weeks followed by physical therapy. So, I have limited options."

Sam shook his head. His right knee popped up and down like a jackhammer. *Uh-oh, I'm losing him.* Instead of raising his voice in exasperation, Sam growled, "How is it the entire DEA can't supply one guy in their 5,000-personnel roster to do this? C'mon, Larry. Kate and Brian are putting a ton of pressure on me to settle in for a while."

Yep, he's pretty pissed off. "Sam, I don't want to put your family situation in jeopardy. Want me to call Kate?"

Travis ignored the question. Obviously, his wheels turned so fast that Larry feared he'd just locked up. Then, he croaked, "When does this op begin?"

"Their intel suggests the target boat will get underway for a seven-to-nine-day sortie the day after tomorrow. This briefing folder outlines the specifics. Plus, here are a couple things to sign, temporarily establishing you as a Special Federal Police Officer again for jurisdictional reasons, and initializing your injured-on-duty health insurance coverage in that role."

Now that the rubber was meeting the road—yet again —and smoke rolled off his metaphorical tires, an increasingly dejected Sam mumbled, "Swell. No time for family or me in between assignments."

"Sam, I give you my word that after this op, I won't call on you for six months. Minimum. Is that enough down time for you to get things right?"

Travis looked up at Jamison. "Okay, I go home, talk with Kate and Brian, get their take. That's gotta be the deciding factor for me."

"Got it, Sam. I understand. My wife's gone because the job came first. Ain't coming back either. I don't want that for you. I got real lucky with Lindsey and aim to keep her around for a million years. Call me tonight, okay, my friend?" He didn't mean to come across so fucking needy.

"Okay Captain. I'll call." He rose from the chair in slow motion. Walked out the door. Larry was choking *himself* on the pressure he put on Sam. He looked at the clock, waited ten minutes before he browsed through his Rolodex. Kate'd still be at work. After two rings, "Kate, it's Larry. Got a sec?"

Her voice sounded sullen. "Hi Larry. Strange to hear from you this time of day. Is Sam alright?"

"Sam's fine. Sorry to call you at work. Listen, Kate, I don't normally ask a wife's permission to send one of my troops out on assignment, but this is the right thing to do. I've asked Sam to go undercover beginning the day after tomorrow. He'll be gone seven to nine days working on a commercial sword-fishing boat, undercover as a DEA agent. The poor guy is worried sick about you and Brian. He's on his way home now and is really distressed about this. He's all twisted up about how you'll react."

A pause. Jamison waited her out. "How dangerous will this be, Larry?"

"I won't lie to you Kate. All undercover work has risk. But Sam can handle this. I'm sure of it."

"Larry let *me* be honest with *you*. I have two big fears. One, he won't come home. And two, he's coming up short as a parent and husband because of his job. Both Brian and I are reaching our limit. That may sound selfish but that's what it is."

"Kate, it's an enormous strain on a relationship. After this op, I offered him a guaranteed six-month reprieve from *any* assignments other than his routine district duties. It's the best I've got. Do you think you can go along with this last op for a while?" He was pleading, not as Sam's captain, but as his friend. Silence for 10 seconds, 15 seconds... he timed it with the second hand on his office's wall clock. *Shit!*

Kate broke the silence. "Larry, we trust you and love the wonderful relationship you share with Sam, with us. But I was praying not to face this yet again, not so soon. You've got to get more people trained and not let these jobs fall on my new husband's shoulders every time. It's not fair to him or to us."

She took a noisy deep breath and blew it out even noisier through puffed-out cheeks before continuing in a slow and deliberate tone into the phone. "Let's try this. We'll talk as a family when he gets home. I know you can order him to do it, but I know you won't let it come to that. If you do, that *will* be a game-changer for all of us. You know that, Larry."

"Fair enough, Kate. I promise you I will not order him to do this. Please understand that this is a serious case, and I'm not asking this of you lightly. The DEA has promised us complete protection including over-flights with private unmarked aircraft. You won't have much communication. I'm telling you that up front. And I give you my word he'll get his break. I'll oversee this myself and not rely on the DEA for intel."

"Okay, Larry, I'm sure he'll be calling you after we talk."

"Thanks Kate. We'll figure this out and get through it."

If only I was as confident as I sound. Heaven help me if anything happens to our Sam!

39

She gently surged against her mooring lines at a commercial pier in Gloucester, Massachusetts. They had christened her the *Miss Guided One* several decades earlier. Back then she was a state-of-the-art commercial longliner—a serious fishing vessel that trailed tens of miles of hooked lines behind her with the equipment to enable that with efficiency. Though well-maintained, this rusty old swordfish vessel still suffered from deterioration in all the usual places. Definitely a hard-core workboat.

She was 72 feet long with a sleek 22-foot beam. She carried up to 70 *miles* of 700-pound-test monofilament mainline on huge machine-operated twin spools bolted to her aft deck—steel, of course. Like most commercial seagoing craft, they constructed the *Miss G*, as they called her, with hundreds of deck bolts securing access hatches that were covered with non-skid material. Every steel surface was sheathed in countless layers of salt-resistant paint.

Once at sea and on site, they'd deploy this longline fishing gear by trailing miles of this mainline behind the boat held near the surface with floats. From this mainline, they dangled drop lines called *snoods* every 100 yards or so with a stout swivel clip. Lashed to these snoods were large razor-sharp J-hooks that skewered a chunk of bait. Each snood supported up to 400-pounds of catch. They descended to various depths down to 150 feet.

Twin Caterpillar engines powered the *Miss G.* These V12 diesel power plants each displaced almost 2,000 cubic inches and produced 1,900 horsepower each. The boat weighed 70 tons empty and carried up to 3,000 gallons of fuel. Loaded, she'd burn ten gallons per hour at ten knots, or 11.5 MPH. That enabled her respectable 3,000 nautical mile range without refueling in ideal sea conditions, but a lesser range during inclement weather.

Portuguese by birth, Captain Afonso Matos descended from a long line of commercial anglers. He hated his family, but he loved the business. His vessel, the *Miss G* hailed out of Pier Seven in the village of Gloucester, Massachusetts. Several smaller Coast Guard vessels, along with a few other sword boats, draggers, and trawlers, also moored along both sides of this stout but aging wooden pier.

Longliners were not long for the Eastern Atlantic. *By-catch* was the major reason for their decline. That's what they called the illegal and unwanted catches they snagged but dared not keep. This awful waste of marine life comprised the killing of marlin, sea turtles, sharks, dolphin, and pilot whales. Any swordfish less than 47 inches long—*short swords*—were also illegal to keep. Shorter than that, they'd kill and toss them over the side. They'd unhook all of this nautical equivalent of road kill and leave it all floating in their wake. If they brought this by-catch into port, they'd be cited with costly violations. Of course, the sword fishermen viewed by-catch as inevitable but minor collateral damage. No big deal. To them.

Many captains' logbooks offered dubious tallies, they said. National Marine Fisheries Service officials often questioned their catch numbers, and federal legislation gave NMFS jurisdictional authority within specific coastal areas called Exclusive Economic Zones, or EEZs. In this part of the world, the Northeast Region EEZ granted the US and other coastal nations absolute jurisdiction over natural resources.

This *federal* authority compelled commercial captains to take monitors onboard during their fishing trips—their sorties—into these rich fishing grounds when required to do so. The captains reluctantly obliged to prevent losing their businesses.

Longliners had already been banned from the US West Coast 40 years earlier. States other than California also banned longliners inside their EEZs, mainly due to their destructive by-catch practices that were devastating oceanic ecosystems. The Canadian Department of Fisheries and Oceans, or DFO, also feared the horrible impact of this by-catch practice by longliners.

The influential DFO enforced Canada's strict fisheries practices. Canadian authorities also deployed monitors aboard any boat they desired, for any reason, and for as long as they deemed necessary. They dealt with violators in the harshest terms: suspension of license, revoking docking privileges, and even banning entry into Canadian waters rich with sea life.

Longliner captains despised the shipboard monitors, but compliance was unavoidable; occasionally, a monitor perished at sea.

40

A crew of five operated the F/V *Miss Guided One* under Captain Afonso Matos. Antonio Sousa served as Matos' First Mate. Sousa was known for his skill, knowledge, and ability to control emergency situations. Matos also depended on him as the vessel's enforcer.

The boat's engineer, Carlos Almeida kept the big twin diesels humming. They thought of him as the shipboard MacGyver. He could fix anything.

Of the two deckhands, Eduardo Braga possessed ceaseless energy. The rest of the crew loved Eduardo, a guy they depended on. The top deck man was Jose Belo. They'd nicknamed him *Cachorro Grande—Big Dog*—or just *Chacci*, for short. His formidable stature was atypical of a Português, because unlike the others from Portugal, he towered six-two and carried a husky but chiseled 230 pounds. Chacci was a beast of exceptional strength and power. He also drank. For that, he needed, but never wanted, supervision. His temper, combined with his strength and a copious non-stop flow of Brazilian rum, made for an ever-volatile recipe aboard the *Miss G.*

And their newest crew member, Andre Gagnon, hailed from Quebec. Andre descended from three generations of commercial fishermen. Captain Matos reluctantly hired the Québécois—the only non-Português aboard—after a former long-time crewman dropped dead on deck. At fifty-seven, the man stroked out, pulling aboard a thirteen-foot great white shark they would kill but not keep.

As his replacement, Andre was a solid man of decent height and weight. He preferred keeping to himself. Partly because while he spoke fluent French and English, unlike the rest of the crew, Andre did not speak the Portuguese language. He was left out of most conversations. But Andre was a competent hand who pulled his weight. Captain Matos considered replacing him with a fellow countryman when he found the right guy. No luck so far. The captain remained suspicious of anyone not of Portuguese lineage. He'd soon learn why.

41

Captain Matos had committed to memory every one of Canada's strict fisheries laws, even though many changed from year to year. He had better, since he fished their waters. And this trip was to be no exception. As required by Canadian law, he kept his EEZ permit number at the ready to notify the Canadian Coast Guard and their DFO twenty-four hours prior to his arrival in the designated but invisible EEZ boundary 12 miles offshore.

He also was poised to notify them again no later than twenty-four hours before departing Canadian waters. Yes, he knew the laws, but that didn't mean he'd abide by them... not all of them, anyway.

The *Miss Guided One* provisionally planned to make port in St. John's, Newfoundland, to take on fuel and provisions for a trip out to the *Flemish Cap*. But only if that became necessary. *The Cap* was the aptly

GK JURRENS & TOM KASPRZAK

named plateau atop an underwater mountain, making for an area of shallow water in the deep North Atlantic. The Cap bore 300 nautical miles east of St. John's. Captain Matos also acquired extra fuel before leaving Gloucester, filling a pair of 300-gallon bladders that he ordered his crew to secure against *Miss G's* hull sides over her gunwales (pronounced *gŭn'əls*).

But before he got underway from Gloucester, he received an unwelcome call from the US National Marine Fisheries Service Supervising Agent in Charge, a Randy Gerrard. "Captain, you may not leave port without an NMFS monitor aboard. He'll be there at sun-up to meet your boat."

Matos protested. Gerrard informed the captain. "Sir, no monitor, no fishing. It is that simple."

Fuck! Now a college yuppie aboard during my operation? They are always snot-nosed college kids, these monitors. He wiped the sweat from his brow. Yeah, he'd take the kid and hide him from anything important. Either way, he was coming aboard. No choice. *Although heading offshore on a working vessel? Risky business.* But disappearing an NMFS employee? *That generates too much heat. No, I cannot afford that. Shit, shit, shit!* This guy would be as welcome as a skunk at Sunday morning mass.

This was going to be a long trip, perhaps up to two weeks. Shorter if the fish showed up in strength. But only his Portuguese crew members were privy to their other mission. His new guy, Gagnon, remained clue-

184

less. He didn't even speak *língua materna—the mother language!*

The vessel was now loaded with fuel, provisions, ice, and bait. She prepared to depart after checking in with the harbormaster and corroborating his float plan. *Now to wait for this punk kid.*

As of a year ago, Captain Afonso Matos *owned* this boat at last, after 19 hard years at the helm. He'd mortgaged his house to realize that dream. But now, with the end of long-lining looming, he'd formulated a new strategy. He knew his next score would be his last, forever settling him into a comfortable future.

Besides, the profit margin on swords shrank more each year with all this damn legislation, as well as diminishing catches. There was no longer any wiggle room. Not like the old days.

He smiled, but no one within sight had a clue why.

42

Sergeant Sam Travis arrived home. *How do I tell Kate and Brian about another operation starting on the coast in 48 hours? For at least nine days?* Larry wasn't fooling anyone. A drug smuggling operation this sophisticated involved dangerous people. On top of that, the DEA asking for state agency help on a case this big? Unprecedented. Especially when sharing a spotlight is not in the feds' DNA.

Sam spotted Kate's SUV in the open garage's shadows and Brian bounced a basketball in the driveway, aiming for the hoop Sam installed last Christmas. Brian had told his mom he wanted to play like his dad. He'd seen some of the old newspaper clippings with the box scores. Travis shot double figures most every game.

"Hi, son!"

"Hey, Dad. Wanna shoot around some?"

"Can't right now, son, but I need to talk to you and Mom about something important."

A disappointed boy frowned and flung his basketball out onto the overgrown lawn in frustration. Sam went to him. Draped his right arm over his shoulders as they walked up the steps to the porch and into the house.

Sounding upbeat, Sam hollered, "Hi, hon!"

Kate returned the greeting. He read her like a book. Something was up. He asked, "How was your day?"

"Interesting and disheartening."

"How so?" The heat of their scrutiny radiated off both of them in waves.

"You've got another case coming up soon. A big one, right? *Another* one away from home?"

"You've heard." He wasn't asking. She was telling.

"We all need to sit down and talk about this. Larry Jamison called me at work and gave me a heads-up about some of it. I can't say I'm thrilled. Working for the DEA isn't a small matter, Sam. This is a dangerous case isn't it?"

"That potential is there, but Larry promised his personal over-watch. And the DEA will watch over the op, too. Back-up will be around just in case."

From Kate's experience as an investigative journalist, she appreciated how dangerous such ops tended to be, over-watch notwithstanding. "Back-up? How far away? And how long to get to you?"

Sam thought to himself, *This woman is no dummy. Be straight with her.* "Yes, they'd be a ways away. I'll have to use my best judgement, keep a low profile, and not cause any commotion or suspicion."

"Pretty weak case you're making here, Sam." Brian sat and listened, with only the slightest frown on his early-teen forehead.

"Just being straight with you. I know this is tough on you two, *and* on me. Yeah, the job, the job.... Both of you know it's what I do, and I do it better than most. When the bell rings I answer it. I have the option to decline. I will not accept it unless *both* of you accept it with me. That's asking a lot. I love you both like crazy and there will be a break once this one is done. Larry gave his word." He felt out of breath belting out these short declaratives.

Kate walked up to Sam and slowly put her arms around him. "I love you Sam Travis. If you're convinced you must do it, then do it. I won't be angry at you, but neither will I be happy about it. But you must promise us you'll come home in one piece, not in a casket, or lost at sea. We need you. Understand, mister?"

"Yeah, babe. I promise. Scout's honor."

Brian squeaked, "You're not a Boy Scout, Dad. I don't like this one bit. But if Mom agrees, then I'll have to be the man around the house for a little while longer."

No, Sam, you don't deserve either of these wonderful people! "Guys, I am *so* grateful for your understanding. I need to call Larry. Then, we'll do dinner. Any requests?"

As if Brian had forgotten the serious discussion they'd concluded seconds earlier, he shouted, "Burgers and dogs on the grill!"

Sam looked at Kate. Hugged her close. Everyone grinned. Then they scooped up Brian into a group hug.

Later that night, Sam packed. He was to meet with DEA's SAC Sawyer and Captain Jamison the next morning for a full briefing in Rockport. This was to be his last night at home for a while. Tomorrow night he'd bivouac in Rockport. He tucked in Brian and did his best to reassure him. His son, unconvinced, hugged his father close and hard. *My boy's getting strong.* Sam did the same. Told him he loved him and he'd be back to being a father after this op.

Kate said she was turning in early so she could send him off in the morning. In bed, they held each other, more like clinging, expressing their love without words.

Five am came too darn soon. The goodbyes were tough.

43

Sergeant Sam Travis picked up Captain Jamison in Framingham on the way to the coast, and they headed to the DEA's Rockport substation. They shared a quiet ride. They met SAC Sawyer in his office. What started as an awkward conversation turned to business in a heartbeat. Sawyer handed a new high-tech encrypted satellite phone to Sam. "Let nothing happen to this, Sergeant. I pulled teeth to acquire it on such short notice."

"Thanks Agent Sawyer. Show me how to use it? And while you're in a giving mood, how about you scare up a small voice-activated recorder with a long battery life? That'll come in handy."

"Anything else?" Sawyer's respect had quickly eroded into sarcasm and was anything but subtle. Sam thought, *Yeah, this guy is no pushover.*

Larry asked Sawyer to program both their

numbers on speed dial since Travis probably wouldn't have the time to search for or dial numbers. Both men assured Sam they'd answer no matter the time of day.

Sawyer also assured Travis of over-flights with private unmarked aircraft on an irregular schedule to keep an eye out. As he programmed both his and Larry's numbers into Sam's new phone, he added, "There's a GPS locator built in, so we'll know your location. Do not needlessly endanger yourself, Sergeant. But get as much intel as possible."

They shook hands and both of the big wigs wished Sam luck.

"Roger, that, guys."

44

Dawn blossomed above a pinkish-red horizon. *Red sky at night, sailor's delight. Red sky in the morning, sailors take warning.* Yes, a storm had developed offshore on their intended north-northwesterly course. But Captain Matos aboard the *Miss G* remained undaunted. They'd get underway within the hour.

They'd taken on extra fuel, so no need to stop in St. John's, after all. He'd need to make a fast working run to 75 nautical miles southwest of the Flemish Cap, the rendezvous point. There'd be plenty of fuel to fish for a few days, make his rendezvous, and return to Gloucester in eight or nine days. That was the plan, anyway. A weathered seafarer like Captain Matos knew plans offshore often went awry.

And a light load of fish? Better fuel economy and a safe return to harbor sooner. Captain Matos felt pretty good despite the setback of NMFS forcing a monitor aboard—a fed. *Fucking Marine Fisheries sticks me with this fruitcake at the last minute? Bastardos!* Nothing he and his crew couldn't handle.

The brightening sky revealed a hard-looking man, not a college kid, boarding on their port side carrying a briefcase. Dressed in jeans, a flannel shirt, and a windbreaker, he also lugged a sailor's duffel over his left shoulder. At the top of the gangplank, he asked Antonio Sousa, first mate, for permission to come aboard.

Sousa snarled, "Can't stop ya, so get your ass aboard. We're castin' off as soon as you get below." Sousa looked up at a much taller man standing nearby as he singled up a midship mooring line to prep for getting underway. "Chacci here'll show you to your cabin." The mate kept his eyes on the newcomer, but nodded toward the big guy. "Chacci, you get 'im squared away and hustle back up here quick-time."

With a nod to his shipmate, Jose Belo, a.k.a. Chacci, looked this newcomer up and down, spit over the rail with obvious disgust, and to lose a cheek full of tobacco juice that'd outlived its usefulness. He hustled forward. As this Nimfy fish counter followed Chacci, Sousa thought, *This Frank Murdock sure 'nuff ain't no college kid. Almost as big as Chacci, and that's sayin' somethin'. Broad shoulders 'n carries himself like a seafarin' man. Why he still a fuckin' monitor at his age? He should be inside some little office at Nimfy HQ starin' at some computer screen. He a threat? Mebbee. We see, sure 'nuff.*

Sousa decided he'd watch this hard-looking stranger.

Sergeant Sam Travis now served as a Federal Police Officer for the Drug Enforcement Administration. His federal designation was temporary for this op to ensure he held cross-state and admiralty jurisdiction. For this assignment as an NMFS operative, his cover name was Frank Murdock, the name of his actual previous EPO partner. Frank was killed a year earlier by a crew of nasty wildlife poachers. Using Frank's identity offered Sam the opportunity for a small sense of poetic justice. Bad guys killed Frank. *What if a Frank Murdock took down these other bad guys?*

This Chacci hadn't bothered to introduce himself. Brought Sam to his cabin, one level below and forward of the weather deck. The only natural light entered through a ten-inch porthole constructed of heavily tarnished brass on the starboard bulkhead as it curved toward the bow. Its green patina made it look older than it probably was.

A single naked sixty-watt incandescent bulb near the center of the small compartment's overhead provided useful artificial light. The cabin also featured a tiny sink with a six-inch square unbreakable plastic mirror behind it. Its optical clarity left much to be desired.

Sam, a.k.a. Frank, figured the quarters to be about six-foot by eight-foot, narrower forward, with a ceiling that tickled his hair if he didn't slouch, and he needed to dodge that damn light bulb so he didn't break it on his forehead. Definitely not the Ritz. He figured he was near the fo'c's'le (pronounced *fōk'səl*), the crew's quarters close to the vessel's bow—the front of the boat.

Sam stowed his gear before searching for a place to hide his service weapon. He used the knuckle of the middle finger on his left hand to tap the bulkheads— the walls—searching for a hollow spot. It took a while, but he found a loose tongue-in-groove panel beneath the porthole where some rot allowed him to pry loose a foot-long section of paneling with his multi-purpose pocket knife. Tore out a few bits of matted and moldy insulation. Tucked in his pistol and pushed the panel back into place. It was a tight pressure fit. A perfect spot.

Sam then scanned the compartment for anything that might raise suspicion: he'd leave his voice-activated recorder out in the open. Just a tool used by a harmless Nimfy monitor to record notes; no badges, only a thin wallet with $200, his picture ID from NMFS, and a false passport in case they'd go ashore in Canada. Solid cover.

His somewhat bulky satellite phone was another

matter—not easy to conceal, and he didn't want to risk getting it confiscated. Sam looked around and saw no easy solution. Grabbed the long side of his bunk's mattress that rested against the bulkhead. He lifted it toward him, and with his knife he cut a slit in the center of the cheap mattress's side just long enough. Pulled out some stuffing, and buried the phone deep inside. It wasn't a heavy phone, so even if they tossed his bed, they still might not discover it. But the slit was a chance he'd take.

Before hiding the phone, he performed a successful comms check with SAC Sawyer and Captain Jamison. Tucked the phone into the mattress and straightened it out on top. Too risky to toss that now-extra bit of mattress stuffing and old insulation from his hides out the porthole while alongside the pier. Someone topside might notice. He'd wait till they were underway offshore. For now, he stuffed that shit under his bunk's mattress. Good to go.

Just then, some hollering topside and the engines throttling up signaled they were getting underway. Then came a grinding sound as the boat's side thrusters pushed the boat sideways away from the pier. He'd check out the rest of the boat next.

45

Sam was alone in the galley—the kitchen—which was a small compartment with a trio of large coolers, a small refrigerator, and a large chest freezer cram-packed with the trip's culinary provisions. To Sam's eye, it didn't look like enough food for a five-man crew plus captain, and now a Nimfy monitor, but they'd also eat some of their catch.

A small yellowish-white three-burner alcohol stove looked brownish around the edges, like it had survived more than one cooking fire. It looked as old as the boat. And like the rest of this old tub, had obviously survived some rugged times.

He snooped around several small latched cabinets by the light of a couple of naked sixty-watt bulbs on the overhead. Not romantic. Not meant to be. Every space was filled with something. From the stores, it appeared they'd eat fish, burgers, an occasional steak, and linguica with Portuguese bread, butter, bacon, boiled potatoes, and eggs. Tightly wrapped sandwiches were piled high in the fridge. Sam knew there'd be nothing wet in them like mayo or ketchup, or they'd be mush in two days.

Cooking duties on most boats similar to this, depending on the vessel, rotated among the crew with each featuring their own specialty. Sam suspected this crew did the same. Of course, meals served depended on sea conditions. Fishing ops and extra lumpy seas prohibited meals. He suspected that sometimes, the only available food would be pre-warmed soup sealed in Thermos bottles *before* a storm hit.

Two hours later, the entire crew, less the captain, ate the first night's meal together in the small compartment adjacent to the galley. They called it the *mess*. Sam introduced himself. Nobody paid attention or seemed to give a shit. So they ate.

Then, the bitching started. Someone threw a piece of food, then another. Sam stood up from the small but heavy wooden table that was bolted to the deck and pressed his back against the bulkhead. He had no interest in participating in such bullshit. Besides, he could barely understand a word. He didn't speak more than a few words of Portuguese.

It stopped when Belo—Chacci—got hit in the face with a slice of linguica pie. First Mate Sousa slammed a razor-sharp cleaver into the solid maple tabletop, narrowly missing a couple of fingers. "Clean this shit up and get to your bunks." The men lost out on finishing their dinner, retiring more hungry than not, and more pissed than hungry. It seemed the tone of the voyage had been established.

On the way back to his compartment, Sam noticed a large, first-aid kit up against the midship *ladder*, a.k.a. interior stairwell. A latched metal canister, marked with a large Red Cross, showed its age with its yellowed-white exterior. He snapped open the latches to poke around. The well-supplied kit included a printed list of prescription drugs kept onboard. They were under separate lock and key.

A boat's captain was usually well-versed in treating the most common wounds and injuries. Stitches, sprains, head injuries, removing hooks from various parts of the body, as well as treating back and muscle injuries were common on working vessels. This wasn't a humanitarian consideration. The loss of one man could determine the difference between a productive trip and a bust.

Carlos Almeida, the boat's engineer, was an expert on fixing most anything aboard the *Miss G*. He knew everything about the boat's hydraulics, electrical systems, especially the captain's most crucial electronic chart plotters, radar, and weather forecasting gear. This included the critical INMARSAT, or the International Maritime Satellite Organization communications device. INMARSAT was the precursor to commercial satellite weather communications services, which were new to the civilian market. They were still too costly for the boat's meager budget. Besides, the older INMARSAT worked fine, but Carlos found it necessary to tweak it occasionally. Carlos was proud of his considerable responsibility aboard the *Miss G*.

Also a matter of pride, Antonio Sousa knew the *Miss G* couldn't run smoothly without his knowledge and influence. His was close to the captain's. When Captain Matos was in his quarters, Sousa commanded the vessel. On the *Miss G*, they called Sousa by his last name. But Matos was *captain* or *sir*.

Sam continued his survey of the vessel. At the end of a short hallway heading aft from his compartment, he made a U-turn to descend a short flight of steps, more like a four-foot ladder with railings, into the hold area where they kept their catch. The holds comprised a configuration of multiple bins with bulkheads between them that ascended all the way to the overhead.

That partitioned them off into various rectangles accessed by latched hatches down here, but were also accessed via overhead hatches that opened to the deck. Most of these bins were six feet wide, eight feet long, and eight feet high. Several smaller partitions appeared to be four-foot cubes. He imagined that's how they'd separate swords from their secondary catch of cod, haddock, and pollock.

They reserved larger bins for their primary catch of swordfish and tuna. Someone had secured two of those larger bins with shiny new locks and hasps. He'd noticed they secured the deck hatches to those holds similarly. Sam wondered why that was necessary. Ice chutes ensured all fish in each hold were easily and thoroughly iced down. *No wonder it's chilly down here.*

When Sam turned around on the grated walkway between the port and starboard holds, there was Jose Belo—Chacci. The big man's bulk filled the narrow walkway behind Sam, between him and the ladder up and out.

In every vessel, a crew member's physical prowess largely defined the boat's pecking order. Sam suspected such a defining moment would come, just not so soon.

Chacci bellowed, "Waddaya doin down 'ere?"

Sam carried his notebook and clipboard in his right hand. He didn't shout, or bluster, but stated, "My job. None of which is your business." Sam needed to establish himself. As good a time as any. "Back off so I can pass, whatever the fuck your name is."

Chacci then used his index finger to poke Sam in the chest with each word. "This is our boat and everything that goes on here *is* our business."

Sam looked down at the finger poking his flannel shirt. Each poke was a mini-punch. He thought, *Easy enough to grab it and snap it.* But he was certain the entire crew would hate him even more for disabling an important part of their small work force.

They stood nose to nose in the narrow passageway, invading each other's space. Sam snapped his head back and then forward in one lightning motion. Medium force. Solid contact between the bone of his forehead and the soft cartilage of this asshole's nose, busting several blood vessels. A measured response. Before the big man figured out what had happened, he was clutching his already-gushing nose.

With the stench of rum on his breath, he charged Sam, who deftly side-stepped the bruiser. Didn't even drop his clipboard or notebook. Tripped him and gave him a push. Hard. Because of his own forward momentum, Chacci went down face first onto the grated-steel decking. He jumped right back up and wound up for a big punch. Sam was ready. Suddenly, Sousa bounded down the few steps into the hold area behind Sam and shouted, "What the fuck is going on down here?" Chacci froze, mid-charge... in... fear?

Sam said, "Just a small misunderstanding. We're working it out."

Sousa pointed to Chacci. "You! Get back on deck and do what you're supposed to be doing. I'll handle this."

Dripping blood from both nostrils, Chacci dropped both arms, letting the blood run down the front of his already soiled shirt. He shoved Sam aside and growled, "We ain't done, Murdock."

"Anytime, Josephine," insulting the big man, showing no fear. Or anger. He then shrugged at the first mate.

Sousa hissed at Sam, "You ain't here to dance or make friends. You'd be wise to stay clear of him when his blood's up, senhor."

"His blood isn't *up*, it's *out*, all over him. I was doing my job. Got assaulted and defended myself. End of story."

"There's something about you that tells me you're more'n a fish counter, senhor. Am I right?"

Sam projected a simple air of casual confidence. "NMFS hired me after I retired from the Navy. That's it. I don't take shit from anybody."

Sousa asked, "What rank? Officer or enlisted?"

"Enlisted. E-8. Ship's weapons specialist. 20 years."

"What weapons?"

"Sorry, classified."

"I, too, spent time aboard ship. We were a small Navy, but well-trained. Served ten years. Watch yourself, Senhor Murdock. Unpredictable things happen on a ship, as you well know. We're done here."

Sam nodded. With that, Sousa stepped aside as Sam passed. He followed Sam up the two short flights to the weather deck aft.

Won't take long for the rest of the crew to hear news of the 'wimpy fish counter.' Sam smirked.

46

The crew sometimes caught lobsters in a small drag net and did not return them to the sea. They'd remove the claws and tails to be stored in a secret spot later to be divvied up for a few delicious meals after making port. They'd scrub the female egg-bearing lobsters of their eggs.

But they didn't hold a license to take *any* lobster, much less eggers. If caught, Matos would lose his license to operate in both Canadian and US waters. That's why the crews exercised extreme care with these illegal lobsters. Risky practice, but they took them anyway.

Of course, Sam discovered this secret, knowing a lot more about lobsters than he did two weeks ago, and the crew knew he knew. If Sam reported this violation, he was messing with the livelihood of the captain and the entire crew. Sam smirked at his own fatalistic attitude, but with 'gallows humor.' *Oh, what the hell. One more motive to toss my ass over the rail. Add it to the list.*

The fish had to be sorted by species and size, then gutted, gilled, and bled before burying them in ice. Incidental by-catches were tossed overboard, leaving a trail of death and destruction in *Miss G's* wake. Sharks loved the vile longliner practice. All Sam could do was record and report. And that he would.

47

In 1944, during World War II, a massive typhoon hit a US fleet of warships. Some called it Halsey's Storm. They named it after the admiral who pushed through it instead of navigating around it. Its real name was Typhoon Cobra.

The sea claimed three US destroyers—the *Spence*, the *Hickok,* and the *Maddox*—leaving few survivors. Two other destroyers—the *Hull* and the *Monaghan*—suffered such damage they became useless for combat. That massive storm either destroyed or took nine ships out of action. Winds of 195 MPH and 80- to 100-foot waves made rescue efforts impossible.

This little chunk of history crossed Sam's mind. Not because the weather was bad, but because it soon would be. The North Atlantic had its own history of not disappointing such pessimism.

Sam returned to his bunk after the shit show of the evening meal. *Don't anyone lift a finger to assist this fish counter in any way* was the unspoken rule of the boat, at least unspoken to him. They had to know the witnessing and pictures he'd take of their everyday by-catch practices would someday play a role in closing the longline industry in the Atlantic. *No small wonder they hate me. I'm messing with their livelihood.*

He peered out of his little porthole at the gentle swells sparkling under a waxing moon. Overwhelmed by fatigue, Sam could barely keep his eyes open. In the twilight before sleep, he thought of Kate and Brian at home in the mountains without him. And he was without them. *Like we're worlds apart.*

After sleep's slow arrival, morning appeared way too fast... and hard. The large and heavy 72-footer shrunk in God's angry ocean as the calm evening gave way to intensifying swells before dawn. The ship's engines wound higher RPMs to combat the ever-increasing rage of Mother Ocean. As the boat's twin propellers found more air than water after cresting a mountainous wave, they cavitated and the engines revved ever closer to their redline RPMs.

Either Captain Matos or First Mate Sousa had deployed the vessel's stabilizers to slow their roll and combat *Miss G's* yaw as much as possible. Better, but still mighty uncomfortable. Sam bolted upright in his bunk. *Yup, the North Atlantic never disappoints.* The little ship heaved as if the sea were rejecting her, like a bad organ transplant. He hadn't undressed, so he combed his short hair back with both hands. Grabbed the tiny sink two feet away for stability, pulled himself vertical, stood, and wedged himself between the sink and the bulkhead to its right. He splashed some water over his face and brushed his teeth.

His right hip banged the bulkhead as they topped the crest of each mammoth wave and slid down the other side. Sam hung onto an overhead grab rail with his right hand. He brushed his teeth with his left.

There's a reason ship builders plant these grab rails everywhere. He pocketed his voice recorder and tucked his newly issued laptop computer firmly under his right arm. That kept his left hand—his dominant hand—free. The old saying suggests *One hand for yourself, the other for the ship.* Especially when the weather kicked up.

Sam headed toward the helm up in the pilothouse, on the loftiest deck of the boat. Caught some heavy spray as he wobbled up the long flight of exterior stairs above the weather deck on the starboard side. He entered through the pilothouse's starboard door and slammed it behind him against the stiffening wind. Matos stood there alone, wedged between his helm seat behind him and the boat's controls close in front. "Morning, Captain. Getting sloppy out."

"Sloppy? You ain't seen sloppy. Know how to read a weather chart?"

"Yes, I do."

"Well, you can see we're in for a 36-hour roller coaster ride. If you puke on any part of my boat you'll lick it up." Sam thought, *Make me.* He said, "No, I don't get seasick. How rough will it get?"

"40 to 50 knots out of the northwest, almost a beam sea." That was the worst, as a beam sea caused a boat to roll from side to side. Skippers often changed course to avoid taking waves directly from the side— from abeam—at all costs, where they're most vulnerable. Sam wondered why they weren't changing course... for 36 frickin' hours? Matos continued, "Even with stabilizers deployed, that'll toss us around like a fuckin' beach ball. Seas to 25 feet, probably more. See how close those isobars are? And they're getting tighter."

That meant rapid *changes* in barometric pressure, so the storm *was* gonna worsen. Sam clutched one of the ever-present overhead grab rails to steady himself on his short wobble to the weather station. He pretended to look at both a paper chart on the high table and the radar screen next to the table. The single-sideband receiver squawked large-scale weather reports. So did the shorter-range marine VHF receiver. Matos also tuned in to one of the local NOAA weather reporting stations. They were still close enough to shore. Farther out, they'd lose those channels.

Plus, the brass barometer bolted to the bulkhead behind the nav station had plunged to near historic lows for this region. The captain focused on his various sources of weather information as well as on the sea conditions through the pilothouse windows with obvious concern. His eyes darted forward before he peered at the waves outside the pilothouse's side windows. *Yeah, he's nervous about this one. Pressure this low is hurricane-like.* Not gonna be the perfect storm, but maybe close to it.

The captain, obviously a competent offshore skipper, even though he was an asshole, needed as comprehensive a picture of his immediate world as possible. For all their sakes. Sam drifted his thoughts back to the 1944 Halsey Storm.

Sam ensured Matos still stared out the forward windows toward their windward side seeking to spot the rogue wave that would ruin their pre-dawn roller coaster ride. He needed intel. So, he wedged his voice recorder under the back edge of the chart table, next to the bulkhead. Without changing the direction of his gaze and both hands clutching the helm, preparing to override the autopilot at a moment's notice, Matos snarled, "Stay below deck. No fish for you to count anyway, so just stay out of our fuckin' way. Got it?"

"Yeah. Got it."

.   .   .

Sam wormed his wet way back toward his bunk, bouncing off both bulkheads in the narrow passageway en route. With only one hand free because of that frickin' laptop, he'd reach for the next grab rail as soon as he released the previous one.

Once he got to his cabin, soaked but otherwise unscathed, he plopped down onto his marginally comfortable bunk and hooked up his lee cloth. That's a heavy canvas sheet that appeared from under his mattress. He hooked its upper corners to the overhead to prevent being tossed out of his berth while he slept, *if* he slept. Tried to rest as best he could.

The howling wind whistled as it sang a siren's song through the boat's wire rigging. It increased in both volume and pitch on its way to a crescendo. The boat danced to the ocean's music as the waves all around swelled and broke over them when their vessel was not tunneling under them. *Yeah, a fuckin' roller coaster ride, alright.*

48

Matos cursed to himself. *40 to 50 knots, my ass.* He glanced at his instruments. The anemometer on the pilothouse's roof sent a signal to his panel. *Sure as shit, 60 and building with higher gusts!* He flipped a toggle to disable the autopilot, spun the wheel to starboard, putting the waves more off the starboard bow. Didn't want to, because that 30 degree turn to head more *into* the monstrous waves took him off course to his rendezvous for which he dared not be late. But better late than broached... and dead. The boat's motion settled down a bit. *Goddamned weathermen. They never get it right. Easier to blame a human than a fickle Mother Nature. That would be bad luck, a sure.*

He reviewed in his mind what he knew about wave action. It's how he kept his knowledge fresh. *Wave height is driven by at least three things: wind velocity, water depth and fetch. That's the uninterrupted distance the wind travels over the open sea, not slowed down by islands or other land masses. The farther offshore, the longer the fetch, and fueled by higher winds pushing over deep water? Fuck!*

Despite his decades of seagoing experience, his nerves frayed. Hard as hell to hear himself think over the screaming freight train sound of howling winds and his engines winding ever closer to their upper limits with tons of green water slamming into them. It bashed non-stop against the hull, the pilothouse bulk-heads, and her stout windows, three decks above the weather deck.

The entire vessel shuddered with each wave taken over the rail, or after the bow ascended skyward, as it slammed down into the next trough between waves. He thought, *It's gonna be a bitch of a ride, no matter what I do. But it'll be worth it. If we make it. Yeah, we'll make it. Might still die if I'm late.*

No matter how many times Matos navigated hellish storms, he'd never get used to it. He guessed the waves had mounted to at least 25 feet already. *Shit!*

A wave larger than the rest did its damndest to jerk Sam out of his berth. *Thank goodness for this lee cloth.* The rest of the crew had to be lying low, too. No walking around in this shit. It still blew non-stop well into the following evening. Too rough to cook. Instead, sandwiches flew out of the fridge and found their way to the crew's bunks. White bread, baloney, and mustard with a slice of American cheese. But it was food—barely—and Sam was hungry. He'd had nothing to eat and little to drink all day. Even too rough to brew coffee. Baloney sandwiches never tasted so delicious.

These waves didn't feel like water. More like hardened steel that had to be cracked by the *Miss G's* knife-edged bow. She'd defeat these barriers by cleaving them with speed and an optimal angle of attack. Taken broadside, they'd tear the *Miss G* apart. Thankfully, Matos had changed course.

Sam realized Matos was a damn decent skipper. But no man had ever conquered the sea. He'd only tolerated by it, but only if he was sharp enough and his will strong enough and his gear stout enough. Even then, the sea tempts and lures and dares man to challenge her. She lulls him into complacency until he discovers she is *still* his master.

49

The weather abated by daybreak 30 hours later aboard the *Miss G*. Captain and crew inspected the entire vessel topsides and down below for loss or damage. Neither was abundant. Of particular importance? Checking for leaks in the bilges, exposed or separated hull plates from the incessant hammering. And to ensure every pump still did its job of expelling the inevitable incursion of seawater. That was business as usual.

Everyone ate a huge breakfast without speaking. The day dragged, but despite the still lumpy weather, they made excellent time toward the coordinates where the captain said they'd find fish. No one knew how he knew. But if he said so, they'd be there.

Sam returned to his compartment and fooled around with his new computer. He needed to learn its software well enough to enter the statistical data for his cover job. Boring, but necessary.

They had crossed the half-way mark—the point of no return, as it's called—to south of the Flemish Cap despite the horrible weather. The *Miss G* now made a respectable 14 knots. The captain was pushing the old tub hard, burning a lot of fuel. Thankfully, the huge fuel bladders hanging over both rails survived the storm. They'd need that fuel. *I wonder what's driving Matos' sense of urgency?*

Barring complications, Matos instructed the crew to be ready for the first set—that is, to fish—by the following evening. Sam checked his camera and his NMFS logbook. He dragged his foul weather gear from his duffel. It would be wet and slippery on deck. He'd stay out of the way, but he'd record and photograph the actual number and relative size of each swordfish caught, as well as the by-catch by species. He'd also tally if they were released alive or dead. His Nimfy cover job. This would annoy the crew, as it should, and while he found this work gratifying, he was there to uncover a possible drug smuggling operation. Meanwhile, he'd be damn good at his cover job, too.

The crew was already prepared for the first *set* — for deploying their longlines. They lashed hooks onto spare drop lines (snoods). They stretched and measured lengths of leader to the proper length. And they readied an array of deck gear for managing the huge twin spools of line near the transom—the back of the boat.

The Cap was shallower than the continental shelf surrounding it. History and the captain's log book taught them that fishing to a depth of 150 feet made for the best catch there. Sam paid close attention to the deckhands' activities.

Chacci sported a large band-aid around his swollen nose, but worked like a plow horse. Andre Gagnon, the Québécois, intrigued him. He hadn't spoken to him yet. He knew what to do and did it with great efficiency. He moved with purpose and confidence. Kept his head down. Sam wished he had access to police databanks to look up Andre and the rest of the crew. He sensed something different about Andre besides his nationality.

A twin engine Cessna flew high above the vessel. No one but Sam suspected it was a DEA overflight. He tucked that away for now. Chow time.

The entire crew, except the captain, who ate and slept alone, bunched into the small mess. Linguica—a fatty and spicy Portuguese sausage made from pork and seasoned with onion, garlic, paprika, and other spices—served as their primary source of protein. When Eduardo's turn in the galley arrived, he vowed to bake linguica into a Shepherd's Pie facsimile. Boiled potatoes, but no veggies, and plenty of fresh Portuguese bread and butter? All delicious. Each crew member received his daily ration of two half-liter bottles of Portuguese Madeira wine. Sam was not a crew member.

After dinner, darkness approached with startling swiftness. Sam stared at the now-slick-smooth sea, a remarkable contrast to the previous night's ferocious gale. With a partially overcast sky and a half-moon peeking out from behind lacy, high-altitude cirrus clouds, *Miss G* glided along like a wraith on her way to an ignominious fate. A curious pod of dolphins rode her bow. Everyone retired early. Sam set his watch alarm for 0200 hours. He wanted to observe the ship's nighttime protocol regarding lookouts or unusual activity.

At 0200, however, Sam had already been glancing at his watch for ten minutes. Pressed the button to disable his alarm before it sounded. Dressed in black, he smeared a little camo grease on his face for subtle concealment. If he got spotted in bright light, his face would just look dirty.

Sam crept out of his cabin with a small but powerful red-lens penlight that he left extinguished until needed. He took shelter in the shadows of the dim passageway outside his cabin. Saw nothing unusual or out of order. Climbed the short ladder aft and up to the weather deck for a quick walk-around. He crept around nets, lines, hatchways, various fishing tackle, and lots of hardware, much of which he didn't recognize. He spotted a man, too dark to ID, the designated lookout, as required by maritime law.

The vessel also met lighting requirements for nighttime running. They displayed a white masthead light above the superstructure, a white stern light aft, and one more white light forward, but not at the bow. The usual side lights—red to port and green to starboard—were also required by International Navigation Rules. When engaged in fishing, they'd require a different light configuration.

Sam's natural night vision worked well, leveraging the boat's lights and the dim moon glow once his eyes had adjusted. Now, for some unknown reason, Sam's sixth sense jumped him to high alert. He didn't hear or see anyone, but he felt a presence. Then, 25 feet away, Sam spotted the toe of a boot visible in the hatchway that led down to the crew's quarters forward. Another man, for sure, attempting to conceal himself. Sam waited him out.

After a long count, the boot disappeared without a sound. *Had someone spotted me? Or... what are the chances someone else is out here besides the lookout after a hard day's work on deck? Slim to none, that's what.* Options raced through Sam's mind until he decided to take no action. Not enough to go on, but he sensed something suspicious... or... dangerous.

He crept in a slow rhythm, leveraging the natural shadows from the deck overhangs and sundry equipment. Made his way back down to his compartment. As he was about to open his cabin door, he caught sight of something shiny in the dim light. He noticed a sturdy, brand-new brass hasp on the *outside* of his compartment door, minus a lock. *Huh. Okaaay....*

Someone had installed that hasp without waking him before his little topside sortie. Wasn't there after evening chow, and he hadn't noticed it leaving his cabin. Probably installed by Almeida under captain's orders. *Maybe because of the incident with Chacci?* He stowed his gear and tried to sleep. That took an hour's worth of tossing and turning in the tiny berth. He wondered, *Who else would be sneaking around on this boat besides me?*

50

Miss G steamed northeast at close to her maximum hull speed. Captain Matos notified the Canadian authorities of his intent to fish near the *Flemish Cap*. He'd radioed them the info they required, and ordered the crew to prepare to set as soon as they reached their coordinates. They arrived by evening and baited hooks as they deployed 20 miles of line from the eight-foot-high reel at the starboard transom. All hands busied themselves with their assigned tasks.

It took three hours to set the last flashing marker buoy, which had a transmitter to broadcast its position. The captain marked it on his chart plotter screen. Those buoys also warned other vessels in the area against crossing the line and severing it with their propellers.

Now, they'd enjoy a period of waiting and resting before the morning haul as they now continued to steam on a course of the captain's choosing while they fished. Matos had slowed to eight knots, which seemed slow for swords, the crew said. It was certain to be a long and exhausting workday tomorrow. Sam took another trip on deck to spot the crew member who had been creeping about at 0200 hours two nights earlier.

At 0100, Sam left his cabin, once again in full stealth mode, dressed in his black outfit complete with his black woolen watch cap. His intense demeanor demanded he dial in every sense, perceptive to the slightest movement or sound. He rounded a corner aft of *Miss G's* pilothouse, where it met the weather deck. There he encountered Chacci amidship leaning against a bulkhead with a rum bottle in his hand.

The big man turned with a sluggish motion. "The fuck are you doin' up 'ere?"

"Getting some fresh air. Cabin's stuffy."

"Dressed up like that? Bullshit. I knew there was something 'bout you I din't like." Sam knew he looked like a damn cat burglar. In retrospect, stealth might have been less important than normalcy.

He looked up into the big man's soggy eyes and asked, "What now?"

Chacci was quick, even when drunk. He punched Sam in the solar plexus. Knocked the wind out of him.

Sam crumpled to the deck with one hand on the railing, holding him up in a kneeling position. Chacci got ready to kick him in the face. But Sam caught his foot and twisted. Chacci lost his balance and crashed down onto the steel deck.

Sam scrambled back to his feet fast and prepared to hit this goon with a left cross. He connected, but not as solid as he'd hoped, or needed. Chacci charged, wrapping Sam in his gorilla arms and pinned him with his face inches from the stench of this drunk's rum-soaked breath. His eyes glistened white... well, more of a rheumy yellow, like his bared yellow teeth.

The man was scary strong. Chacci continued charging forward, pushing Sam backward. They hit the port rail with force. *I need to break this guy's hold, or I'm dead.* He slid his arms inside, with his elbows almost touching, and up to Chacci's face, far enough to jam his thumbs into both of the drunk's eye sockets. After he worked the fingertips of both hands toward the back of this guy's melon head, Sam squeezed with every ounce of strength he still mustered, driving his thumbs deeper into the monster's eyes. Chacci howled in pain.

The big man tried to slab-hand a punch to the side of Sam's face. In a lightning-fast move, Sam released his hands from Chacci's eyes and dropped to a squat. Grabbed the bruiser's legs, wrapped them up and lifted him off his feet using his back against the bulkhead. In one fluid motion, he flipped the 230-pound rummy over the side. Sam saw the splash, but heard nothing over the thrumming engines and the foaming bow wake. Besides, Chacci had already disappeared into *Miss G's* considerable wake astern.

The man didn't scream for help. But Sam saw naked panic in his face as he descended to his death. He sank below the black water four boat lengths back in wicked turbulence generated by the boat's propeller wash. Chacci was just... gone.

Sam rubbed his rib cage where Chacci had slammed him into the rail. With a quick scan, he surveyed the deck for any witnesses. In the fo'c's'le's entryway shadow, up near the elevated bow, stood Andre Gagnon, staring at Sam. *Shit!* Andre wheeled on his heels and disappeared below without a sound. Sam waited for an enraged crew to emerge and throw *him* overboard. He'd brought his firearm, and kept it ready at his side. But... *nothing happened.*

Puzzled, Sam scanned the deck again before making his way back to his cabin. He'd made sure the nearly empty rum bottle was still on deck. The oval-shaped two-liter wobbled in the gentle wave action, but refused to roll overboard. *Good.*

Behind his locked compartment door, he took stock. *Not much of a lock, here. A single slide bar that a sixteen-year-old could break open with a shoulder shove.* Slipped out of his black clothes, stowed them, wiped the camo grease from his face, neck, and hands, changed into his civvies, and waited. And waited. *Nothing happened.*

He pulled up the t-shirt he'd just thrown on to probe the purple bruise on his left-side rib cage. It was shaped like Chacci's mammoth fist. Another matching bruise on his right anterior torso from being slammed into the railing. No first aid kit in his cabin. *Push through the damn pain.* He recalled one of his favorite lines by Patrick Swayze in the movie *Roadhouse* where the actor played a battered bouncer. He'd said, "Pain don't hurt."

Sam eased back into his bunk. He theorized Chacci had had the night watch and just got drunk while doing so, surrendering to his irrational intoxicated anger. Before he fell asleep to welcome a few nightmares, Sam reminded himself to tend to that hasp.

The vessel's engines wound down from 14 knots to about 6 or 8. It was the time the crew customarily kept busy grabbing breakfast. Sam wasn't there for it. He'd forgotten to set his watch alarm. He'd overslept. *Shit!* A commotion on deck awakened him. He grabbed a jacket and went topside. The captain and four members of the crew were there.

Captain Matos stared into Sam's eyes. "Did you see Chacci last night, Murdock?"

"No, I was in my compartment—sleep of the

GK JURRENS & TOM KASPRZAK

dead." Sam watched Andre, who said nothing. This further puzzled him. He'd make it a point to speak with him.

"We searched the boat and all we came up with was his rum bottle."

"Well, maybe he got sick, leaned over the rail to puke, and...."

Matos interrupted. "Not likely. Chacci loved his rum, but I can't picture him goin' over. It's obvious he's MIA and presumed drowned. Fuck!" Matos swiveled his stare to his remaining crew. "Alright men, we're now down a man and we gotta haul our gear, fill our holds, or no payday. Get to it."

51

Sam returned to his cabin to retrieve his notebook and camera. He tried not to jar his wounds. Barring that, he anticipated a perfect day to snap photos of the by-catch and tally the numbers: mortalities, species, and approximate size.

The giant reel hauled in the heavy line. The close-in marker buoy was first aboard and stowed. Then, the snoods they'd baited the night before began coming in. They unhooked each snood and its attendant flashing buoy from the mainline after bludgeoning each fish with their *thumpers*—like short bats—as they hauled them in, if they weren't already dead. Too dangerous to allow a live fish to thrash around on deck, even if they intended to release them moments later.

Then, Sam watched as one white marlin, a couple of sailfish, and several huge sea turtles get hurled back over the transom or over the side after one of the crew —usually Gagnon—beat their brains in. Some had already expired, but some were killed so they could safely extract their precious gear. Sam took copious photos and recorded it all in his notebook to document this by-catch, the unintentional, undesirable, and unlicensed catch, kill, and release.

The crewmen didn't appreciate Sam's intrusive cataloging and documenting their brutality. *Tough shit, boys.* Men like Sam—Nimfy monitors—were proving that long-lining *was* brutal to creatures of the deep and would shut this practice down someday, like they already had on the west coast and elsewhere.

Sam intercepted their thoughts by observing the naked hatred on their faces: *We're gonna lose our livelihood, and this bureaucratic fish counter is gonna help 'em make that happen!* Plus, the crew was now down a man and had to work even harder. It was likely they blamed Sam for this bad luck, too, irrational as that might be —as far as *they* knew, anyway.

By early afternoon they finished coring 52 swordfish, as well as gilling and bleeding out a dozen tuna. By that same time, they'd released four dozen dead carcasses over the stern. That left a trail of bludgeoned fish and marine mammals floating in their wake... chum for the sharks they hadn't caught and killed. They took a lunch break and repeated the process, replacing bent or lost hooks, retying leaders, and reattaching snoods. By dinner, they prepared to deploy another set.

The captain continued to steam northeast, heading ever closer to the Flemish Cap. The crew took advantage of their downtime by grabbing chow. Burgers with cheese, bacon, fries, and coleslaw. Sam sat at the table with the crew. They still gave him the cold shoulder. He expected that. *Whatever.*

The abusive treatment of monitors by crews had been well-documented. It had almost become a tradition. Most monitors were young college boys who did whatever they were told. Those who resisted received harsher treatment. Like little or no food, and/or physical abuse... it varied by boat. But this was a man's business, not for women or kids. If shit-heel monitors —kids—chose to be aboard? They took it. Sam was no kid. Some crews said the food was only for the crew. *You non-crew wanna eat? Bring your own damn chow.*

As a result of all of this, it became more difficult to find aspiring young biologists willing to be monitors aboard these hard-core commercial boats. But most programs included at least one mandatory trip aboard such a vessel either during their sophomore or junior year at the University of Maine, for example. So far, because of Sam's age, size, and attitude, they hesitated pushing this particular shit-heel too hard.

Clear skies held. A wind freshened out of the southwest. A warm wind like that often indicated the arrival of another front from the northwest in a day or two. They ran a course on the edge of the Gulfstream —a major offshore current that ran along the entire North American coast—where water temps hovered around 70 degrees. A far cry from the waters in the Gulf of Maine where 25 or more degrees colder caused different weather patterns.

This current flowed generally from north to south. If the wind blew from any southerly direction, against that current, the sea got very lumpy very fast. So far, the wind wasn't strong enough to punish them with a nasty *stream slap*.

The ship's horn sounded, and everyone geared up for another set, a well-practiced choreography of men, equipment, and a tolerant sea. Sam marveled at their efficiency. *A hard way to make a buck.* After several more hours of hustling, the set was down for the night, and the crew settled in. They'd begin hauling it back in before the next morning's first light.

By the time the fish started coming aboard, it would be light enough to see. This was too dangerous a job even with an illuminated deck from the brilliant Xenon spotlights mounted high above. Obviously recent upgrades, those lights.

The following morning, their second set produced more swordfish, fewer tuna, and about the same number of turtles, sharks, dolphins, *and* a small pilot whale. They released the whale with a 10/0 J-hook left lodged in the corner of her jaw. That hook would rust, deteriorate, and fall out. Sam recorded it all. He smiled. *Hey, I'm pretty darn good at this Nimfy gig!* The baited 20-mile set disappeared beneath the dark North Atlantic surface, 30 feet behind *Miss G's* transom. But the periodic small orange plastic buoys, each containing battery powered flashers and marking each snood, seem to march off over the horizon.

After the gear had been hauled back in, and Sam finished recording, he needed to speak to the captain. Climbed the exterior starboard ladder—steep stairs—to the pilot house. He found the captain lounging in his commodious chair aft of the helm. Matos turned just his head and grumbled, "Waddaya want?"

"Captain, I'd like permission to use your sat phone to call my office. They expect me to check in every forty-eight hours, and I'd also like to touch base with my wife and son." There was no expectation of privacy, so Sam would talk with the captain listening.

"Alright, but make it short." Sam retrieved the phone from its bracket on the dash forward of the helm so Matos didn't have to reach for it. A sign of respect. Handed it to the captain to punch in the four-digit security code. Sam watched and made a mental note of the code. He didn't want the captain to know he had his own phone. They'd confiscate it until they made port in Gloucester.

Sam called DEA SAC Chuck Sawyer at his private number. He'd taken the time to memorize it before boarding. "Checking in, boss. Everything's fine aboard the *Miss G,* except we lost a crewman at sea. A tragic accident. Recording all info for debriefing upon my return." Matos didn't hear what Sawyer was saying.

After a pause, Sam said, "No sir, the crew is treating me fine. I'll check back with you in forty-eight." Sawyer briefly answered. Sam responded, "Yes sir. Good day."

Then he dialed his home and reached Brian. "Hey, son. Just checking in to see how you and Mom are doing."

Pause.

Sam continued. "Yes, I'm fine and things are going well. Glad everything is good there, too. Where's Mom? Shopping?"

Pause.

"Okay, kiddo. Tell her I called. Remember, you're the man of the house while I'm gone. Gotta go."

Pause.

"Me, too. Bye." Sam signed off and returned the phone to its cradle. He thanked the captain, who grunted something in Portuguese.

Probably called me an asshole.

52

Sam needed some time alone with Andre Gagnon. Something wasn't right about that guy. Why didn't he report that he saw Sam throw Chacci overboard? He ambled down to the weather deck from his overwatch railing aft of the pilothouse and one flight up. He approached Andre. But the other crew members were too close. Instead, he'd wander below and leave a note on his bunk. But where?

There were no locks on the cabin doors from the outside, and he didn't want anyone else to see the note. He hid it inside the Canadian's pillow case. The note asked for an 0100 meeting aft of the fo'c's'le— where he'd seen Andre that night.

Sam tried to sleep. It did not come. He'd dressed and crept up on deck by 0045 hours. He ducked under the starboard-side overhang and waited. 0100 - no Andre. At 0115, Sam heard a soft tapping on the bulkhead around the corner. Sam rose from his hide, saw Andre, and approached him. "Thanks for meeting me."

"What do you want?"

"First, I appreciate you not reporting what happened to Chacci. Why didn't you?"

Andre muttered in a neutral voice, "He assaulted you and you defended yourself. Chacci was a drunken pig and a bully. I don't miss him."

"But what prompted you to be out on deck at that hour?"

"You ask too many questions. Be satisfied you got what you got."

"Whoa, no hostility needed here, Andre."

"You ain't seen hostility yet."

The guy's reaction surprised Sam. "Yet? You got a lot of pent-up anger, dude. What's up?"

"I told you to stop with the questions. I see I fucked up coming here tonight."

"How so?"

The two men faced each other in the darkness. A medium swell rolled the boat under a million stars as she skidded along. Andre hissed, "Let me make this real clear for you." He caught Sam off guard with a cheap shot, a straight right to the jaw. Sam dropped, shocked by the unexpected punch. He couldn't let this stand. He wouldn't.

Andre hovered over him, close. Sam swung his left leg to sweep Andre's legs out from under him. He hit the deck. Both men rose to their feet with their fists raised. Sam did not expect this at all. But he was in it now and had to finish it. A moral imperative... or something. They danced and swung punches. Some connected, some missed. The guy's training revealed itself in his feints, his moves. This was no ordinary deckhand.

Andre's boxing skills were a level above Sam's, but Sam possessed greater power and size. Time to get him on the ground. Sam stepped inside of a big right. He grabbed Andre's shoulders, put his right foot behind Andre's left, pushed him while lifting his legs with his right foot, and brought him down hard. Andre's head struck the deck, stunning him. Sam put his elbow under his chin and pressed down with significant force, limiting his air supply.

Sam sensed he also possessed superior hand-to-hand experience, strength, and endurance. Gritting his teeth and placing his mouth close to Andre's ear, Sam whispered, "Who the fuck are you?" Sam kept applying pressure to Andre's neck, but saw the man was on the edge of passing out.

After realizing he'd been beaten, the Canadian croaked, "Awright, awright, enough." Sam eased up a little on his neck. Andre said, "I'm an undercover operative for the Canadian Department of Fisheries and Oceans."

That shocked Sam. Didn't believe him. Sam looked around. Nobody else to be seen. He hissed, "Who's your boss? Where do work out of? Names and numbers."

Andre gasped through gritted teeth, now almost breathless. "You're not what you seem, either. Who are you? Who do *you* work for?"

"Seems both of us need to be convinced to trust each other. I work for the US National Marine Fisheries Service and was deputized for this role. My real job is a state environmental police officer. What about you?"

Andre squeaked, "Can you loosen up the elbow, please? No tricks."

Sam forgot he still pressed pretty hard on the guy's windpipe and backed off the pressure. He remained uncertain of Andre and his story. But how to verify his credentials? He loosened his grip. They sat on their asses side-by-side with their backs propped against a bulkhead. Sam said, "How do we verify our information?"

Andre said, "I've got a sat phone hidden in my cabin. We can use it to call each other's agencies for verification, like tomorrow night. No way we do this during the day."

"Agreed," replied Sam. "What is your assignment here?"

Andre told Sam his agency had been monitoring this vessel and another large cargo ship via satellite. "Too far out for our choppers to reach. Even then, no way to board. These vessels rendezvous once every six weeks or so, supposedly to pick up bulk bait."

Sam found this information useful. "Have you boarded them?"

"We did, by boat. Couldn't find a damn thing. But something is rotten about this whole deal. So, the DFO got me aboard and I've been with this crew for about three fuckin' months. I've watched this boat rendezvous once with a French freighter. Their bait transfer appeared legit. But something isn't right. Likely gonna do it again, but didn't we bait up in Gloucester? Then why at sea, now? By a *French* cargo ship, no less? I'm missing it. With both of us on the job we might find what we're looking for. What about you?"

Sam replied, "About the same thing. The DEA assigned me to this boat undercover because drugs have flooded the region. They know it's coming in by fishing boats but not sure which one, or how. So, they put me in at the last-minute as an NMFS catch monitor. This boat was the most suspicious. So, here I am. Like you. Seems we both had suspicions about each other. When I tossed Chacci over, you saw it, and didn't report it. I knew then you weren't what you seemed."

Andre tapped his right index finger against his chin. He said, "Well, let's leave the verification until tomorrow, but we'll have to be real careful."

Sam offered his hand. They shook. Sam remarked, "You know you're pretty edgy, Andre. You should get that under control, man. It never should have come to blows between us. Is this your first undercover op?"

Andre said sheepishly, "Yeah, and I've been on this stinking tub for almost three months, working my ass off, with nothing to show for it. So, yeah, I *am* edgy and you're right. What are the odds of two UCs from two different countries on the same boat? Look, Murdock, or whatever your name is, I know it's a high-level case. Thanks for the advice. How long have you been a UC?"

"Quite a while. But I'm also getting a bit worn down from the constant pressure. Forever watching my language so I don't sound like a cop, always looking over my shoulder, and knowing these are bad guys, trying to make friends with 'em just to betray 'em. One wrong move, and you're gone. My wife and kid are fed up with my job, too. For now, let's stay professional and help each other whenever we can. We can't be seen talking. Even these late-night meets are risky as hell. We need to limit them to important information exchanges. Agreed?"

"Yes, absolutely."

"Use your sat phone and call this number. Chuck Sawyer is my DEA guy in charge if you want to verify my identity. The codeword for access is KSB. I remember it as *Kiss Sawyer's Butt*." Sam winked. "I'll use my sat phone to verify your identity. Give me your supervisor's name and number and any code word so they will answer my questions."

Andre took out a pen with a couple of scraps of paper. They each wrote out their contact numbers and codes. While Andre wrote, Sam whispered, "Let's try to verify each other after the next haul and new set. They'll be exhausted."

Andre sounded defeated and depressed. He mumbled, "Okay."

They retreated to their cabins ten minutes apart. Sam got some ice from the chute in the hold below his cabin to reduce the swelling from Andre's sucker punch. When he returned to his cabin, he worked on the hasp they'd put on his door.

Sam ensured the area was clear, retrieved his trusty multi-tool knife, and unscrewed the hinge. He used the Philips screwdriver shaft and blade to widen the screw holes so they'd still hold the hasp. But one shoulder shove would pop them out. If he needed to get out fast, he'd now be able to do so.

No fuss, no muss.

53

Tomorrow would be a hectic day for the crew, especially since they were down a man. Sam lay in his bunk, wondering about Kate and Brian. He missed them far more than he feared. *Nope, not gonna take any more of these ops for quite a while.* And he meant it.

The bruises from Chacci and Andre were throbbing as twin reminders of this op's physicality. Made it impossible to sleep. Got out of his bunk, retrieved the phone, and called Andre's contact number. A woman answered after three rings. She said, "Code in."

Sam read from the slip of paper, "Oscar-Foxtrot-Golf-Numeral One."

"Wait one." Sam waited three. She returned and asked who he was. He told her he was an undercover operative for the DEA aboard the US-flagged commercial fishing vessel *Miss Guided One*. And that he was verifying the identity of Andre Gagnon as an operative for the DFO.

A long pause later, she said, "Not knowing who you are, and, if we had an operative aboard, you could have tortured him to reveal the code. I can neither confirm nor deny any person or assignment. We have protocols and we follow them. Good-bye."

Click.

Well, that didn't get me anywhere. Sam wondered if Andre's call to the DEA was gonna be the same. He then called Jamison, who picked up right away.

"Are you okay?"

"Yeah, for now. Little time to talk. There is a man aboard who says he's from Canada's DFO as a UC. I was unable to confirm with his agency. Call Sawyer and tell him. If a person gives my code and says his name is Andre Gagnon I'm not sure about divulging our plan. Recommendations?"

"Sam, do you trust him?"

"Not sure. This is his first UC assignment and he came apart at the seams until I put him down and questioned him. Sounds legit, but I don't trust him yet."

"Trust your instincts, Sam. That's my advice. He has too much information as it is. Pump him for more info if possible. We'll verify him from our end. Give me the number and code. Sawyer and I will run this down. Give us a day and then call when it's safe. Meanwhile, stay loose and play it cool. Sawyer's computer geniuses are confident you're on the right boat. You better go. Talk soon."

"Roger that. Out." Sam thought this through, and it made sense. A deeper mistrust wiggled his psychic antenna, though. He re-examined his cabin and secured his phone. Not a safe place. *Hide it in plain sight somewhere on deck? But what if they find it and seize it? Then I'll be without comms if everything turns to shit.*

Sam stuffed his mattress again. He needed to pump Andre as much as he dared and report back. His altercation with that guy still gnawed at him. *So unprofessional, even if it **is** his first assignment. The Canadians gotta be training their UCs better than **that**.*

Now, though, he was tired. But his mind raced through tactical options on how to proceed. He'd ask Andre if he got through to Sawyer, though he speculated the DEA's response to him would be the same. A stand-off. Sleep came at last.

Sam was roused at 0400, after less than three hours of sleep.

54

The *Miss Guided One*—the *Miss G*—retrieved their third haul in four days. They neared 15 tons of sword-fish in the holds. They'd only need one or two more days to fill every hold if decent weather and the fishing held up, they said.

Sam recorded the by-catch, fish kills, and the number of legal swords with passionate attention to detail. Only four holds left. Three more for swords and the restricted area. The weather held, but sea swells were building. More lousy weather on the way. A twin engine Cessna flew high over the boat. DEA overwatch.

Hauling in the catch progressed without incident until an enormous swordfish they estimated at over 600 pounds flopped around on deck, slashing his deadly sword. Andre Gagnon tried to knock it out with his thumper as it came aboard, per their practice, but he either missed or his blows had no effect on this monster. Eduardo Braga hustled into the deck wash station and came out with a handgun. Sam recognized the powerful ten-millimeter semi-auto Glock with a standard 15-round magazine.

The entire crew watched as Braga approached the sword that was still slashing his deadly bill—his *sword*—around the deck, fighting for its life. That fish's tiny brain would be a tough target, even up close. It was going crazy. Braga fired twice, missing each time, only to kick up small chunks of the heavy oak-planked working deck. He moved closer to the fish. Too close. The swordfish's huge eyes seemed to sense this opportunity.

With a wicked effort, the fish sped up its slashing and moved forward on the deck as if swimming. Scraped his bill on the planking and used that as a launch platform to raise that jagged serrated sword almost two feet above the deck as it quick-wiggled forward. With a lightning strike, it impaled Braga clean through his right calf and stayed there. Braga howled in pain and dropped the gun close to the fish as it continued thrashing, now hauling poor Braga with it.

Sam reacted while the rest of the crew appeared paralyzed in disbelief. He reached for the gun with a swift snatch, tucked 'n rolled, timing the giant fish's vicious slashes. Once armed, he approached the fish from behind, not head-on. He fired three rounds into the fish's brain, killing it in an instant. Like somebody had turned off its life switch. The fish and Braga froze in position as if part of a single body.

Applying an after-action instinct, he smoothly slid the gun inside his belt in the middle of his back and covered it with his shirt in one uninterrupted motion. No one noticed. They focused on their crew mate writhing and bleeding on the deck. His blood soaked into the wet planking, slightly punky from age and wear. Braga's blood mingled with the pink fish blood already there.

Braga kept screaming and squirming in pain, clutching his right calf with both hands. Must have missed the artery, as they weren't seeing a lot more pumping blood. First mate Antonio Sousa woke up from his standing trance before the others and ran to retrieve the first-aid kit just outside the compartment they used as a sick bay.

The sword had penetrated Braga's right calf through-and-through. But they couldn't easily back it out, especially with it still attached to quarter-ton fish. Braga and the fish had merged. He'd also suffered several other abrasions during the thrashing, but the calf would was the most serious, by far.

Carlos grabbed a meat saw used for coring. He cut off the now-dead fish's bill, as big as a large man's forearm at its base, six inches from Braga's wound. Antonio remained unsure of how to remove the now-amputated bill from Braga's leg. He looked to Sam, knowing *Murdock* had combat experience and likely triaged many wounded men during his Navy days.

Sam said, "Eduardo, we can't leave it in because of infection." To Sousa, he said, "We'll have to medivac him off the ship."

Antonio whispered to Sam, away from Eduardo, "We can't delay our schedule."

From that, Sam confirmed an important rendezvous on a rigorous timeline regardless of any crew member's condition. Antonio slipped a double-thickness of two tongue depressors from the kit into Eduardo's mouth to bite down on as he prepared to remove the remaining eighteen-inch piece of the fish's jagged bill. From one deck up outside his beloved pilothouse, Captain Matos shouted. "Do it!"

Sam held Eduardo's leg while Antonio grabbed the serrated bill with gloved hands and slowly pulled. It took considerable force. Eduardo emitted a curdling scream again and stiffened before he passed out. The crew looked away. Pieces of Eduardo's flesh remained attached to the serrations on the fish's bill. Blood now gushed out of the three-inch hole in Eduardo's calf. Antonio started to wrap the wound. But Sam told him he'd bleed out if they didn't first tighten a tourniquet on the leg above that wound, and *fast*.

Antonio said, "No idea if we even have one!"

"Well, fucking *make* one!" yelled Sam. He took *his* knife and slashed a large piece of Eduardo's jeans. While doing so, he screamed in the general direction of the other three crew, "Get me a dowel or piece of wood or metal at least a foot long. Now!"

Gagnon handed Sam his thumper. Sam then tied the strip of blue jean cloth around the leg with a simple overhand knot close above the wound. He then tied another knot around the middle of the thumper. Sam rotated the stubby bat slowly, which tightened the tourniquet. The blood flow lessened considerably. Sam used another strip of the sturdy cloth from Eduardo's jeans to lash one end of the bat to Eduardo's thigh to prevent the tourniquet from unwinding and loosening itself. The ragged hole through Eduardo's calf was plain enough for everyone to see. Sousa then bound it with a pad from the kit. Gagnon headed to the rail to puke overboard.

The captain appeared with two syringes—one loaded with antibiotics and the other with morphine. First, he jabbed Eduardo in the arm with one needle, depressing the syringe's plunger. He repeated the process with the other needle. He commanded, "Get him to sick bay, remove his filthy clothes and Sousa, you clean him up. We have to loosen the tourniquet every so often, so he doesn't lose the leg. Murdock, you go with him and assist. You've had obvious experience with both handguns and emergency first aid. We can see that. I'm asking for your help."

That visibly astounded the crew. The captain did not order him. He *asked* him. Sam guessed they had *never* heard him *ask* something of *anyone*, especially aboard *his* vessel.

Sam simply nodded. The captain shouted to the rest of what remained of his crew. "Get these fish cored, stored, and iced. Fast! We've got eight more miles of line to haul."

They snapped out of their trances, including Andre, as he had done nothing other than offer his thumper and projectile-hurl over the side. His inexperience was obvious. Sam thought, *Untrained and untested.* That made him even more suspicious. Now, he wished he had said nothing about his assignment to the fickle Canadian.

Antonio and Sam carried Eduardo to the compartment they used as a sick bay and stripped him. Sam grabbed a bottle of hydrogen peroxide from the first-aid kit that Antonio had brought back in with him from Eduardo's triage on deck. He also left to fetch alcohol swabs, surgical dressings, and anti-bacterial ointment. He yelled to Antonio, "get a roll of duct tape too, Ant."

They cleaned and flushed the wound. Extracted visible pieces of the fish's bill that had lodged inside the wound. Flushed it again. Like a large-caliber hollow-point bullet's jagged exit wound. Only it was oval, not round—stringy and ragged. Antonio never made eye contact with Sam while tending to the wound. He said, "Happened so fast. I shoulda been the one to do what you did. But you were fast. Thanks for your quick thinking and sharp shooting. Your Navy experience? Very obvious. Saw action too, didn't ya?"

"Yeah, I did, Ant. Too much. I never wanted to see anything like it again."

After they did everything possible for Eduardo, Antonio asked Sam when to loosen the tourniquet, and for how long. Sam answered in a casual tone, "Leave it tight for an hour and then loosen it a bit. A little longer is okay, but I'm concerned about tissue damage if we leave it too tight for too long. My biggest concern is infection, though. We also need to get fluids in him by starting an IV. Do you have plasma?"

"I don't know."

"Well, do we have a record of the crew's blood types?"

"I don't know these things, Frank."

"Then ask the men if they know their own blood types. We'll rig up an IV arm-to-arm. I'll come by in a while and check on things. Gonna clean up first. I'm supposed to be recording what's coming in on deck. But that's gonna to have to wait."

"Okay. Obrigado, Murdock."

"De nada, Antonio."

Sam went to the main deck's wash station. Rinsed most of the blood from his hands and arms, even his face. Splashed his face and neck with water and toweled off with the damp and dirty rag that dangled on a nearby hook. He headed to his cabin to change clothes when Carlos Almeida approached him and said the captain wanted to see him right away.

55

Sam wasn't sure why Captain Matos wanted to see him, but he remembered the Glock in the back of his waistband. In the confusion, no one noticed Sam had picked up the gun and hung onto it. He clumped up the stairs to the pilothouse. His boots suddenly felt like twin anchors. Matos sat at the helm. "You asked for me, Captain?"

"Yes, sit down." Sam sat in the adjacent navigator's seat closer to the boat's port side, often occupied by the first mate, and swiveled it to face Matos just to his right. "Murdock, your quick action saved the life of one of my crew. I am grateful."

"I'd do it for anyone." Sam reached behind his back and pulled out the pistol. Matos reacted with surprise and... fear? Sam turned the gun around and handed it to Matos, butt-first. Matos took the firearm with cautious deliberation and put it on the console. Sam muttered, "I picked it up after I shot the sword. Kept it to return to you. We may need it again."

"You had me fooled for a moment, Murdock. You were quick."

"Well, I trained for 20 years in the Navy so it didn't require a lot of thought. I reacted to a situation for which I was trained. Do you hold any medical records of your crew?"

"Why?"

"Because we need to get fluids into Eduardo or he'll go into shock. Lacking plasma, if I had his blood type, and that of the crew's, I'd hook up an IV man-to-man if there's a match."

"You're clever, Murdock. Impressive. But yes, I keep that information in my safe. But it's beyond my medical knowledge. I'll get the files. Wait here."

Sam used the time to sneak a peek at the captain's nautical chart. He saw a plotted rendezvous for 0300 hours tomorrow morning. *Aha!* A few minutes passed and Matos returned with several files. Each was marked *Medical Record* followed by a crew member's name. The captain laid the files on the chart table aft of their helm seats. "We got lucky, Frank. Eduardo has A-positive blood and Carlos has the universal donor blood type O-negative."

Sam mused, *No medical knowledge, but he knows the universal donor type is O-neg? Hmmm.* He said, "Excellent. With your permission I'll transfuse Almeida's blood to Braga. I must tell you, though, he's far from out of the woods. We need to medivac him off the boat and get him to a hospital."

"That long of a delay to our schedule is impossible. If we do the transfusion, how much time to save him *after* our rendezvous with the bait-provisioning ship?"

"You're telling me that taking on bait is more important than a crew member's life?"

Matos snapped, "Yes, I am! I cannot get into the reasons, but it's critical." His tone softened a notch. "Please do what you can to save Eduardo with what's onboard. I'll order Carlos down to the sick bay for the transfusion."

"You are now down two crewmen, but Carlos won't be down long after the transfusion, if at all. You've got 30,000 pounds of swordfish by my calculations. Another 15,000 would put you in excellent shape for the trip. This isn't making much sense to me captain."

"Look, this is *my* vessel. We will do what *I* think is best for all aboard. Mind your own damn business and stay out of my way. Is that clear enough for you, Murdock?"

"Yes, it is, captain. I will make note of it all in my reports to NMFS."

The captain snarled, "You're dismissed after your check-in call to your office. It's been forty-six hours. Do it now so I don't have to deal with you again in two hours." He retrieved the phone, punched in the security code, and tossed it.

Sam thought, *You ungrateful son-of-a-bitch.* He dialed Sawyer's number.

Pause.

"Yes, boss, the info is recorded. This computer is a bitch. For your information, we had an accident on board. The bill of a sword penetrated the calf of a crew member. I provided the best first-aid I could. I plan on additional medical efforts to keep him alive."

Pause.

"Yes. I will stay within the scope of my training. Total catch so far is near 15 tons of swords, 5,000 pounds of tuna, all tagged, and smaller amounts of other legal sea life like cod and haddock intermingled."

Pause.

"Yes, sir, four or five days longer. Will you plan to pick me up at the dock? I'll contact you as we get close to port."

Pause.

"Yes, thank you. I will need some help from our techies to download the data. I don't understand the intricacies of this new computer and its software like the old one."

Pause.

"Yes, sir. I will keep you advised. Out."

Sam hoped Sawyer understood his coded message —"*help from our techies*" was a call for significant back-up upon his return to Gloucester.

He then called home. Kate answered. He turned his

back to the captain and spoke in a hushed tone. "Hi, hon. We're still at sea for another four or five days."

Pause.

"Yes, I'm fine. How are you doing? Brian? Bobby? Hey, give Larry a call and ask him to meet me with a tech guy at Pier Seven. Sawyer said it was okay."

Pause.

"Aw, just block out the bill part. I'll deal with it when I get back. Ask Larry to bring you and the boys. Can't wait to see all of you.

Pause.

"Love you, too."

Kate would indeed call Larry right away and tell him something was wrong. There is no Bobby. "Bring the boys" she'd deduce that Larry needed to bring plenty of back-up to the pier. "Block out the bills" was something Kate wouldn't understand. She'd call Larry and relay the message. Larry would decipher what Sam was saying—"blocking out" is road-block preparation. This way, he'd have more time to organize the men and coordinate numbers, placement, and road blocks.

Sam handed the phone back to Matos. "Thank you, Captain. Please ask Eduardo to meet me in the sick bay for the IV."

"Done." Matos smiled at his own cleverness as he thought, *Ha! Almeida does **not** have O-Negative blood. He's B-Positive. That'll kill Eduardo, but that's one less share to split, if I split the take at all. I'll just blame Murdock.*

56

Matos paged Almeida over the ship's loudspeaker, "Carlos, get your ass to sick bay. Braga needs your blood." But Carlos knew they needed him on deck to help bait 20 miles of longlines. Giving blood? That just creeped him out. But he went to sick bay as the captain ordered. Everyone heard. He got a few pats on the back on the way down. That felt good.

Sam kept busy setting up for the transfusion. He didn't have all the necessary medical equipment, but he remained confident it would work. He told Antonio—first mate, enforcer, and now nurse—to raise the other bed for Carlos to its highest position, and to place Eduardo as low as possible. Gravity helped induce the blood transfer.

He then loosened the tourniquet to the now-conscious Braga. "Drink, Eduardo. You need fluids." He just grunted and offered Sam a weak wink. *What a trooper.*

The morphine wore off. Braga drank water, as he was told. He suffered despite his brave face. Carlos entered the compartment, now too small for the four men. Sam briefed him. Then he asked, "Carlos, do you know your blood type?"

"Uh, no idea."

The transfusion took 20 minutes. Afterwards, Sam gave Almeida a bottle of water and said, " Go easy for a couple hours." Almeida nodded and slumped out. He didn't appear happy about the entire affair. But he seemed glad to help his mate. As he passed their patient, he croaked, "Hang in there, Eduardo." Braga winced again and offered his mate a weak slow-motion nod.

Sam took Braga's temperature. It ran high. Infection. Sam looked at Antonio. "The transfusion should give him a boost to fight off the infection." Sam dumped the equipment into a shallow tub of straight alcohol to sterilize it in case he'd need it again.

Antonio asked, "What do you think?"

"Should help him." He took Eduardo's temperature again 15 minutes later. Still spiked up. *Odd,* thought Sam. *Why isn't it stable or edging down by now?*

His troubled expression caught Antonio's eye. "What's wrong?"

"His temp is still going up." Sam ransacked the memories of his medical training. *His temp surged upward after the transfusion. Hemolytic transfusion reaction, maybe? His body's red cells are attacking the new blood cells and are killing them? His body's response to... the wrong blood type? His immune system is rejecting Carlos' blood!*

Sam took his temp again. 104.5 degrees. Up from 103.1 just 20 minutes earlier. Sam said, "The captain told me Carlos had the universal donor blood type O-negative. He lied."

"Why? Kill his own crewman? Ridiculous! Did you screw up, Frank?"

"No, absolutely not. Look at the wound, Antonio. It's swelling and the tissue around it is turning bright red. Get me some ice. Let's wrap his wound in it. We'll put some on his head, too, and wash him down with ice water to get his temperature down." Not sensing any movement, Sam yelled, "Move!"

Sousa hurried off. Sweat now *poured* off Braga's forehead, neck, and chest. Sousa returned less than a minute later with two large buckets of ice. They wrapped the leg with towels filled with ice while Sam held ice against Braga's head and neck. Sousa swabbed his body in cold water that ran off, soaking the thin mattress, and pooled under his cot.

Time ticked away with only two crew left on deck. It seemed Eduardo Braga's life also ticked away.

57

A call squawked on the intercom from the captain. "Antonio on deck, now. Urgent. Gagnon to the helm. The summons surprised Andre. He climbed the ladder up to the pilothouse and entered, closing the door behind him. Captain Matos stood there, staring at him with a gun in his hand and the barrel leveled at... him!

Andre gulped. "Captain?"

"Andre, you have been with me for over three months. I have watched you. So has the rest of the crew. We suspect you are a cop."

Andre froze. Then his voice quivered as he spoke, mustering indignation. "I am *not!*"

"Carlos spotted you and Frank talking on deck late one night. Want to tell me about that?"

"Well, we ran into each other as we both were on deck at the same time. I recall my cabin was stuffy that night, and we talked about both being new to the boat. He asked how long I'd been aboard, if I liked it, nothing else, Captain. I swear. I went back to my bunk. That's it."

The captain raised the Glock to the center of Andre's chest from three feet away. A cold sweat dripped down the middle of his back inside his shirt.

Ten long seconds later, the captain put down the Glock, and Andre breathed easier. "Since I am now down two crewmen, I'd like to offer you a full-time position aboard this boat with more money and every benefit the others receive."

"Uh, well, thank you sir. I am definitely interested in continuing on with you. What other benefits beyond pay and insurance?"

"See this cargo ship?" He pointed to a photo of the *Grand Francaise* laying on the chart table to Andre's left. "Why do you suppose we meet that ship?"

"No idea, but our holds are near full and we're taking on bulk bait? It makes little sense to me, but I keep to myself. Whatever it is, it's none of my business. I do my job, nothing more."

"Let's say it's additional profit from a transaction you've witnessed before. I've had you followed ashore, Gagnon. Nothing unusual about where you go or what you do. That's good. So, I'm offering you a full share. That'll be about $250,000 for each of us when our business is complete. No strings, but confidentiality must be absolute."

. . .

Andre imagined he'd hit the jackpot. *Tabarnac!* Loosely translated from Québécois to English? *Holy shit!*

The captain continued as the wide-eyed Andre stood there, mute. "You will receive a similar share for each successful trip. Antonio and I will show you how and where to deposit your money into an off-shore account so no government will track it. When this run is complete, for example, you will be free to buy what your heart desires. But in small, reasonable increments so you don't arouse suspicion that will endanger yourself *and* the rest of us. Is this something you want? And are you willing to abide by these conditions, Gagnon?"

Andre absorbed what Matos just asked. This was a one-time offer. If he declined, he'd die. So, he mused, *I could still go back to DFO for a while, and then retire because the job is too risky, especially with a growing family. Resign, get passports to some place with no extradition treaty with the US or Canada, buy off a few locals in return for silence? Yes! Except...* Frank Murdock.

I've already told Frank I am a UC for the DFO. So, Frank's gotta go. It's the only way. With this melange of thoughts swirling topside, he said, "Yes, Skipper, I'm with you all the way. I'll do as you say and my silence will be absolute."

Captain Matos grinned, offered his hand, and said, "Welcome aboard, Andre." They shook. Andre thought, *Is this the time I tell him that Frank is a DEA UC? No, because Frank would rat on me. I'll dispose of him myself.*

58

Now Sam was convinced the captain intentionally sabotaged Eduardo Braga's chances of survival. *That rat bastard!* He had done everything possible, but Braga's temperature kept rocketing. He'd already exhibited a dangerous temperature of 105.0. Braga would lapse into unconsciousness, then a coma, and death.

Sam was powerless, and that pissed him off. But that was nothing compared to the disgust he felt over the captain's contempt for his own crewman's life. He found it nearly impossible to control his seething anger. *One of his own loyal crew members and a fellow countryman! Matos orchestrated poisoning the guy and got me to do it for him.*

He analyzed the situation. The captain was at the helm, and the three other crewmen remained crazy busy on deck. All he could do was analyze. Nothing more to be done for Eduardo except to keep him as comfortable as possible. He strapped him onto the bed in case a convulsion caused him to buck off.

So, Sam snuck down to the hold marked *RESTRICTED AREA*. This was an opportunity not to be wasted with everyone else occupied topside. This hold appeared identical to the others, except for a heavy steel door featuring a serious combination lock. This lock looked plenty sturdy, not to be popped with a crowbar. But it was unlocked, open to the empty hold. So, why the security? Sam would have to get back down here after the captain's urgent but mysterious rendezvous with another vessel.

He returned to the sick bay without being noticed. Eduardo's irregular pulse raced. He'd be dead within twenty-four hours. And there wasn't a damn thing Sam could do about it. Except to exact revenge. His head worked triple-time, putting together all the pieces. Poor Eduardo. Sam's blood smoldered, but his hatred boiled. *This wasn't supposed to be a part of it all along. Or was it?* He'd reserve judgement until he collected more information.

This warranted another trip up to the pilothouse. Sam intended to advise Matos of Braga's dire situation and to start a fight. Facing the felonious captain, he hissed, "What will the men say about you when they discover you engineered a lethal transfusion for Braga?"

The captain smirked. "They're never going to know because you will not tell them."

"And what's to stop me?"

"Because I'm going to tell them you screwed up, *Doctor* Frank. I overheard you say you wouldn't exceed the scope of your training. Well, I'm going to tell my crew that's just what you did and caused Eduardo's death. Who are they going to believe? Me, their captain or you, the government fish counter? And consider what they'll do to you before we make port. An accident, perhaps? Who knows?" Matos exuded confidence. Or was it arrogance? No, it was both.

"Well, I'm sure the Coast Guard's investigation of two disappearances of your crew and another death during a single trip will prove beyond suspicious. You lost Chacci and now Braga. Then, me too? Yeah, I'll take my chances."

"Yes, you *have* been taking chances. Maybe too many. Maybe you became despondent over the loss of poor Eduardo and ended it all. It will be the end of your job as a fish counter *and your life.*"

Sam responded, "You fucking wish." He turned his back on Captain Matos and stormed out of the pilot-house, slamming the door so hard it failed to latch. He scrambled down the ladder to the deck, and then below to the sick bay. Sam found Braga convulsing uncontrollably. So he administered the last of the morphine. At least the captain now knew for certain that Sam was a dangerous man.

The crew had cored, iced down, and stowed in the holds the last of the fish from the latest haul. Sam had no idea how many because of his preoccupation with the captain and with Braga. The three exhausted crewmen came to the sick bay to check on their mate. Each gasped to see Braga so pale and his breathing so ragged.

They then stumbled in shock from there to the mess, where they wolfed down tens of thousands of calories in retaliation. Sam sneaked down to the restricted area once more. Now, though, it was locked.

Sam then re-joined the crew for fresh cod that was baked with potatoes. He had gone the whole day with only some water. After a full meal, he still stopped back by the galley to grab a couple of sandwiches and a bottle of water for later. Good nutrition kept the mind alert. He intended to call Larry after returning to his cabin. But then he decided against it. There'd more to report after the rendezvous early tomorrow morning. He locked his door from the inside and fell asleep.

He awoke at 0300. Went into sick bay. Checked Braga's pulse. None. Travis shook his head and looked away. Covered Eduardo's face with a clean towel. *Poor bastard.* He felt grateful for his solitude, unable to hide the murderous expression that betrayed his desire for revenge. His face was painted with it.

59

The next day gave birth to a flat gun-metal-gray dawn that was only good for a steady rain and treacherous decks. Sam took cover by the rail under the overhang aft of the pilothouse to observe the working deck eight feet below his feet. He counted the night's haul. They had not re-baited the hooks. Instead, they'd secured the main and drop lines, as well as the leader/bait lines. No fishing today, but they'd still be working till sunset.

Sam retreated to his cabin after advising the recently roused crew he'd start compiling his report and the catches. He locked his door and dug out his DEA satellite phone. Decided to call Larry after all to give him a quick briefing. He asked, "What did you find out about Andre Gagnon?"

"We had a hell of a time getting any info—nobody trusts anybody—but it seems he's a legitimate UC for the DFO. They asked about you, too. We made sure you're okay with them. The DFO is re-tasking a satellite to record what they believe is the sixth transaction between these two vessels in the last nine months. They'll record this one as well. Looks like the rendezvous is indeed early tomorrow morning, and we'll have full DEA backup standing by on the dock in Gloucester starting four days from now.

"Our own EPOs will parole the perimeter to block off any escape. We will not inform the local police to mitigate the risk of a leak. We'll decide whether to call them in as the situation develops. Getting those coded clues to me yesterday bought us some valuable prep time. And Kate, well, she's a trooper. She understood and played along. Thanks for the early heads-up."

"That's great, Larry. I'll call again tomorrow, if possible. The captain threatened my life, but that's under control... for now. Please reach out to Kate, again. See if she needs any help with anything around the house. Tell her I really am okay and things are going as planned. Out."

Miss Guided One scudded along under thinning clouds, backlit by a full moon. Despite an earlier long-range forecast, no wind and a calm ocean should offer perfect conditions for an offshore rendezvous. Captain Matos spotted the large freighter on his radar and got a visual in the distance at 2330 hours. Ahead of schedule. He'd have turned off his AIS earlier and cranked his radar to its fifty-mile range. They'd need to know if any other vessels approached. The crew prepared for a boarding operation.

The freighter loomed larger and more intimidating by the minute. She towered over the *Miss G* like a cat over a mouse. They traded shouts over the railings and then exchanged short and cryptic radio calls on short-range VHF radio.

Antonio Sousa appeared large and intimidating as Sam rounded the corner of the fo'c's'le from the portside deck, where they nearly collided.

"Murdock, get to your cabin and wait until called upon."

"Why?"

"Captain's orders."

"You do know Eduardo is dead, don't you?"

"We moved the body to the hold and covered him with ice."

"He needn't have died, Ant."

Antonio lowered his head for a moment. Then, he jumped back to business. "Maybe. Most unfortunate."

Sam entered his cabin and heard Antonio lock the door. He wasn't supposed to see what was happening with the freighter. Sam waited ten minutes before nudging the doctored hasp loose. He wondered how he'd re-insert the hasp from inside with the lock still dangling from the hasp. He could say that NMFS requires all at-sea transfers must be documented to prevent the poaching of swordfish. That might work.

Tucked his sidearm in the small of his back inside his belt. Not ideal for a quick-draw, plus sitting down like that was always a literal pain in the ass. Sam hung to the shadows. He watched a flat black rigid inflatable boat—a RIB—with an outboard motor, being lowered from the towering ship, two-thirds of the way back from her bow. Spotted a French flag hanging limp from the freighter's flagpole at her transom. They displayed no navigation lights.

Four armed men aboard that RIB with two medium-sized camouflaged duffel bags? *Why are they armed for a bait transfer? Has to be drugs.* Clouds buried the moon. He'd still try to identify the ship's name if he were able.

Carlos Almeida stood on *Miss G's* deck, ready to receive the freighter's burley foursome and their duffels. But something wasn't right, even though things were going according to the captain's plan.

60

Puzzle pieces fell into place for Sam as he gained confidence by covertly watching this felonious little ballet unfold. He finally felt like a winged predator riding the thermals high above his prey, unseen, but potentially lethal. Only... *listen to the alarm bells, Sam. If you don't, you're gonna get yourself killed.*

At that moment, however, he descended closer to the real action aboard this tub of malfeasants. Four paces away, around a corner from Sam's shadow hide where he glued himself to a bulkhead, Captain Matos emerged from his cabin only accessed from the pilot-house. He descended the ladder to the weather deck passing by Sam, still unseen. In his wake, like they were in tow, Antonio Sousa and Andre Gagnon each lugged a large duffel bag. *Gagnon is part of this transaction? Either he's crooked as a bent penny or he doesn't know what the fuck he's doing! Another puzzle piece?*

The four men from the freighter's RIB deftly scrambled up the eight-foot rope ladder Carlos had flung over *Miss G's* starboard side moments earlier. They'd slung their MP5 machine-pistols over their shoulders to more easily lug *their smaller duffels* that didn't appear to be all that heavy. Sam was sure they muttered something in... French? That made sense, given Gagnon's information about the previous rendezvous.

One man took up a position to cover Sousa, Almeida, and Gagnon, with his back to the gunwale— pronounced *gŭn'əl*. A black-clad Frenchman motioned them to the aft portion of the vessel's working deck by waggling the barrel of his nasty little machine gun. They did as directed—no words needed. *Do they even speak English? Or does Matos speak French?* Two others led their boss in a protective V formation toward Captain Matos.

Sam watched as their boss shook Matos' hand. They spoke briefly in soft tones. *I'm betting it's English. Wish I could hear.* One of Frenchie's minions stooped down to unzip and spread open each of Matos' large duffels for a moment before zipping them back up. Sam spotted a flash of cash bundles. Lots of 'em. Looked like US dollars.

Boss Frenchie then signaled to two of his minions, toting their smaller duffels to allow Sousa to inspect them. A quick nod later from Sousa to Matos, two of boss Frenchie's escorts slung a large duffel with ease.

This despite their obvious heft. Sousa took possession of the two smaller French duffels. *What's inside, I wonder? Too small for drugs to justify such an elaborate rendezvous at sea.*

The Frenchies heaved their acquisitions over the low railing down into the RIB. It still obediently bobbed in the nasty chop that had developed almost eight feet below the *Miss G's* starboard gunwale. The boss climbed down the rope ladder, the first to re-board their RIB. Then his two escorts followed. And last, the fourth man backed toward the rope ladder with his weapon remaining at the ready, trained on *Miss G's* crew.

While he climbed down, the crew already in the RIB trained their weapons upward to cover his retreat. Not a lot of trust there. But Sam observed nobody tested any product, despite the flashy weaponry. *Has to be clear evidence of an ongoing business relationship. Another puzzle piece.*

The RIB's engine roared to life just as the last guard dropped onto the only hard bench seat amid-ships. The others sat on the inflated gunwale's and gripped integrated handholds. Once they roared the short distance to the freighter, they snap-shackled the RIB's one bow and two stern lift points to the tackle dangling over the freighter's side near the water. The freighter's onboard crew raised the RIB with speed and efficiency, using a motorized davit (a small crane) that then pivoted and swung the small boat aboard.

Several crew members guided the RIB into its on-deck cradle.

The four men climbed out and disappeared into the ship's interior through a nearby hatch (door), where Sam assumed the money in Matos's duffels would be quickly machine-counted. Sam guessed neither boat would get underway until they'd counted the money and Matos received confirmation. *Would that be it? Nothing more?*

Several minutes after the four men disappeared, someone quickly flashed the masthead light twice aboard the freighter. Sam looked up to see the same signal issued by Matos, once again at his precious helm. Both parties were satisfied? Engines fired up, and the distance between the vessels closed to within a few feet before holding steady. A crane above the freighter's forward hold hoisted a net that engulfed three medium-size wooden crates marked *BAIT*. They lowered them into *Miss G's* forward-most hold through an already open deck hatch—the restricted area.

Less than ten minutes after that and two more sets of quick masthead flashes later, the two vessels eased away and headed out on reciprocal courses—away from each other, at speed. Until the next time?

Sam read the freighter's name in large letters on her transom, the *Grande Francaise*. Visual confirmation. *And yet another piece of the puzzle plops into place.* He hoped the Canadian surveillance satellite recorded this rendezvous, but it wasn't necessary. He remained in a quandary, though, deciding his best immediate course of action.

What was in those French duffels? And why were they taking on thousands of pounds of bait when their holds were already nearly full? Seemed like a rather shabby cover story, unless.... *They don't care! Not yet, anyway. OR there's a double twist here somewhere! Are they that clever?*

No doubt Sousa would soon come to Sam's door to check on him. Only he'd find the hasp and lock on the floor outside of his compartment, the one that was supposed to keep him locked away. He planned to confront Sousa forcefully. Tell him he was not a prisoner and would not be treated like one. He'd be taken to the captain and interrogated. But he'd deal with this shit storm one minute at a time. *Can't plan for the unknown, but I'll prepare for the worst. Gun or no gun?*

Gun.

You're military-trained in weaponry, Sam. You always go armed.

Take the initiative.

Bluster.

Shout.

Show no fear. Only aggression.

61

15 minutes drifted by. Sam laid in his bunk. He kept his gun lodged in the small of his back. Fucker was cold and uncomfortable as hell. His door swung open without warning. Sousa stood there holding the hasp. "What the fuck have you been up to, Frank?"

"No, what the fuck have *you* been up to, Antonio?" An aggressive Frank Murdock leaped out of his bunk, ready to deal with the first mate in case he wanted to dance.

"Upstairs. To the helm. Now. We have questions and you have answers. We're gonna get 'em out of you." Sam glared at him. Antonio shouted, "Move!" Sam took his time to demonstrate defiance.

In the pilothouse, Captain Afonso Matos held his Glock-10 trained on the door through which Sam entered. "What are you up to, Frank Murdock, if that's your real name?"

GK JURRENS & TOM KASPRZAK

"Murdock *is* my name and when I realized someone locked me in my cabin with no explanation I felt entitled to know why. The activities aboard this vessel are my business too, whether you like it or hate it. That's your problem, not mine." Sam wasn't yelling, but his voice left no doubt he wouldn't be taking any shit. "Read the rules and regs that entitle me to go into any hold to inspect for illegal catches, transfers, or actions contrary to US regulations."

Antonio seethed. "So, what did you see, Frank?"

"I saw a large cargo ship rendezvous with this vessel and an exchange of some sort was made. Your business, since no evidence of illegal transfer of fish or fish products took place. Why are you taking on bait when our holds are full? Makes no sense."

He'd finished answering Antonio's question, and glanced over at Matos with a down-glance at the barrel of his pistol still trained on his gut. "But you know what, Captain, whatever else you got going on I really don't give a shit. Once I saw there was nothing of concern to me, I headed back to my cabin. I did not record, photograph or notice anything that pertained to my mission, nor did I make out any conversation that involved illegal fisheries activities. I won't be a prisoner aboard this or any other vessel. Best you let this go."

Both men stared at him. "Nice response, Murdock, but I'm not buying it."

"Buy it or don't buy it. I do not give a flyin' fuck,

Captain. And point that gun somewhere else or I'll take it away from you and shove it up your ass."

Matos looked surprised. "Oh, you think you can do that with two of us here?"

"You need to ask yourself with my 20 years in the Navy and more time to practice hand-to-hand combat than most anything else, is that a probability? Or a certainty? I'd love to show you."

"You're bluffing." The captain's helm seat gave Matos limited ability to move. Antonio was two full steps to the left and beside him, flat-footed, trying to look cocky and confident more than remaining vigilant. Sam moved with lightning speed—a left elbow to Antonio's face dropped him. In the same fluid motion, Sam snatched the muzzle of Matos's Glock with his own right hand. He lifted, bent it backward and upward with Matos' finger still inside the trigger guard. Matos yelped in pain and released the gun. In one fluid motion, Sam one-handed flipped the weapon and pointed it at Antonio, then back at the captain.

The next words out of Sam's mouth emerged with what had to sound like unnerving calmness. "Ant, go stand next to the good captain." Sam took a few steps back and smiled. Ant's nose bled profusely and had already started to swell. A moment later, he'd retrieved a kerchief from a pocket in his dungarees and held it against the flow of blood.

"Now where were we? With this thing," Sam down-nodded to the captain's pistol with his own finger laid parallel to the barrel beside the trigger guard, "I can turn your face into something that looks like it French-kissed a landmine, Captain. Antonio, I'd shoot *you* in the balls and let you squirm around on the floor bleeding out from where your dick once was. How does that sound?" Their only response was genuine and obvious fear.

"Look, guys, I have no desire to harm either of you. But let's get something straight. If you try anything funny with me, I will kill you. Plain and simple. I'm here to monitor your catch and by-catch with access to your holds. *All* holds. This includes anything you've taken the trouble to label *restricted*. That is what I'm interested in. Nothing else.

"Whatever you're doing on the side, I just do not care. Better you shoot me or throw me overboard if you think you're able, and then live with the federal shit storm that *will* follow. Is that really where you wanna take this little party? Look, I want a sturdy brass lock on my door with both keys to keep you out. No locks to keep me in. While you're at it, put another combo lock outside my door. I don't trust you with keys. I wanna keep me and my own shit secure.

Matos hissed, "You think you're at a fucking Ace Hardware?"

"Well, guess what, Captain, they don't pay me enough to get involved with any non-fishing bullshit. Are we clear?"

The captain and Antonio looked at one another.

Their restless body language broadcast they were deciding how to respond.

Finally, Matos said, "We can live with that arrangement, Murdock. It's clear we underestimated you and your skills. But what guarantees do we have you'll do as you say?"

"Guarantees? You think I'm a fuckin' washing machine or a TV? I don't come with a warranty or guarantees. I give you my word I will not interfere with your operation here. Just wanna do my fuckin' job and go home. And one last thing. You are responsible for the death of one of your crew members. He didn't have to die. There's that hanging over your head. I'm sure the autopsy will show the two different blood types you lied to me about. That's murder. And if Eduardo's body disappears over the side, I'll swear to your destroying evidence. That alone is enough to suspend your credentials, Captain."

"You don't leave us with much choice Mr. Murdock. We have one more day of fishing and then we're headed back to port."

"I'll need to check in. I'll do it right in front of you so you see and hear for yourselves I won't mention any of this. Nor do I intend to, later." He waggled the pistol to take in their detente. "Either on the phone or in my report. Best deal you're ever gonna to get. Take it and be grateful."

He turned his back and was standing right next to

the weather station. He retrieved his recorder with a sleight of hand. Neither Sousa nor Matos caught that.

The captain and first mate looked at one another with resignation and agreed. Sam pulled the Glock's magazine and dropped it onto the deck at his feet before he racked out the single cartridge in the chamber that flew off to his left. Turned the empty pistol around and handed it butt first to Captain Matos.

"We have a deal, Murdock. You do your job, we'll do ours, and we'll try to get along."

Sam asked, "Antonio? You good with this arrangement or not?"

"Yes."

"Yes, to what, Ant? I want to hear the words."

"Yes, to the arrangement that Captain Matos agreed to, Frank."

This from the enforcer, the first mate, the big guy who, out in the open, could give Sam a run for his money. "Ok then, gentlemen. Let's get to it. Please have Carlos install those locks within the hour."

With his voice heavy with sarcasm, Matos asked, "Anything else, Your Highness?"

From the chart table, Sam grabbed a protractor with a two-inch sharp anchoring pin. Slammed it down, stabbing the sharp end into the wooden chart table one inch from Matos' thumb.

"I won't miss if there's a next time, and I'll be aiming for your eye, not your hand." He wheeled on one heel and left them speechless in Matos's pilot-house. Took the gun with him, even though he still had his own tucked in the small of his back.

Sam went to the galley, looking for something to eat and drink, and to find a place to puke... not necessarily in that order.

Matos and Sousa didn't know what hit them, but both agreed to abide by the terms... at least for now. Matos said, "Antonio, keep your eyes on him. I don't trust him one bit, but for now, let's play his game. He mentioned murder. You think he will say something to the authorities?"

"What do we do about that, sir?"

62

In the galley, Sam microwaved a plate of leftovers from the night before. He reviewed his plan to remain alert —twenty-four/seven—somehow. He'd now pushed his cover as far as he dared. Long UC experience had taught him that. Time to contact Larry, not Sawyer, and brief him on the day's action.

Returning to his cabin, he found Carlos already there with tools and a new lock. It looked stout. They did not speak. When Carlos finished, he slapped the keys for the inside lock and the instructions for the exterior combo lock into Sam's palm. Sam waited five minutes inside the cabin, and put his ear to the door before opening it and looking out, half expecting a knife to the gut. Clear.

He closed and locked his cabin door, retired to the only place to sit—on his bunk—and pulled out the recorder. Kept it at a low volume and close to his ear as he listened to several conversations on its tiny built-in speaker. That's the moment he got stabbed with the metaphorical knife in his metaphorical back. He listened in shock to Matos' entire recruiting conversation with Andre Gagnon. "Geezus H! This'll cause a shitstorm."

He retrieved his phone and called Larry, who picked up on the second ring. "What's up, sailor boy?"

Sam briefed him on the rendezvous, the exchange of duffel bags, and the name of the French freighter. Told him of the confrontation with the captain and the first mate. He also said to hold off on notifying the French authorities until he was in port or close to port. Maybe have the Canadians keep a satellite eye on them.

Then he dropped the bomb on Larry. "They flipped the DFO agent for money on the drug deals, boss."

"Whoa! Are you sure he wasn't setting up the captain?"

"Yes, I'm 100% positive. Oh, and the captain is responsible for the death of the crew member that got impaled by a gigantic sword's bill. Fucker intentionally gave me bad blood-type info on the transfusion. This is gonna get messy, Lar'."

Sam heard Larry's prolonged inhale and noisy exhale. "Shit, Sam. What else?"

"Larry, set the DEA up on the docks when *Miss G* comes in, EPOs armed to the teeth and ready to rock. I still have no idea where the H is. But it's onboard.

Gotta be. They've discovered a way to store it and off-load it without detection. Keep the perimeter tight. We may have to go into the water after these guys, so be prepared for that, too."

Larry took notes. Then it was his turn. "How many men? Firearms? Any usable secondary evidence? When are you due in? Where do I hook up with you? Suspicions? Gut feelings?"

Sam told Larry that the relationship he now had with the captain and his men pushed his cover to the limit, and then some. As a result, he'd likely forced them to play this landfall differently from their others. That was when criminals made mistakes.

"It'll be a last-minute thing. Consider them armed and dangerous—Captain Matos, First Mate Antonio Sousa, Engineer Carlos Almeida, and the flipped Canadian UC Andre Gagnon. I'll try to get my recorder back to the helm, but they're now watching my every move. And yes, Larry, I'll be careful. My normal check-in with the captain's satellite phone is due in about an hour for a very different type of update to you and Sawyer, obviously. Please call Kate and let her know I'm okay."

"Sam, *are* you okay?"

"Lots of loose ends, Lar'. Still gotta discover who the heavy hitters are, in what I believe to be a substantial drug operation. As clever as Matos is, he and his little North Coast Fisheries mob aren't big enough or sophisticated enough to honcho a trans-Atlantic smuggling op, much less a North American distribution network. This is tricky shit, Larry."

"Stay frosty, Sam."

"Gotta go. Will call when I have more for you. Of course, relay to Sawyer what you want him to know."

"Roger. Out."

Sam returned the phone to its hiding place before massaging the pain in his gut.

63

Mealtime was graveyard quiet. The only thing missing were the crickets. Andre avoided eye contact with Sam. *Awkward.* The three crew members retreated to their bunks, as did Sam. They'd deployed a twenty-mile set for their last haul in the morning. So Sam had to be up early as well. The weather held, which allowed outstanding fishing. A low-pressure area loomed two days out, but filling their holds swiftly might allow them to evade that front. They'd steam southwest for two days to Gloucester.

Sam was convinced they'd retrieved their drugs, and if they went home with a three-quarter load, who'd care how much they presented at auction?

Captain Matos and Antonio met in the captain's quarters. Deep in thought, Matos considered how Murdock breathing down their necks had complicated this trip. "Are the goods packed like earlier trips?"

"Yes, but I'm not sure that's gonna work this time. Captain, we need to distract Murdock so Carlos has time to weave his magic."

"Ideas?" said the captain.

"Sir, I have a way, but we need to work it right."

"Let's hear it."

"A fire—big enough to muster all hands on deck except Carlos who will do his thing. We say he's in sick bay because he hurt his back. We persuade Murdock to pitch in with fighting the fire."

"Excellent, Ant. Scope it out and start prepping for it. Make it late at night. How about an overheated winch? Do we let the crew in on it?

"No, Captain. We let it play out for real. Murdock is sharp. He'd see through a staged fire. We need honest reactions, confusion, finding and deploying hoses, pumps, and hooking them up. This boat is history after this run anyway, so what do we care?" He sent a co-conspirator's wink toward the captain.

"Okay, then. Make it happen at night. You know I told Andre he'd get a full share. But he ain't gonna get shit. Something about him makes me suspicious. But I played it well enough. Here's what I've planned."

They talked into the early hours, planning out their *real* op.

"Tomorrow will be a long and exciting day. Get some rest, Antonio."

"You too, skipper." He clomped down the ladder to his bunk below the weather deck.

64

First Mate Antonio Sousa did not see Sam hiding around the corner watching him head for his bunk. It was one in the morning. They'd have made a new plan to work around him... Sam was sure of it. He considered the possibilities after he returned to his own compartment.

Whatever was going to happen would be after the haul. Too much going on during, especially since they were now so shorthanded. And Sam believed this would be the last set and haul of the trip. By tomorrow, they will have been out seven days, plus the two-day run back to Gloucester, making this trip a nine-day run. That was almost identical to this boat's previous sorties.

He harbored zero doubt that whatever they transferred from the freighter was aboard their boat right now. He guessed they'd make the transfer during the sale of the fish at auction, or right after.

Next morning, the last of the haul came aboard, and it was a good one. They'd be heading back to Gloucester now, for sure. Sam suspected the crew looked forward to the next trip without a nosy monitor on board. Too many weird things happened this trip. They'd blame him. *Well, fuck 'em.*

They had cored the fish, stored them in the cargo bays—the holds—and iced them down. They left the restricted area unlocked, as if to show Murdock they had nothing to hide. Sam noticed it, and that puzzled him. *Where the hell are the drugs?* He searched every cubby hole, every storage area, the food stocks, every compartment, and the engine room. He came up with nothing.

Sam didn't give up, though. He examined the three large crates of bait transferred from the freighter; none had been opened, even though they had finished fishing. He found a crowbar and pried open the top of the crate labeled *HERRING*. Yup, herring, alright. Ice packs topped the fish. He used the crowbar to stir around in the crate's contents. About two feet down, he hit what sounded like wood. Another two feet or more remained. Sam stopped to analyze the situation. He had little time, as the crew kept close tabs on him.

So, he focused on the box itself, its construction, and convinced himself the H was hidden inside. Levered the crowbar underneath that heavy crate and pushed down hard, using a small toolbox as a fulcrum. It lifted one side of the crate eight inches off the floor. Got down on his knees with his head close to the deck, pulled out his red flashlight pen, and studied the bottom of the crate. There! He discovered a removable panel someone had cut from a nearby corner. He braced the canted crate to prevent an accident. *No need to get my arm crushed underneath this baby.*

Sam discovered a tiny latch that secured a hidden waterproof area. It was rectangular and maybe 40 inches high, 18 inches across, and 24 inches deep. It had been left open. And empty. He imagined every crate featured the same hidden chamber. This was where the H *was* hidden, but was no longer there. *Gotta be thousands of places to hide this shit on a 72-foot fishing boat. It just has to still be aboard, and it must be offloaded. But how, how much, and when?* He cleaned up his mess. Returned everything to the way he found it, and headed back up to his cabin. *I need to think.*

65

Sam stretched out on his bunk. He considered possible dope hides: luggage, trash, or working bait containers that were now empty, or close to it. *How much are we talking about? Most certainly in kilos, and a lot of 'em. Hundreds? What gets offloaded, but is not carried by members of the crew? Swordfish. But just how are they doing this?*

For each question for which Sam theorized an answer, another popped up. He'd need more eyes on this than just his. But where to position them? Backups? Commercial fishing vessels advise the auction house of their types of fish, how many pounds, date of arrival, and off-loading requirements. That's called their *hail.*

He locked his cabin door and called Larry, who answered on the second ring. "Let's go, shit-magnet. You okay?"

"Here's a dump for you, boss. They smuggled what's gotta be H from a French freighter onto this boat inside three sizable wooden crates with false bottoms marked *BAIT*. Secret panels down low are secured by a latch. Hides are about 40 x 18 x 24 inches each. The dope is gone and I'm without a clue where it went. But here's my supposition. They will hide it in plain sight. Inside the swordfish, maybe? But how? And isn't that too obvious? They also took aboard two small duffel bags. No clue what's in 'em. Gotta be in the captain's cabin, and I'm stuck with no access."

"Whew, that's a pant load of intel, Sam. Is your cover holding?"

"I've got them intimidated, but they're watching me real close. Lost a deckhand to a hemolytic transfusion reaction. A crew member got himself impaled by a sword in the calf. We removed the bill and used a tourniquet, but he lost a lot of blood and dropped into shock. I started an IV and in less than twelve hours he was dead. The captain murdered him. He offered up a donor with the wrong blood type."

"Son-of-a-bitch!"

Sam said, "I'm sure you've got ideas on how to proceed."

"Well, we'll need DEA agents at the dock when you arrive. They'll offload the catch and search the boat. EPOs will serve as a second line of defense. We'll also need an EPO boat close by cruising the harbor in case they make a break or get picked up by other accomplices."

"Okay. These guys are no dummies. My gut says they're smuggling in a substantial amount of H. Maybe dozens, or even hundreds of kilos. I'll keep working on how they're doing it. Questions?"

Larry said, "Yeah. A few hundred. For starters, how many DEA agents and EPOs are we going to need? Where do we station 'em? Will any specialized equipment be necessary? How about drug-sniffing K-9s? Tell you what, you think on all that. I'll cover most of it with Sawyer, and we'll have that place buttoned up tight. You worry about getting back here alive. If you're even close to your estimate of the volume of H we're dealing with, Sawyer says this'll be the biggest operation we've encountered so far. Ever. Well done, Sam. Again. Cover your six. We'll be in touch. Out."

Larry would get it right. If they were bringing H ashore from the *Miss G*, it must be headed for high-level buyers soon after landing. Nobody ever left that stuff lying around for long. They'd keep it simple—exchange cash for the drugs. Then they'd go their separate ways... without delay. *We need to put a tail on the captain because all this ain't happening right there on the docks. Also, a tail on the buyers. Or take them both down as the exchange takes place. If we can find 'em. Options. Lots of 'em. Too many.*

Sam strolled topside to observe the last batch of swords being cored. He counted and photographed the carcasses, including the by-catch they once again cast adrift in their wake. *What a waste!* They had stacked and iced the last haul of fish in the holds and locked the doors. As Sam approached, Antonio was there. "What's your total, Ant?"

"About 40,000 pounds of sword, plus a couple thousand ground-fish and tuna. That match up with your numbers?"

"Yeah, pretty much. I also have eighteen marlin, six turtles, five dolphin, and a bunch of sharks that I haven't totaled by species yet."

Ant chuckled that off. "So what? There's plenty of 'em out here. We didn't even dent the population. Fucking bean counters in DC. If they'd just get real."

The crews secured all lines and equipment, sprayed most of the salt off the spools, winches, lines, and rinsed down the decks with fresh water from their onboard water tanks. Now that the holds were full, they knew for certain they'd make for Gloucester. Good money, plus the other benefit package that would now be split four ways instead of six.

Sam headed up to use the captain's satellite phone to report in and deliver his preliminary numbers.

"Captain?"

"Yeah, yeah, I know. He retrieved the phone, punched in the code, and handed it to Sam.

Murdock dialed, waited for the connection, and said, "Good afternoon, sir. We are loaded with about 40,000 pounds of sword and heading in. ETA Gloucester is forty-eight hours."

Pause.

"Yes, all went smoothly. I'll check in when our ETA firms up. Seas are medium chop, partly cloudy skies, and maybe some rain tonight."

Pause.

"Roger that. Murdock out."

Sam then called home. Spoke with Kate for a couple of minutes to reassure her he was well. Brian played outside with friends. "Give him my love. I'll be home in about fifty-five hours. See you then. Love you. Murdock out."

He handed the phone back to Matos. "Thanks, Captain. Looks like everything's okay back home."

"Just great, Murdock." replied the captain in his most facetious tone. Sam flipped him off when he wasn't looking. He noticed Andre coming up the pilot-house ladder and made way for him.

"Hey, Andre. How's it going?"

The Canadian UC ignored Sam's question. Was he

playing his undercover role, or had he truly gone dark? Sam returned to his cabin and locked the door. He reviewed in his head his theory about hiding the H inside the cored swordfish. *But with 40,000 pounds of fish, which ones?* Keeping the *RESTRICTED AREA* door unlocked carried significance. *But what? What the hell is the message they're sending me?*

66

Antonio busied himself preparing for the serious fire designed to break out at midnight. The crew observed his unusual activity, but knew better than to ask. Something was up, and they were sure it involved the cargo and Frank Murdock. Except for Antonio, everyone enjoyed a stout dinner of fried cod, coleslaw, and seasoned tater tots with Madeira wine. Frank, too.

The crew's mood seemed lighter than previous nights because they and the boat headed for port, and for a payday. They retired early. With two men down, that meant more back-breaking work for the remaining three. Sam, a.k.a. Frank did not offer to help. *Fuck 'em.*

Sam fooled around with his computer and debated whether to call Larry. He really wanted a shower. It had been days, and he'd grown pretty ripe. He fell asleep with the computer on his chest, only to be awakened by sirens and fire alarms just after midnight. Lots of boots clomping around on the deck above him, too. There was no mistaking the urgency, even panic in the captain's voice over the boat's PA. "All hands-on deck, all hands on-deck, including Murdock. Fire in the aft winch area. Report to Antonio for your assignment. Now!"

Nothing gets a crew's attention like an offshore shipboard fire. Sam threw his feet to the floor, slipped into a pair of jeans hanging over the sink next to his bunk, pulled on his deck shoes, and mustered aft as ordered. A substantial blaze had consumed the machinery associated with the huge reel of line on the port side just forward of the transom. Everybody shouted. Chaos reigned.

Sousa and Gagnon had each already deployed a hose; they held brass nozzles still closed, and both hoses remained flat. Sousa then dropped his nozzle in place near the blaze and scrambled to fire up a stand-alone diesel pump stored on deck and strapped down near the starboard rail, just forward of the working deck. Its huge inlet hose already dangled over the side to pump ocean water onto the boat. Sousa hollered at Sam. "Pick up the nozzle I dropped and aim it toward the base of the flames!"

Sousa fired up the pump. He connected both hoses, and flipped the levers on two bronze gate valves. Both hoses stiffened once they pressurized with sea water water. That pump now pushed a beefy 800 GPM (gallons-per-minute) on demand. Sam and Gagnon aimed their nozzles toward the base of the fire and pulled back on the yoke atop each nozzle. The reaction from the suddenly charged hoses now releasing pressurized sea water onto the flames tried to kick them back. They planted their feet and stood fast.

The pump grunted. Its RPMs dipped as it bore down behind them to meet the hoses' demands. An instant cloud of sticky saltwater steam engulfed them. It stunk like rotten eggs. Though they now saw little, they heard the wet blaze hiss like it was pissed at being challenged. Sam heard that hissing even over the insistent thrumming of the rather loud diesel pump less than 15 feet behind them.

Sam shouted, "Where's Carlos?"

Without looking up from his finicky pump's controls, Antonio shouted, "Sick-bay. Strained back."

As Sam waggled his nozzle sideways, then up and down to douse the flames, he yelled back, "When did he do that? He looked fine at dinnertime."

Antonio still didn't look up from the pump. "He lifted a sword by himself after it slid out of the hold. The idiot should have asked for help."

Strained back? Right!

67

Before the fire started, and hidden from prying eyes in his cabin, Captain Matos handed over the latest shipment of heroin—their biggest yet—to Carlos. Now, his engineer would do his part. While the fire raged aft, Carlos made several hurried trips down to the hold. He then sealed a plastic bag containing a brick of heroin inside a cored swordfish that was ready for auction. Each brick comprised half a kilogram—over a pound each.

With a nine-inch razor-sharp filet knife, he made a precision cut from the vent of each cored sword down its center to the bottom of its tail. He inserted a bag. Wiped the edges of the cut dry, and then super glued them back together. Perfect. Did this a couple hundred times. He hurried while the others fought the fire.

The street value of 100 kilos of pure uncut heroin from Afghanistan was worth at least twenty-two million US dollars. But to get that much, they'd need a distribution network, dealers, and a lot of risky hands-on overhead. Instead, they'd take a fraction of that from a buyer, like before. Still, that was several million dollars, now to be split only four ways. Not a bad week's work!

The rest of the crew had arranged the carcasses, so it would be easier and faster for Carlos to do his work without jockeying fish around too much. Antonio, and even the captain, told him his artistry was amazing. He had done this many times. Carlos was making excellent time, but moving, packing, gluing, and replacing each of 200 heavy fish still made for exhausting work.

The fire still raged, fueled by the stinky incineration of hundreds of small plastic floats used for marking the longline at every tenth snood. Twenty gallons of accelerant started the fire, but now it had spread to the greasy equipment that operated the port side eight-foot-diameter longline reel. They hadn't counted on that. Now, the danger was all-too real on the small boat, still 60 miles offshore.

Still, the men worked with the captain to both keep Murdock occupied while watching for Carlos, *and* now battling a suddenly serious enemy that threatened to sink their boat.

They drowned that fire with thousands of gallons of seawater pouring over the top and around the flames. This took almost two hours. Fortunately, that water drained back overboard from the canted deck through a dozen scupper holes located around the edge of the deck. The captain shouted out, "Make sure you allow no embers to rekindle. Keep wettin' her down till she cools!"

By 0300 hours, they had doused the fire and the threat to the boat. The captain said, "Secure hoses, pumps, and all other fire-fighting equipment except for one hose just in case. Antonio, hang around a while to make sure it doesn't restart."

Sam said to no one in particular, "Now I *really* want a shower."

Captain Matos looked around. "Yeah, go, Frank. Thanks for your help."

Murdock wandered off to his compartment looking dirty and dead-tired—as planned. Matos nodded to Antonio before making his way forward and below decks to the holds. He startled Carlos, still busy stuffing fish with bags of dope. "How goes it, Carlos? You 'bout done?"

"A half-dozen to go, Captain. Just markin' *the*

specials with the somewhat lighter blue ink for each core's weight stamp."

Matos stood guard at the hold's entrance. Carlos finished and gave the captain two thumbs up. Carlos had worked his magic. He retired to his compartment. Sousa and Gagnon came down to help Matos rearrange the layer of ice atop the fish so it looked like it did BC—*Before Carlos*. Then, when it seemed none of them could keep their eyes open a second longer, everyone hit the rack.

68

At 0400 hours, Sam fell into his bunk at last. *The captain might grant a couple extra hours of sleep after spending most of the night fighting that strange fire.* Too soon, though, the captain's annoying voice squawked over the loudspeaker, "Grab yourselves a ten-minute breakfast. Then, all hands-on deck for clean-up."

Sam brushed his teeth. His clothes from last night still lay in a pile on the floor by his bunk. They still wreaked of burning plastic, rancid smoke, and salt water steam. They'd never dry until he rinsed them with fresh water. He dragged his large backpack from underneath his berth. Grabbed a fresh change of duds —the last of his clean laundry—and threw them on. That helped a lot.

. . .

He scored two breakfast sandwiches and a large coffee from the mess. Settled in his customary position above the deck but below the pilothouse's aft bulkhead over-hang—his station where he commanded a clear view of everything happening down on the oak-planked working deck. They'd already tossed the detritus of the fire overboard except for the faulty corroded wiring on a winch pump that had allegedly caused the fire. He wanted to inspect that winch's equipment more thoroughly.

He wondered about the fire. How convenient. When he first arrived at the scene, he immediately helped battle the flames. Now, after some time to think about it, he harbored reservations about its cause. On the pretense of taking a leak, Sam approached the port railing close to the burn area. With as much nonchalance as he could muster, he wandered over and examined the winch's wiring. He noticed a burned red wire pulled from its junction box, detached from its wire nut and laying against the grounded winch. *That* created a dead short. And *that* resulted in an *intentional* fire.

"Whatcha doin' over here?" said Antonio.

"Sort of curious about what started the fire. Aren't you? Is that a problem for you?"

"Ain't your business, so get back to your fuckin' fish counting."

"Hey Ant, kiss my ass. Not my fire to fight, yet I

helped you. I've got as much right as anyone on this tub."

Antonio sneered, "You and me got some personal business to finish before you head for shore."

"Anytime, Ant-man." *What is his breaking point? I'm getting close to my own.* Sam's confidence bloomed in the face of this formidable foe. He snapped a photo of the winch's wiring and marched back to his station. There, he pulled up the picture he just took with his Nikon Z. He expanded the shot and examined it closely. Yup, intentional, alright. But why? *To keep me busy last night, the final night before making port?* Sam admired their creativity.

Sam finished his sandwiches and most of that horrible mug of muddy caffeine. Wobbled down to sick bay faking a headache. Empty, and no sign of anyone having been there since he'd tended to the dying Eduardo Braga. So, Carlos supposedly had been in sick bay with a bad back. He now knew that wasn't true.

69

A half-hour later, Sam then snuck down to the fish holds and searched every nook and cranny. He found nothing unusual except for quite a lot of ice scattered on the deck. Yesterday it had been dry. *Another puzzle piece.* He cut open several cored swordfish to inspect their insides, but found nothing unusual. No way did he have the time to examine every one—there were hundreds. An impossible task. And so far, they'd discovered no probable cause for an exhaustive search of every fuckin' fish.

He sensed a presence behind him and ducked low on instinct after hearing a big inhale through their teeth. A sweeping right hand passed over his head like the sudden wind of a brooding storm. *Whoosh!* Antman. He'd finally boiled over with Sam's relentless attacks on the captain and him. A left also missed. With a crushing grip, Sam grabbed the big man's balls now right in front of him and dug in. Antonio howled. Sam stood up fast to drive a solid left elbow up into his right cheek. He connected with brutal force.

Following that pile-driving elbow which put the man on his heels, Sam hammered Sousa's liver with a vicious right hook. That shot buckled him. Sousa hadn't landed a single blow yet. Sam had him on the ropes but dared not let up. Ant's size and strength meant he was still damn dangerous. And Sam sensed Antonio meant this encounter to be lethal.

So, he bludgeoned Antonio's face with a cruel left cross and drove another right to his gut. Adrenaline now raced through Sam's system. He rallied primal instincts fueled by eons of evolution. His survival now depended on the same animalistic impulses that allowed cave dwellers to defeat a superior foe in order to survive. Sam embraced the rage from deep within his lizard brain as it now roared through his psyche. He feared losing the control he'd been able to leash so far, mostly. But now....

Still, he paused to assess the big man's condition. Hurt, but not out. A bone-jarring upper cut from Antonio sent Sam reeling on his heels. *Next time, don't fuckin' let up until the man's out cold. When are you going to learn?*

A staggering but still dangerous Antonio closed the distance in that narrow passageway that divided the port fish holds from those to starboard. Not much room to dance. The floor this close to the ladder, aft of the holds, was always wet and slimy, despite the grating. The lighting in the room sucked. He shivered at his own counsel. *Use these to your advantage.*

Sam's earlier onslaught had slowed Antonio. That made his moves easier to anticipate and to counter. He easily blocked Antonio's right cross with his left arm. Sam continued the follow-through with his left fist by landing a rock-solid blow to Antonio's right cheek. He then followed through by peppering the big man's face with a flurry of fierce jabs.

Antonio now bled from a deep cut above his right eye. *Okay, any head wound bleeds like crazy. That'll blind him on that side. He's gonna have to wipe it to see my lefts.* So, Sam concentrated on Ant's right side with his vicious jabs and solid body punches. He wanted to open that cut further and to keep him off-balance. Now, Antonio's punches lacked his usual speed and follow-through.

Sam kept up his relentless onslaught, using his bony elbows, forearms, and knuckles. He wondered how much more whoop-ass he'd need to deliver. He grabbed the man's ears like they were handles and pulled his head down to meet his ascending left knee. *Crunch.* That murderous blow finished him.

Both men's chests heaved. Antonio was now down *and* out cold, at last. Sam put him in the rescue position to prevent him from drowning in his own blood. *Geezus, I've fought more rounds on this op than a pro fighter in a championship fifteen-rounder.*

He slumped on the metal grate decking next to the unconscious brute, leaning up against one of the hold's cold metal bulkheads. Felt good. Sam suffered a couple of wounds, but nothing major. His jaw hurt from Ant's upper cut, but he was glad he'd seized the early initiative because this guy outweighed him by a good 25 pounds. He gained an advantage by leveraging this space, too. These cramped quarters constrained Antonio's primary advantages—his reach and power.

A few minutes passed. Sam suddenly realized the captain, Carlos, and Andre now stood over them. He'd regained his breath and stood with some effort. The captain spoke first. "What the fuck is this?"

"I was down here doing a count and Antonio started swinging. I defended myself. Nothing more than that. I don't know why he wanted to fight. I wasn't doing anything other than my fuckin' job."

Matos seethed. "You took out my first mate. I'm throwing you in the brig until we get to port,"

"No, captain, no you are not. And if you think that Glock you're holding is the answer, guess again, You already have two dead crewmen to account for. Make that three? Bring your toothbrush, sweetheart. You'll go away for a long time." Sam pointed toward Andre and Carlos. "And if you two birds have any ideas, forget 'em. You'll be joining him. I'll flood this boat with more badges and guns than you've ever seen, in port or out. I have a right to defend myself anywhere, anytime, when attacked. Ask Antonio when he regains consciousness. If he's man enough, he'll tell you the truth. Jumped me from behind. Get him to sick bay and get ice on his swollen parts, including his balls, and bandage up his lacerations. Now get him out of here and leave me the fuck alone."

Captain Matos had no doubts Frank Murdock would make good on his threat to rain law enforcement hell down on him. He couldn't afford that. Neither could he afford a third body on this trip. He'd relent to complete his mission. At least for now.

Goddammit, this guy is a pain in my ass! His time is coming.

70

They steamed southwest to Gloucester. The men remained in their bunks. Captain Matos stayed glued to his helm. Sam wondered how much time that man spent up there alone and who he might be contacting. Hadn't been able to get his recorder placed again. He'd also retreated to his cabin, locked the door, and pulled out his phone from its hide inside his mattress.

He brought Larry up to speed. "I haven't solved the puzzle yet."

"Okay, Sam, but I suggest you cool it with the fisticuffs and make it back without getting your butt tossed overboard, or worse. Preparations for your arrival are underway. Had a productive meeting with the DEA. We established set-up positions in Gloucester, assigned back-ups, supervisors, and formulated cross-agency communication protocols. I'll be with SAC Sawyer, the overall commander of the op."

"That sounds great, Lar'."

He signed off feeling a little better and called Kate. Told her he'd be home soon. "Love you and miss you like crazy, babe." He hung up without saying goodbye when he heard someone approaching his cabin door. Stashed his phone in haste. Turned out to be a false alarm. *Yeah, the jitters are gettin' bad, soldier. Get control over these emotions.*

After what seemed like a non-stop chain of physical and emotional eruptions over the past week, Sam now prioritized a few quiet minutes to ponder the big questions. *Where have they stashed the contraband? And what was in those duffel bags the Frenchies brought aboard if the H was in the bait crates before they emptied 'em?* It always came back to swordfish—the only transient commodity on the vessel. *What in this particular hell am I going to do? Should I pester the captain again and ask for his final tally?*

The captain would need to call the dock master and advise him of his position, ETA, and all species he'll be offering for auction—his hail. *If our numbers tally, great. If not, then what?*

Sam took his Epson laptop computer with him to the pilothouse. But he'd never give up his paper notebook. Took that, too. When the captain saw Sam enter, he said, "Now, what the fuck do you want?"

"Since we'll be in port in less than twelve hours, I need to compare notes with you on your haul. It's required under ICCAT rules and regulations that we coordinate our numbers. Might as well get it done now because upon arrival you'll be busy with unloading and the auction."

"Oh, for crissake, Antonio handles all that for me. I secure the boat, complete the captain's log, and then go to the auction house."

"Okay, but from what Ant provided you for your official log, I need swordfish numbers in pounds, not in quantity, please." Sam figured it couldn't hurt to be polite.

The captain mumbled an eloquent litany of creative profanity under his breath, most in Portuguese. He thumbed through several folders in a slotted bin between his helm seat and the chart table to its rear. He split his attention between this interruption and his duties at the helm. After some page-turning in his logbook, the captain grumbled, "I'm going to hail 35,000 pounds of swordfish. Plus, we got 4,000 pounds of yellowfin, and about 300 pounds of cod, haddock, and pollack."

Sam scrunched his forehead and scratched his chin with the hand not holding his notebook splayed open on top of his still-closed laptop computer. He used it like a portable desk surface crammed in the crook of his right arm. "Um, I've got *40,000* pounds of sword, and Ant agreed. The rest are close to my numbers. What gives on the sword number?"

An awkward silence ensued. Then, "A customer, a friend in Newburyport, wants 5,000 pounds for his dealers. I been doin' business with him for 15 years. A short stop there to offload. Take an hour or two."

"Huh, first I've heard of this unscheduled stop."

Matos said, "Look, Murdock, I don't have to disclose shit to you about *who* I sell to. No regulation about that. I checked. You only need to know we've accounted for the catch."

Matos was right. He didn't answer to Sam. But this unscheduled stop at a port in another coastal town to drop off 5,000 pounds of swordfish? *Another puzzle piece falls into place. This is the play!* Specific fish for a specific friend at a specific but unscheduled place and time. "What's our Newburyport ETA?"

Matos said, "About three hours. Which puts us there at about 1900 hours. That's seven pm for you lubbers." He sneered at this pain-in-the-ass bean counter. Or fish counter, in this case.

Sam interpreted this new stop as a serious threat to solving this case. *Is this a diversion to throw me off with the real stuff going to Gloucester? And what about Andre? Where and what will he feed me, if anything? Is he still a Canadian UC since he's a confessed accomplice now? Or was that part of his cover? Is he that clever? I'll deal with his ass later.* He'd need extra caution with Gagnon.

Sam nodded to the captain in silent thanks and

returned to his compartment to call Larry on his own secret phone. "A change in plans, boss. Captain just informed me he's making a delivery in Newburyport first—5,000 pounds of swordfish. Then he'll head to Gloucester with the other 35,000. I know this is fishy —sorry—but we need a second team there. Pronto. We're only three hours out of Newburyport. Someone from NMFS and DEA needs to inspect every single one of those damn fish. I think that's where we'll find our contraband."

Larry murmured, as if distracted... or frustrated, "I'll get right on it. We'll be ready... somehow."

It was uncharacteristic of Larry to just hang up. *But he's gotta scramble tail over teakettle on this Newburyport wrinkle. I hope I'm not hanging out alone when we get there!* Sam packed up his gear to prepare for landfall and to get the hell off this murderous tub.

On second thought, is Matos feeding me misinformation? This Newburyport twist sucks resources away from Gloucester. A double fake? Is he that shifty? An insistent knock on his door shook him loose from the questions rattling around his overstressed brain. Sam opened the door. Andre, the Canadian DFO undercover agent, or whatever, stood there with wide eyes.

Sam growled, "What do you want?"

"We need to talk since everyone is busy readying for landfall."

"What about?"

Andre whispered, "What are you plans for the

landing? I'm betting you'll have teams ready to hit this boat once it arrives and unloads."

"I have you on tape, Andre. You're colluding with the captain and are now one of his accomplices."

Andre's eyes darted around before he responded. "Shit, that ain't worth nothing. The fourth Amendment to your Constitution protects people from electronic surveillance without consent. It's worthless and will be suppressed in court."

"Yeah? You think you know our Constitution? The Fourth Amendment applies to US citizens, not aliens. You are not a US citizen. I checked. Your words are admissible." Sam wasn't entirely sure here, but he need this guy doubting himself.

Andre paused, but said nothing. He turned on his heel and marched out. That puzzled Sam. *Is he friend or foe?* But Sam resigned himself to trusting his gut. Andre didn't offer to work together, or assist, or even deny he was now Matos' lackey. He also hoped he was right about the Newburyport drop, that it was the key to solving this smuggling operation—yet another important piece of this puzzle.

Beyond his gut, though, he wasn't sure about anything other than *this is the boat*. And that the entire crew was a part of the operation, including Gagnon. There could be no doubt about that, at least.

71

DEA SAC Chuck Sawyer and EPO Captain Larry Jamison analyzed the news from Sergeant Sam Travis, EPO and temporary undercover Federal Officer for the DEA, Sawyer said, "We'll split the teams up and get 'em in place, *but* with insufficient scouting. Don't like it at all, Larry."

"How far away is Newburyport from Gloucester?"

"Maybe 24 miles? 40 minutes by vehicle, at least, even with lights and siren."

Larry scratched the top of his head, and ruffled his hair in frustration. "Shit. That means another boat and crew for a possible water exit. That's mine. Another K-9 ashore, too? Can I assume you got that, Chuck?"

"Not on this short notice, I'm afraid."

"Olay, I'll call the local PD for a dog. Or the State Police."

Chuck said, "One more thing. Can Newburyport handle a 72-foot, 70-ton sword boat?"

"No idea. I'll call the harbormaster's office." The op had suddenly accelerated to light speed. And they were losing tactical control.

Sawyer asked, "Are boat-to-boat transfers allowed by commercial fishing regs?"

Larry searched his memory. "Whew, that's a tough one. That's called a *landing*. As long as the fish are dead and will be used for consumption, it's legal. I get where you're going with this. We'll keep the *Miss Guided One* under surveillance as soon as she enters state waters. If a transfer takes place, we'll board the boat under the guise of a safety check with no further probable cause. If we find something... yeah, that works. A little tricky, is all. Let's get the *Miss G's* location and get a bird aloft. How much time to get all this in place?"

Sawyer said, "There's a bird at Hanscomb Field and another at Logan. I'll get the one at Logan up if it's available. If it's not, I'll call Hanscomb."

72

The *Grim Reefer*, a sixty-foot commercial dragger, hailed out of Newburyport. She headed out of the Merrimack River to coordinates already locked into her GPS and autopilot—about three miles offshore. Franz Heileg, the *Reefer's* skipper, planned to arrive after sunset for the rendezvous. He looked forward to receiving, ship-to-ship, his special order from that Portuguese pirate Afonso Matos.

The weather sucked. Some low fog and drizzle with the temps in the forties made everything dank and cold. A steady 15-knot offshore wind cut through one's soul and tossed it about in a bitch of a chop. These conditions guaranteed a complicated transfer.

The *Reefer* made 16 knots. Her windshield wipers squeegeed the drizzle with a syncopated rhythm, but they helped little in the lousy visibility. One hour out. He clicked his radar over to its five-mile range.

The captain's two crewmen scurried around the deck so slick it was as if it had no non-skid surface at all. The biting wet and cold even penetrated their Grundéns—head-to-toe rubberized fishing apparel—that they wore over their flannel shirts, wool sweaters, wool socks, and heavy dungarees. Their insulated and rubberized gloves ascended all the way to their elbows, where Velcro sealed them against the cold sea spray and rain.

Captain Heileg had painted on his radar a few small fishing boats returning to the harbor. Only he was headed out. But nothing large like the *Miss G* yet appeared on his scope to seaward. The appointed time drew near. Heileg shouted to his crew above the shrieking wind, "Make ready the winches, and for crissake, don't slip and fall overboard!"

Sam reclined in his bunk, suspecting that a legal boat-to-boat transfer *was* likely to take place soon. He worried about allowing that transfer, doubting whether his own agency and the DEA were flexible enough to adjust to his last-minute intel. But he remained powerless to stop what would happen next. He was about to lose the contraband and maybe the whole case.

Sam walked out on deck, thinking his extra layers of clothing would protect him from the weather. He was wrong. His nervousness added to the chill in the air as his teeth chattered, like they possessed a will of their own. He was early and scanned for any sign of another vessel. Hopeless. Fog obscured everything. Yet the stars were out. He'd wait, but not patiently.

---

30 minutes later, Captain Matos neared the rendezvous coordinates. Antonio scratched at the edges of a couple of bandages on his face as he prepared to supervise the transfer. Spotted the *Reefer* 100 yards away and closing. The large woven-rope fenders he slung over *Miss G's* starboard side prevented damage to both vessels in these vicious conditions. The *Grim Reefer* drew near.

Each captain maneuvered with their twin throttles. As they drew closer, they used their bow and stern thrusters to fine-tune their approach. Those thrusters battled wind and waves. The two vessels, now parallel to each other, closed to a few feet. Two crew on the *Reefer* tossed over bow, stern, and spring lines. Carlos manned the bow winch and cranked in the *Reefer's* bow line. Andre tended the stern winch to receive the stern line opposite the damaged longline spool winch from the earlier fire.

After snugging it up, he caught a spring line that would stabilize their fore-and-aft positions relative to one another by running from the *Reefer's* bow to another of the *Miss G's* stern winches. They had now drawn the two vessels together and compressed the huge, rope fenders between them. Two vessels had become one, at least as far as the wind and waves were concerned.

Antonio then set and lashed the short gangplank with help from the *Reefer's* two-man crew. He thought, *Time to do some business.*

73

Sawyer and Jamison failed to complete all the arrangements in time to intercept the Newburyport rendezvous. Plus, the lousy weather further complicated matters.

Two EPOs were underway in their twenty-five-foot patrol boat. Sawyer pulled two DEA agents out of the Boston office to assist dockside at the small Newburyport harbor. A K-9 and his handler from Boston's Logan Airport's State Police detachment provided the quickest access to a drug dog. Who knew if smelling dope inside a dead fish was within a K-9's repertoire? His handler said it most assuredly was.

And they transported in by trailer three fast Coast Guard rigid inflatable boats called RIBs. Two large outboards on each pushed these pursuit craft along at a respective fifty knots if necessary. Each of these twenty-five-foot chase boats carried an armed and experienced three-member USCG crew. The multi-agency task force commander, SAC Chuck Sawyer, tasked them with escorting both subject vessels into custody at the Coast Guard station near their Water Street Headquarters.

A representative from four agencies—Coast Guard, DEA, Massachusetts Environmental Police, and the Massachusetts State Police—planned to perform an exhaustive search of both vessels. Plus, they'd need *all* engaged law enforcement personnel to muscle around 5,000 pounds of hefty fish.

First, they'd put the K-9 to work. Next, a visual search for contraband would follow. But this magnitude of cross-agency collaboration and resource requirements at this new location on such short notice? Of course, they'd do the best they could.

Miss G and the *Grim Reefer* achieved their rendezvous at the appointed time five miles offshore in adverse weather with no radio contact. Captains Heileg and Matos used nothing but their new GPS navigation technology and handheld spotlights to arrive together at their predetermined coordinates. They took pride at accomplishing this feat on this foggy night with a brutal chop running. The conditions punished them, and they were worsening.

Captain Heileg of the *Reefer* crossed the gyrating

gangplank to the *Miss G*. He nearly got tossed over the side—twice. Captain Matos greeted him with an awkward but businesslike handshake. Each used their other hand to steady themselves by clutching *Miss G's* starboard railing.

The decks of both boats were now lit up like high noon. No choice. In this weather, that was the only way to raft up in the dark of night and make a transfer. Such an ostentatious display was against the better judgement of both skippers. But they also appreciated the shitty weather to hide them.

74

The Coast Guard notified the DEA of their radar fix on the two boats. Their chase boats and the EPO boat planned to approach the two vessels from three directions. The task force assumed the drug transfer had progressed significantly by the time their boats approached. The two boats had already remained connected for 15 minutes.

That's when it happened.

Sam watched and counted the fish transferred. Only 21 lousy fish? He felt defeat. Where the hell did they hide the damn dope? And the larger transfer of fish Matos described was... nothing but a... smokescreen? Carlos and Andre emerged from below, each carrying a smallish black duffel bag. Must be the ones from the

French Freighter *Grand Francaise*. They handed both across to Heileg's crew. Heileg shook hands with Matos, and that was it. He scrambled back to his own boat. *What?*

Matos unlashed and withdrew their stubby little gangplank. Gagnon and Almeida tossed off the *Reefer's* lines and pulled in their fenders. It seemed they'd completed their transfers to the *Reefer*: less than two dozen cored swordfish, two small duffels, and the money to pay for the transfers had passed to the *Miss G*. But something smelled... fishy.

Nothing to do but let that happen and trust the K-9 and the DEA agents to bust them. One more leg to go. Sam remained optimistic... almost. The vessels separated, killed their spots, illuminated their navigation lights, and got underway.

* * *

The Coast Guard tried to maintain their radar fix on the two suspect boats. Surface clutter from choppy conditions partially obscured their fix, but they could tell when the two boats separated and were underway, even though each frequently disappeared in what's called surface clutter, or noise, on their radar screens. Lousy sea conditions. Even worse, minute by minute, the fog grew more dense. Upon receiving word from cross-agency task force commander, SAC Sawyer, the two Coast Guard RIBS planned to approach the vessels along with the single EPO vessel. So they notified the DEA.

The Coast Guard and EPO boats located and stopped the *Grim Reefer* about two miles from their rendezvous point. The *Reefer's* captain radioed *Miss G*, informing them of the boarding. They were being escorted to the Coast Guard Station in Newburyport. Captain Matos smiled. He'd thrown up a red herring and they bit. Plan B had worked like a dream. He now knew for certain that there'd be a greeting party in Gloucester, too. Who was the rat? Andre or Frank?

Time for Plan C. They'd bought Carlos enough time to move their 100 kilos of H from the marked swordfish into three waterproof dry-bags. Clever to keep Murdock busy topside by allowing him to snoop on their rendezvous with the *Reefer*. That's when Carlos accomplished yet another switch. Each dry-bag weighed in at a hefty seventy-five pounds.

A short time later, Sam learned in a quick debrief from Larry on his phone that the State Police K-9 unit got a hit on the duffel bags aboard the *Reefer*. Fifty pounds of hashish in each bag. Must have been a special order. No H, though. They'd allow the *Miss G* to dock and then tear the boat apart at their leisure. Better than a cursory search at sea. Or so they assumed.

The fog had lifted, and a billion stars now illuminated the night sky. Sam stood on deck surveying the lights of Boston's skyline, peeking over the horizon off their starboard bow. The ocean's obsidian wilderness to port stared back at him. He asked himself, *What have I missed? Something.*

A brilliant quarter moon hung in a now clear and twinkling sky. Conditions change swiftly at sea, and tonight was no exception. *So, if the contraband we're looking for didn't pass to the Reefer, then it has to still be aboard this vessel.*

They'd reach Gloucester in about half an hour, ready to offload, weigh, and sell their catch. They'd store the catch on ice in a refrigerated room until the auction began at 0500. The winning bidder planned to deliver their purchases to distributors or to large markets that did their own final processing. *We're nearly out of time.*

Gloucester Harbor's outer marker, a lighted bell buoy, came into view. That and the rest of the channel markers would guide the *Miss G.* The vessel slowed not long after entering the shipping channel. They passed close aboard a small island. Sam recognized the lighthouse on Ten Pound Island. He thought, *Why is Matos slowing down way out here? We're still over a mile from the pier.*

75

Below deck, Antonio had already donned his quarter-inch-thick neoprene wet suit, hood, and booties. Next, he slipped his arms into a vest worn by every scuba diver. They called that vest a buoyancy control device, or BCD. He'd carry his mask, snorkel, and fins until at the rail. For this short but cold swim, he'd not need a compressed air tank, just his snorkel attached to his mask's head strap. He did not relish strapping on this damn mask. Gonna sting where it put pressure on his bruised face thanks to Murdock's beating. *O bastardo!*

The heroin was now in three waterproof sacks called dry-bags often used by divers to protect their valuables. He strapped one to his back. Secured each of the second and third to a black life jacket. He tethered them to his waist. Swimming with such a configuration, even with his strength, threatened to be a challenge. He'd drag a hundred keys—220 pounds—of dead weight. Even in the mild harbor chop? No picnic. He'd sink like a rock if he didn't deploy life jackets on the dry-bags, even with his scuba BCD inflated *and* with some air sealed tightly within each dry-bag.

The captain passed their target island close aboard. He slipped both engines into neutral. Antonio slid down the hand loops on a line that hung down into the water near the raised bow with his cargo. He remained concealed from the location where that fuckin' Murdock always hung out. Ant began his 100-yard swim toward the tiny island with his *special cargo*. He scanned the shore where a small twenty-footer was to pick him up. As soon as he hit the water, *Miss G's* engines spun up again. He grinned. Plan C.

Captain Matos had already made the call to his buyers, Pierpoint Exporters, Inc. They'd meet in a local Gloucester warehouse that had been vacant for years. Located close to the seafood auction site, Pierpoint had purchased this waterfront building several years ago.

After off-loading his catch and collecting the money from the auction, Matos planned to walk toward the warehouse, ensuring no one followed. Then Antonio was to pick him up. Matos smiled. He had run rings around the feds for the last several years, and each time he'd beaten them.

This—his last run—unknown to his buyers, would be his most profitable. The sale of *his* 100 keys of heroin would fund his retirement nicely. Matos suffered no guilt at keeping all the money. The crew was an expendable means to his own ends. His only reluctance was Antonio. But he dared not leave any loose ends.

DEA SAC Chuck Sawyer and EPO Captain Larry Jamison watched their mission disintegrating before their eyes, despite their best efforts. The report from Newburyport yielded no heroin... only an interesting seizure of hashish. Captain Matos had outsmarted them. So far, anyway.

Both men grew angry and frustrated. Sawyer grumbled, "Let's follow through with the plan, go to the auction, and examine the offloaded swordfish. Every last one."

Jamison shrugged. "Okay, but it's gonna be a monumental waste of time. We got outsmarted, although I have no idea how. I gotta see what Travis thinks."

Sam stood on deck, troubled. He'd witnessed the transfer of a few swordfish to another boat and had convinced himself they'd find the heroin in those cored swords. But that transfer was nowhere near 5,000 pounds necessary to conceal and camouflage a large shipment of heroin. Not inside 21 fuckin' fish. They'd since verified that. No H.

So, Matos had baited him and he not only bit at the bait, but swallowed the whole damn hook, leader, and sinker. He needed to talk with Larry to discuss options. *Did I just piss away a pretty fuckin' dangerous week of my life for a few pounds of hash?*

Sam reached his quarters and dug out his phone. He called Larry whose first words were, "Whatcha got?"

"I missed something boss. I keep bouncing it around in my tiny brain. We're almost docked and there's no dope on this rust bucket. They beat us somehow, Lar'"

"No, Sam, they haven't beaten us yet. We are *not* done. What's your gut telling you? Go deep inside for the smallest detail somewhere in your brain. What felt... *off?* It's there, Sam. Dig it out. Until then, we follow our agreed-upon protocol with the DEA. But it's up to you to find the key to locking up these murdering drug-dealing bastards."

"Okay, boss, but I'm out of ideas."

Scolding, Larry said, "No, you are *not* out of ideas. Think closer to Gloucester without letting that rendezvous shit confuse matters. That was nothing more than a smoke screen. So, forget it. Focus on the recent past, up to right now. It's there. But we have little time left."

Sam knew Larry was right. After he hung up, he lay in his bunk. *Okay, after the transfer, what happened? Nothing. We headed for Gloucester. No stops. What was unusual from that point?*

Five minutes flew by, when he recalled the engines had decreased RPMs as they entered Gloucester Harbor, just for 15 seconds. He also remembered that for a moment or two his feet pressed against the bulkhead, toward the bow, as the loaded boat lost its momentum. She had dropped into neutral—different vibrations throughout the entire boat. Near that small island with the lighthouse... Ten Pound Island. *Why did Matos do that?*

His brain now fired on all cylinders with no distractions. *He must have slowed to drop off someone! Then he bumped the boat back up to harbor cruising speed. Gotta check for everyone that's supposed to be on the boat without them knowing I'm looking.*

Sam jumped out of his bunk with new purpose. He sauntered out on deck, where Andre and Carlos prepared to make port. Looked up and spotted Matos's shoulder as he leaned close to the pilothouse window scanning the harbor for traffic. *But where's Antonio?* He walked up to Andre. "Where's Ant?"

"Dunno. Around somewhere. Can't be anywhere but on the boat." Sam sensed the lie in an instant. Hell, he read it on Andre's face. Now he *knew* they'd flipped

Andre. Another puzzle piece confirmed. The skipper had slowed the boat down to drop Antonio off near that island close aboard *Miss G's* starboard side. He swam there, and a boat picked him up. The only explanation.

But to take him where? A different boat ramp somewhere in Gloucester Harbor? *Shit! That's how they do it! At least for this trip.* They'd then meet the buyers somewhere close by. *The swords don't have the heroin in 'em at all. Maybe never did. Antonio Sousa muled it to another boat!*

After the off-load, Matos must plan to meet up with Ant, and they'd proceed to the buy. *Okay, that works, but how do we counter that? Where the hell is Ant headed?* He quick-timed it back to his cabin, locked the door, and called Larry. Told him about his premise.

Larry said, "That's gotta be it, Sam, but how do we know where Sousa and the heroin are headed?"

"Don't know, Lar'. Say, have the EPO boat check their radar. Ask 'em what they see. I'd bet that boat is making flank speed to clear the area ASAFP. Have 'em scan for a fast mover. **Now**, Larry."

Jamison hailed the EPO boat on his portable radio with Sam still on the phone. Told them what to look for. Given the estimated elapsed time, he suggested they look out to 25 miles. Larry kept his portable's speaker close to the phone.

Sergeant Davis aboard the EPO boat said, "I'm heading in at the mouth of Gloucester Harbor. Made decent time coming down from Newburyport. We're monitoring our radar. Standby." Larry waited for Davis to respond. Then, "I see several vessels, but only one fast-mover. I'd estimate they're making thirty-five knots on a course toward the state boat ramp. ETA no more than five minutes."

"Thank you, Sergeant. Please make all possible speed to that ramp. I'll get a cruiser over there to back you up. You and your partner must secure that vessel and standby for instructions."

"Roger that, sir."

Larry continued in a solemn tone. "Sergeant, consider whoever is aboard that vessel, armed and extremely dangerous. Got it?"

"Yessir. Out."

Sam and Larry sensed they'd just resuscitated new life into their case. Larry said, "Good work, Sam. We're on it. Stay safe. Out." Sam grinned like he'd hit the jackpot at the MGM Grand casino in Springfield. He stashed his phone in a jacket pocket, grabbed his duffel, and waited to go ashore as they closed in on the pier. He didn't speak further to anyone aboard the *Miss G.*

I can't wait to get off this curs-ed tub.

Chuck Sawyer and Larry Jamison also headed for the public boat launch in Sawyer's unmarked DEA cruiser. Larry told the task force commander what he'd learned from his UC aboard the *Miss G*. They used no lights or siren to avoid alerting anyone, but they broke the speed limit, anyway. Larry said, "We'll get there in time with a little luck in tow. We're overdue for some a that, Chuck."

"Roger that, partner!"

76

It was high tide. As soon as the *Miss G's* starboard gunwale kissed the wooden pier. Sam took a giant step down ashore, even before Carlos and Andre secured any lines. He quick-walked toward the auction house and its outdoor bleachers where groups of bidders already gathered, anxiously awaiting the fresh catch.

Sam scanned for anyone who might be a UC. First glance revealed no undercover DEA agents. He approached one possible, but no joy. Sam kept searching for anyone on the waterfront who looked slightly *wrong*. Especially this early in the morning.

As he neared the auction house, he focused his own UC-trained eyes on another possible. Walked over to him. "I'm Sergeant Sam Travis, Mass EPO, working undercover for the DEA on a smuggling case. Are you an operative?" His dead-serious demeanor left no doubt. He was *not* joking.

At first, no response. Then, the guy flashed his DEA badge down low. "What do you need, Sarge?"

"You and a car."

"Follow me."

"What's your name?"

"Agent Daniel Johnson at your service. SAC Sawyer briefed us about you and the op."

"Head for the state boat ramp as fast as possible, Agent Johnson. No lights, no siren. If anyone from law enforcement tries to stop you, keep going. We might need their company. We're looking for one male in a wet suit, or changing out of one, at the ramp's dock, and at least one other asshole. They are our targets. Do you have comms with Sawyer and Jamison?"

"Yes, Sergeant. Use this."

"It's Sam, Agent Johnson."

"Roger that. I'm Daniel."

Sam nodded. He grabbed a miniature portable radio from the bench seat of Daniel's Crown Victoria sedan as they sped toward the state boat ramp. He called Larry to describe his situation and offered an updated description of Antonio Sousa.

Then Sam recognized Sawyer's voice. "Any agent or EPO, these guys are likely armed and dangerous. Do not apprehend. Follow and advise only."

Sam piped in. "This is Travis with Agent Johnson. We're converging on the target's suspected location at the state boat ramp."

Then, Larry's voice: "Jamison here with Sawyer. Let us know if you pick them out at the ramp."

Sam said, "Roger that. Standby."

Then Sam heard two other parties report in:

"Two, copy."

"Three, copy."

So, there were at least six more minds racing as they converged on the target's suspected location, anticipating next moves. Sam thought, *About damn time!*

Captain Matos watched with interest. Sword prices at the auction were up. His load would sell for a handsome price. At eight dollars a pound, 35,000 pounds was going to net him $280,000. He muttered to himself, *Nice pocket change.*

The 5,000 pounds he'd had the boys ditch at sea to legitimize the Newburyport ruse was chump change. That turned out to be tricky without Murdock catching on, but what remained of his highly motivated crew got it done. He headed back to the boat to change clothes, retrieve his personal gear, including his Glock ten-mil, and the two nine-mil Sig Sauers for Antonio and Carlos. As for Andre? Well, he was on his own, wasn't he?

Matos dressed casually in chinos, boat shoes, a dark-colored shirt and a medium-weight jacket he wore partially open. He zipped it up just enough to conceal his Glock in an under-the-pit holster.

The eastern sky now tinged pink. His dreams were coming true. One more big step and he'd be home free, set for life. He'd leave Logan Airport bound for Simon Bolivar International Airport in Caracas. His flight departed at 0900 hours, five short hours from now. A long flight with one stop in Dallas to change planes. He'd packed everything he needed: a carry-on bag stuffed with a change of clothes, his passport, his sat phone, and his computer. One last hurdle to clear and then to the life he deserved.

Matos took one last long look around his boat. Left the keys in the ignition. He fingered the plane ticket to Venezuela in his pocket for the third or fourth time in the last ten minutes. Both to make sure it was still there, and to bolster his nervous stomach at what must happen next. *My ticket. One way. One person.*

Time to meet Antonio at the intersection of Center and Harborwalk. *A short walk toward my future.*

Sawyer and Jamison made it to the state dock in time to see a large, muscular man with a badly damaged nose stepping out of his wet suit. A late model gray four-door Chevy Silverado 3500 pickup parked next to him, with a driver waiting behind the wheel. They waited, too. The big man, now in loose-fitting cotton pants and a sweater, tossed three large backpacks into the Silverado's rear seat.

There it was. The heroin *and* at least two of the men responsible for smuggling it into the US. Now, they needed the buyers. Would this Antonio Sousa lead them right to the big prize? Sawyer called in two of his men with stealthy cruisers and set up a detail to follow the thugs with the drugs. Larry knew these agents were well-trained for the task. This is what they did.

Following anyone who has something to hide is difficult. They'd be watching for the same vehicle or vehicles. And they'd take many turns to identify and shake any tails. They'd remain vigilant to anything that even hinted at surveillance or pursuit.

Sawyer set it up effortlessly. In addition to his own sedan, his DEA agents drove a pickup, another sedan, and an SUV that rotated in their pursuit. Their instructions? Stay on Sousa and he'd find Matos, who'd then lead them to the buyers. They presumed. Sawyer pulled his men from the auction and positioned them a block apart in this small city of 30,000, awaiting orders. He also ordered EPOs to stand down. The markings on their cruisers made them worthless for surveilling their targets.

Sawyer watched Sousa climb into the Silverado's passenger seat with an unidentified driver. He eyeballed the guy behind the wheel. He transmitted, "Sam, what's the physical description of your Canadian guy, Andre Gagnon?"

"Five-ten, one-eighty, fair skin, short black hair, brown eyes, no distinguishing marks or tattoos. Moves like a cop. And sharp."

Click click.

Larry said, "Looks like a different guy driving, Chuck. No idea who he is."

Sawyer said, "We'll take lead first. Johnson, you and Travis pick 'em up when we veer off after his first turn. Kramer, you're third in your truck. Hodge, you're last in the rotation in your SUV. Nobody follows for more than one turn. Use extra caution after they pick up Matos. My gut's telling me they're not going far. When they turn and you're following, you know the drill. Keep going and the next vehicle picks 'em up. All units confirm." All four cars responded.

They drove through the narrow streets near the small city's harbor district. After their target turned left, Sawyer and Jamison broke off by continuing straight and radio'd their status. Sam and Daniel picked up the Silverado. Sam sat low in his seat and slapped on his Red Sox cap. After a couple of lights and intersections, they broke off, too. Next, the pickup tracked the target. The agents called off its location by intersecting streets as each followed at a discreet distance in the light traffic. Three blocks later and another left turn, agents in the DEA SUV slid in behind.

Sawyer and Larry then jockeyed for a position to pick up their target when it slowed, now back near the docks again. Sousa and his driver had traveled in a big zig-zag circle to see if anyone followed—savvy counter-surveillance. It looked like their targets hadn't spotted them. Now, Sousa and his driver stopped at a red light on Water Street near the Riverdale Park area, once again within three blocks of the docks. They turned into a small parking area. Then, out of the shadows, Captain Afonso Matos appeared. He opened the pickup's rear driver's-side door and hopped in.

Sawyer and Jamison had pulled over less than half a block back to see what would happen next. That's when a flash inside the cab of the truck accompanied a muffled bang. The rear door opened and Matos jumped back out. He jerked a limp corpse from behind the truck's steering wheel and dragged the body behind a dumpster in the wide alley where they'd stopped. Matos then returned to the big pickup and hopped into the driver's seat.

Larry flat-handed the dash with a loud *thwack*. "Son-of-a-bitch!"

Chuck muttered, "One less share, one more murder charge. We got some cold fuckers right here, Larry."

The Silverado eased out of that small parking area

between those two waterfront buildings. They were close to warehouses and a commercial section of town where they apparently intended to complete their business.

Without taking his eyes off the road, Sawyer snatched his portable and held it close to his right cheek while mashing the push-to-talk button. "All units, approach the Water St. and Riverdale Park area. Stand by for further instructions. Acknowledge." Since this was a surveillance op, everyone understood without being told: no lights, no sirens, full stealth.

The DEA's teamwork and coordinated communication skills impressed Larry. Everyone knew what was happening. Each unit responded and had awaited the approval to converge on their targets.

Sam and Daniel parked less than a block away. The target pickup stopped in front of an old warehouse that appeared to be a derelict structure in dire need of some TLC: 57 Riverdale Park Avenue. Two black Mercedes sedans sat a half-block north on the same street. Sam thought, *These boys aren't too subtle.* A big man dressed in a tailored gabardine suit stood guard at the door of the warehouse with his head on a perpetual swivel atop his shiny threads. *Geez, even less subtle.* Sam reported what he saw.

Jamison remembered the old adage, *Criminals are stupid by definition. Some succeed despite that. For a while.*

Sawyer jotted down the license numbers of the Mercedes sedans and called them in. He told the dispatcher, "Run 'em."

"Roger that, sir."

Both came back to Pierpoint Exporters, Inc. out of Boston.

77

Matos parked the Silverado pickup in front of the warehouse, near a pair of Mercedes, one of which he recognized from previous meetings—Alfredo's ride—*the man*. He crawled out of the truck, lugging one of the large backpacks. He thought, *Heavy son-of-a-bitch. Ant makes it seem so easy.* Antonio clutched the other two packs, one dangling from each hand by their straps.

As agreed, Almeida and Gagnon had walked their own circuitous anti-surveillance route from the pier to the warehouse to meet them here on the sidewalk. Matos handed Antonio the 9mm pistol he'd carried from the *Miss G,* and the other to Carlos.

The four men from the *Miss G* entered the ramshackle old warehouse together after passing the guard, who opened the creaking door for them and closed it behind them. Antonio had to look up at that monster's squinted eyes. He thought, *Serious muscle. First time they've brought this animal.*

The building's expansive interior carried the stench of despair and distrust. Like previous times Antonio been here, only now more like the stink of, what? Death? Broken windows, graffiti, and lots of evidence that homeless wharf rats took regular refuge in this abandoned structure. None there now, though. Had Mr. Muscle cleared such poor souls out? Or worse?

Everything felt damp. The entire place reeked of oil and industrial waste, plus maybe other kinds of waste, too. In the center of the cavernous building stood four more men, three armed with MP4 automatic 5.56mm military style rifles.

Matos, Sousa, Almeida, and Gagnon walked in. They, too, brandished arms. Matos noticed that Andre now dangled a 9 mm Beretta from his right hand. *Where did that come from?* Reading the room, Antonio handed one of the heavy backpacks to Carlos to free his own gun hand. Despite their yellowed and cracked surfaces, three overhead skylights beamed down onto a chest-high tabletop. The air twinkled and shifted with dust motes floating in the diffuse sunlight.

Matos spoke first. "Hello, Alfredo. We meet again. This time we have the real deal. 100 kilos of pure Afghani heroin. Exactly like I promised. Not cut or stepped on. Test it."

Alfredo just nodded. Antonio slung his seventy-five-pound backpack containing a third of their haul up onto the stout table. One of Alfredo's companions slung his strapped MP4 over his shoulder, stepped up to the table, and brought out a miniature test kit from an oversized exterior jacket pocket. He flipped up the backpack's cover flap, slid out its contents with some effort, and unfolded the dry-bag's seal. Pulled out a brick-sized plastic-wrapped package—one of many.

The expressionless gunman opened the double-edged knife that appeared from nowhere with a flick of his wrist. He cut a small hole, not much more than a pinprick, in the brick's taped-up plastic wrapping. Dipped his knife blade in and came out with a minuscule amount of white powder. He tipped it into a small vial containing a nitric acid re-agent, popped a waterproof cap on top, and shook it. Bright purple.

Eyebrows lifted.

78

Undercover DEA Agent Jim Estes smelled and looked like a homeless boozer. He stumbled up to the gigantic guard outside the warehouse door. Pulled out a half-smoked butt and asked for a light. The guard told him to get lost. Not with words, but with a shove down the three concrete steps to the sidewalk. He stumbled and tumbled.

Meanwhile, a second agent in a suit stole in from behind and delivered a brutal blow to the back of the monster's neck and collarbone area with his expandable baton. Figured the guy warranted a home-run swing. That did the trick. The guy went down like he'd just slid under the grill of a Mack truck at cruising speed on the Interstate.

Sawyer deployed two agents at the warehouse's front door and two more at the rear. Meanwhile, two more flattened a front and rear tire on each Mercedes.

Sawyer crouched with Larry while Daniel and Sam led their approach to the warehouse door. Only slightly bruised from his tumble down the steps, Estes brought up the rear with yet another DEA agent.

As they crept into the warehouse with weapons drawn, they stepped with care over potentially noisy refuse. They used busted up old office furniture for cover. The place stunk like a desiccated stew of old waste. They listened but only made out a muffled conversation.

Sawyer whispered in his mike, "Rear entry group, standby."

Matos assured Alfredo that since this product was pure, he needed more money.

"How much more?"

"Four million dollars."

Alfredo looked at Matos with one eyebrow hiked up toward his slicked-back ebony hair. "Beyond the five we agreed to wire to your account." Not a question. "I understand purity carries value. I will offer you seven million total—*if* it's all like that sample. That's my offer."

Matos' expression broadcast his disappointment. Carlos hoisted onto the table a second backpack beside the first one, also stuffed full of heroin bricks.

The same man picked a random sample and tested another packet. It also tested bright purple.

Sawyer and his crew inched forward until they heard the conversation. Stacks of soggy collapsed boxes and a pile of rusted metal cabinets provided them necessary cover. They continued to pick each step with care.

Matos knew if he didn't accept the offer, Alfredo's mob would probably kill them, take the heroin, and keep the money. He grew angry and close to committing a foolish move.

A nod from Alfredo and two of his men hefted large black duffel bags up onto the table beside the two packs already there. Antonio was closest, so he opened both. Nice, neat bundles of hundred-dollar bills. Alfredo said, "Five million."

Matos whined, "What about the rest of it? And I thought we were doing a wire transfer."

"Money is money, yes? We'll arrange another meet and complete our business together for the remaining two mil."

"No, no more meetings. We'll just keep two mil worth of product and you'll still get more than your five mil worth."

Alfredo appeared calm, deep in thought. He purred, "I'd like to confer with my associates to see if that is acceptable."

Carlos knew this was going badly, and getting worse by the second. He drew his Sig Sauer P365-9 mm with 15 rounds, plus another in *the bucket*.

Antonio dropped the truck keys, stooped, and came up with his firearm. He was ready, too. But Matos could not reach his Glock. He was much too close to Alfredo's bodyguards.

The men broke their brief discussion and, without warning, Alfredo and his three men turned with weapons up and opened fire on the crew of the *Miss G*. Antonio took one round to the shoulder, but took down one guard. Andre hid behind Matos, who took one round in the chest and another to his left arm. Andre downed two more. Carlos took three in the chest from a fully automatic MP4. Two of the four men from the *Miss G* were down.

Matos mused as he lay on that filthy floor, bleeding out. *We were never gonna walk out of here. This wasn't a meeting to make a deal. This was always a rip-off....* His final thought? *Shortest retirement ever....*

Sawyer broke cover and yelled, "DEA! DEA! Put your weapons down and get on the fuckin' floor!"

Andre spun around and shot Sawyer in the stomach, but not until Sawyer got a round off. Almost in that same instant, Sam and Larry wheeled their pistols toward Andre. Sam's big .357 boomed first, then Larry's Glock. Both cannons struck Gagnon in the same place in the chest. That was a millisecond *after* Sawyer's round hit Gagnon full-on in the face. The head of this corrupt undercover operative exploded. He died on his way to that same killing floor. His gun spun away.

Antonio tried to get up, but failed. He was on his way to his grave with a pumping arterial wound. While on the floor, the wounded Alfredo DiMazzi pulled a small .38 Special from inside his fancy tailored suit jacket and casually shot Matos in the forehead. For good measure? Because that was good business? DEA Agent Daniel Johnson fired and hit Alfredo with another non-lethal shot to his gun arm before he got off another round. He was the only bad guy in the room left alive. The rear entry group breached. No friendly fire possibility today.

It was a bloody mess. Agent Johnson whipped out his cell to call 9-1-1. "Officer down, old warehouse at 57 Riverdale Park Avenue. Abdominal wound and still conscious. Profuse bleeding. Please hurry."

Sam and Larry huddled around the badly bleeding Sawyer. The blood pumping from *his* exit wound appeared very dark. A liver shot? Sam applied a lot of pressure. The DEA agents looked worried. Their frustration at seeing their boss gut-shot was obvious. So, they kept busy picking up weapons and checking pulses. Those who weren't dead would be soon, save Alfredo who had surrendered. Sawyer barely remained conscious. He said with a raspy rattle, "Did we get 'em all?"

Still applying pressure so hard it made it almost impossible for Sawyer to speak, Sam said, "Don't talk, sir. Ambo is on the way. You did great... for a feeb."

Larry looked at him and frowned, "There's no slack in you, is there, *Federal* Officer Travis?" Everyone was overdosing on adrenaline. Sam hunched down on his knees, exhausted, but he refused to let up on the all-important pressure on Sawyer's wound. EMTs arrived and relieved him. He thought, *He's in good hands, now.* Crime scene techs were on their way, too. They'd sort out this mess.

Both Sam and Larry now sat cross-legged on the cruddy floor of that revolting warehouse, too frickin' tired to get up. Sam hung his head. Raised it just enough to catch Larry's eye with a crosswise glance. "I need a vacation, boss."

First responders worked on Sawyer. They slid him onto a gurney seconds after arriving and rolled him out the door to the ambulance, waiting with its doors swung open on Riverdale Park Avenue.

DEA Agent Daniel Johnson came over to join Sam and Larry. The agent introduced himself to Larry. He kneeled beside them. "Nice shooting. We sure got the guy that hit Sawyer. I hope Chuck'll be okay. He's a great agent and a good man," Johnson caught Sam's eye, "for a feeb." They all smiled, too tired to laugh, and too nervous about their task force commander's chances of survival to comment further.

Johnson retrieved his official voice. "We'll collect all the evidence: the money, the heroin, and the firearms after the techs clear us. Then, we're gonna head over to the hospital. We'll need full case reports and statements from each of you —especially you, Sam. You came through in the nick of time with that RPM drop. It was key to catching these fuckers. This was a major operation and we took them down. We'll get search warrants for wherever their cover business is and go through everything with a fine-toothed comb. Thanks, men."

Larry said, "Okay, Agent Johnson. Nice to meet ya. Sounds like you have the scene wired. We'll head to the hospital directly. See you there."

"Roger that." Johnson stood and first patted Sam on the shoulder with a grateful smile, and then Larry's. They still sat slumped among the detritus on that filthy warehouse floor.

Larry and Sam then mustered the physical and

emotional strength to drag themselves to their feet. The two EPOs took in the gruesome scene: the bodies, the money, the heroin—a bullet had pierced one brick that dusted the table, and the surrounding floor. Techs wore masks as a precaution.

Sam and Larry peered at each other. Their eyes misted over. They hugged. They needed no words. Seven men were dead, one agent wounded and en route to surgery, one bad guy in custody, and the guard outside was now barely conscious and in custody.

After hugging out some of their adrenaline overload and they finished pounding each other's backs, Larry squared off, facing Sam. He squeezed both of Sam's shoulders, looked him in the eye, but said nothing. Finally, he croaked, "It'll be all over the news all day. We should get the fuck out of here unless you wanna be asked the same questions twenty-five times."

Sam smirked. "Nope, let's head out. Do we have a ride?"

"There's a few EPOs still around. We'll bum a ride from one of them. After all, they *do* work for me!"

79

Larry and Sam headed straight to Anna Jaques Hospital on Highland Avenue in Newburyport. They sat—or more accurately *fidgeted*—in the waiting room. Sawyer was in surgery. Two hours later, they'd still heard nothing.

Jittery DEA agents crowded into the smallish waiting room. They suspected more were on the way. As they showed up, everyone introduced themselves to one another, complimented the great work by Jamison, Travis, and Johnson. Word had gotten around. Some grabbed shitty 'n gritty hospital coffee. Someone ordered pizzas. And a few six-packs found their way around the waiting room. A close-knit fraternity stood by for word about one of their own.

Three hours later, a surgeon emerged from a set of double-swinging doors they'd all been staring at and spoke to the group. "Your friend is out of surgery. It was successful. We'll watch him in ICU for the next couple of hours. He's strong, fit enough, and relatively healthy, so I give him a decent chance to come out of this okay. His liver was pretty messy. We patched that up. I suggest you all go home and get some rest. I'm sure you have a critical incident response unit if you need to speak with someone. Taking advantage of it is my best advice. 'Night, men."

Everyone breathed easier. That status report from the surgeon released a helluva lot of tension. The beer helped, too. The room of a dozen agents and a half-dozen EPOs breathed a collective and noisy sigh of relief. Everyone shared a rowdy round of handshakes and back-slapping. Could have been any of them.

Of course, none of them even considered calling the critical response unit. This sort of thing was part of the job. So was sucking it up and getting on with it. That therapy shit was not. Two agents stayed behind.

Sam hadn't slept in over thirty hours. He called Kate. "Hey, hon. Guess who?"

"Oh, Sam, some major shoot-out in Gloucester this afternoon is all over the news. Was that you? Seven men dead? In a drug deal gone bad?"

Aw, shit. "Uh, well, yeah, today sorta sucked, but I'm okay. I'll tell you and Brian about it later. Okay, babe? Right now, I'm... beat," he said, surprised that a lump had formed in his throat. And his words came out shaky. He looked down at his shooting hand. It shook, too, and would not stop. "I'm fine, but I wanted to let you know I'm headed home. Love you, hon."

"Oh, Sam...." She started... sobbing? *Oh, fuck me.* Rather than risking breaking down himself, he hung up. *It's the adrenaline crash,* he told himself.

He shook hands with Larry one more time. Their strong bond had grown stronger because they'd stumbled through hell together and came out on the other side unscathed. Again. Physically, anyway.

"Boss, I'm gonna take a day or two off and then I'll start working on the case report. I took pretty good daily notes, so reconstruction of the events should be easy."

"Okay, Sam. There'll most certainly be a civilian review board. And fair warning, we'll have to endure whatever else the DEA has in their protocols. Who knows? Maybe another frickin' award."

Sam really did not want another award. He simply wanted a life. He dropped Larry off at his home in Framingham. It felt good someone was there for him. Lindsey Magnus, his former high school sweetheart, was now Larry's life partner. And he'd become a different man now that he had someone to love and someone to love him back.

Now to do the final leg on the Mass Pike back to *his* Berkshires. The peaceful, beautiful Berkshire Mountains. ***And*** *my family. I* ***am*** *going to be a better husband and father.*

Sure, Sam. Keep telling yourself that. The next case is right around the corner. Always is.

80

The US Coast Guard now held a veritable trove of solid new evidence with which to cite the French freighter captain of the *Grand Francaise*. This evidence allowed the DFO to detain the ship before it departed Halifax, Nova Scotia.

The French courts later indicted Captain Jacques Laurent and his second-in-command, Commandant Javier LeCompteau, for the international smuggling of narcotics and suspicion of murder.

Within a few months after that, both Laurent and LeCompteau forfeited their Merchant Marine licenses, and soon thereafter, each began serving a thirty-year sentence in a French prison. Upon their release, however, each counted on enjoying a comfortable retirement thanks to years of successfully transporting *special cargos... if* they survived. They'd discover that question needed answering anew every minute of every incarcerated day. After all, they had cheated Sur-Rapide and their investors from their last voyage's profits. That affair had not yet concluded.

More bad news for the bad guys, too. This DEA case became the linchpin for a sweeping domestic *and* international investigation. The DEA struck a deal with the wounded Alfredo DiMazzi, the surviving boss of Captain Matos' intended heroin buyers. His cover company, Pierpoint, distributed drugs across the entire eastern seaboard of the United States of America. And his arrest cut short a deal for his company going national in partnership with Sansa Trucking, *his* distributor. Sansa planned to expand their operations not only in the east, but from coast to coast with a planned expansion into the Canadian market. No longer.

The DEA, in cooperation with the FBI, made a dozen arrests as a result of DiMazzi's deal. In return, DiMazzi received a reduced sentence. Instead of life for murder, among other felonious charges, he'd be eligible for parole in 20 years—a *rare* deal to shut down the biggest drug operation in US history. Unfortunately, even though they had been partners in crime, there was no love lost between DiMazzi and the well-connected president of Sansa Trucking, Carmen Kilbane. This ruthless and vindictive Irish businessman had come up from the bitter streets of Belfast.

Animosity between Sansa and Pierpoint escalated exponentially after DiMazzi cut a deal implicating Kilbane and his company. Kilbane had loyal "friends" everywhere, including in the Souza-Baranowski Correctional Center in Lancaster, MA.

Even though SBCC was a maximum security prison for men, Kilbane had friends among both the inmates *and* the guards. Less than a week after DiMazzi testified and had taken up residence in the general population at SBCC, they found he'd hung himself in his cell. No one grieved. A cursory examination ruled his death a not-so-tragic suicide.

The US Coast Guard and US Drug Enforcement Administration, in cooperation with Les Garde-cotes Francais, the French Coast Guard, tightened their collective perimeter. Their case swept an international law enforcement net, which also engulfed the *Grand Francaise's* owners at Sur-Rapide, as well as the rest of their fleet's unscrupulous captains and crews.

France's Unified Judiciary's Court of Cassation,

equivalent to the US Department of Justice, also opened a massive investigation into the operations and funding sources—the investors—of Sur-Rapide Exports. Recent surveillance evidence provided by the American Drug Enforcement Administration, and eyewitness testimony of one temporary US Federal Police Officer named Sergeant Sam Travis, cinched it.

The government prosecutors presented a solid case. Especially as supported by the posthumous written testimony of one Hooglie Maisé, a Grand *Francaise* crew member who'd been lost at sea under the most dubious of circumstances. As insurance, he'd sent his testimony to his solicitor (attorney) before leaving France. His instructions were to send it to the French Coast Guard in the event of Hooglie's death.

So, considering this massive body of recent evidence, they expected to indict officials and investors of Sur-Rapide Exports on charges of international smuggling and conspiracy to commit murder. The indictment swept up the captains of several other ships in their fleet. Collaborating international agencies remained confident in their case, even though Sur-Rapide had powerful allies in the French government. But they'd be sacrificed for political convenience. Even figuratively throwing their captain of the *Francaise* overboard did not save Sur-Rapide. The company's dubious investors shared the larcenous limelight, too.

The French authorities suspected this might break the back of the most significant trans-Atlantic drug-smuggling ring in history. Many of the offenders... disappeared... before receiving the benefit of due process.

Upon hearing this news from their *feeb* friends at the DEA, EPO Sergeant Sam Travis mentioned casually to EPO Captain Larry Jamison, "Quite the catch, eh, boss?"

Larry peered into his friend's eyes. Sam looked so... tired. He said, "At least it wasn't lethal, for you, anyway, even though the odds of you surviving what you did were against you. You have great instincts, my friend."

Larry smiled. Sam didn't. He looked forward to spending some uninterrupted time with his family. And he'd cook some damn fine gourmet meals for Kate and Brian. Plus, on occasion, he looked forward to cooking for a few of his closest friends, whether they'd still recognize his face was a question. *Yeah, that'll be nice. Low threat level events for a change, eh, Sam?*

The newly minted Sergeant Sam Travis was no

longer newly minted. He sucked a noisy inhale through flared nostrils, blew it out through puffed cheeks, and nodded at his boss's boss.

They had saved a lot of lives.

The End (For Now)

CAST OF MAJOR CHARACTERS
(IN ALPHABETICAL ORDER)

- **Carlos Almeida:** Engineer aboard the commercial fishing vessel F/V *Miss Guided One (*a.k.a. *Miss G).*
- **Phil Armstrong:** Coastal EPO on the lobster poaching case.
- **Jose Belo:** a.k.a. *Cachorro Grande* (Big Dog), or just *Chacci.* Deckhand aboard the sword boat, *Miss Guided One.*
- **Eduardo Braga:** Deckhand – *Miss G.*
- **Richard Cellini:** Wildlife poacher and father of two boys who ruffed up Brian Travis.
- **John Comeaux:** EPO in a district adjacent to Sam's.
- **Edwin (Win) Davis:** – EPO patrol boat Gloucester Harbor, Sgt.

- **Alfredo DiMazzi**: Drug dealer kingpin of Pierpoint Imports.
- **Jim Estes:** Undercover DEA operative, Rockport, MA.
- **Sean Fielding:** District court judge Gloucester, Massachusetts. Presiding Judge over the lobster poaching case.
- **Andre Gagnon:** Undercover operative aboard the *Miss Guided One* from Canadian Department of Fisheries and Oceans (DFO).
- **Randy Gerrard:** NMFS SAC.
- **Mark Gerraine:** Coastal EPO Supervisor, Lt.
- **Grand Francaise:** A 400-foot freighter of French registry with a 65-foot beam (width) and a draft of 22 feet (depth of water required when she was empty).
- **Grim Reefer:** a sixty-foot commercial dragger out of Newburyport, MA.
- **Franz Heileg:** Captain of the *Grim Reefer* – buyer of *Miss G's* hashish.
- **Ronnie Jackson:** Desk Officer, Trooper, Massachusetts State Police (MSP).
- **Lawrence Jamison**: a.k.a. Larry, Academy Commandant of the Massachusetts Environmental Police and hand-to-hand combat instructor, Captain.

- **Cameron Kilbane:** President of Sansa Trucking and partner in crime with Alfredo DiMazzi.
- **Brad Kowalski:** MSP Barracks Commander Mass Turnpike, Lt.
- **Jacques Laurent:** Captain of the French freighter *Grand Francaise.*
- **Javier LeCompteau:** Second-in-command aboard *Grand Francaise.* Referred to as Commandant.
- **Lindsay Magnus:** Jamison's life partner and ex high school girlfriend.
- **Hooglie Maisé:** Veteran loader aboard the *Grand Francaise.*
- **Afonso Matos:** Captain of *Miss Guided One, a* drug-smuggling sword boat.
- **Miss Guided One:** a.k.a. *Miss G*, a 72-foot long-line commercial sword-fishing boat (longliner) out of Gloucester, Massachusetts. Also called a *sword boat* since its primary quarry is swordfish.
- **Katherine Miller:** a.k.a. Kate. Sam Travis' wife.
- **Manny Pizzelli:** Coastal EPO on the lobster poaching case.
- **John Riley:** Grounds manager of the Tanglewood Resort.
- **Roxie:** EPO Dispatcher.

- **Chuck Sawyer:** Estes' Boss and DEA Special Agent in Charge.
- **Bobby Silverman:** MSP Barracks Commander, Lt.
- **Antonio Sousa:** First mate, *F/V Miss Guided One.*
- **Barbara Travis:** Sam's deceased wife and his son Brian's biological mother.
- **Brian Travis:** Sam's almost-fourteen-year-old son.
- **Sam Travis:** Newly promoted, Sergeant, a Massachusetts State EPO (Environmental Police Officer).

GLOSSARY

- **Abeam:** Used to describe wind or waves that impact a vessel directly from its side (its *beam*).
- **Backstraps:** Tenderloins of wild game, the choicest parts of the animal.
- **Beam:** The width of a vessel. Also describes the orientation of waves relative to a vessel (e.g., a beam sea).
- **Below deck or below decks**: Downstairs.
- **Bow** - The front of the boat or ship (usually "the pointy end").
- **Bridge Wing:** The area adjacent to the railing on either side of the pilothouse of a boat or ship that provides a clear view of a dock or pier from which a vessel is about to moor or depart.

- **Broach** - When a ship flips over sideways and probably ends up bottom-side up ("turtled") and/or subsequently sunk.
- **Bulkhead:** An upright wall within the hull of a ship or boat.
- **Bulwarks:** Extensions that rise above the main deck, designed to protect passengers, crew, and cargo from falling overboard and to shield the deck from waves during rough seas.
- **Close aboard:** Nearby one's vessel.
- **DEA:** US Federal Drug Enforcement Administration.
- **DFO:** Canadian Department of Fisheries and Oceans.
- **EEZ:** Exclusive Economic Zone - a 1982 United Nations Convention on the Law of the Sea, is an area of the sea in which a sovereign state has exclusive rights regarding the exploration and use of marine resources.
- **Fore:** Toward the front (of a boat or ship). Also, in front of.
- **Aft:** Toward the back (of a boat or ship). Also, behind.
- **Rafted up:** When two or more vessels tie up to each other side-by-side for a period of time, for any purpose.

- **Forecastle**: Pronounced fōk-səl, often written as fo'c's'le, is the area on a boat or in a ship where sailors sleep and congregate while off duty. The fo'c's'le is located in the forward part of the ship (the bowz0, and in front of the main mast. The fo'c's'le serves as accommodations for regular sailors, while officers of the ship are housed in other areas.

- **Grundèns:** Rubberized outer wear worn by commercial fishermen as protection against wind, waves, and cold temperatures.

- **Gunwale**: Pronounced *gŭn'əl,* and sometimes written as *gunnel.* The upper edge of the side of a nautical vessel, where the (vertical) hull meets the (horizontal) deck.

- **Hashish:** A drug. Resin prepared from the flowering tops of the female cannabis plant and smoked, chewed, or ingested to induce euphoria.

- **Head:** A restroom on a boat or ship.

- **Headway:** The speed of a vessel necessary for steering or maneuvering. Sometimes also called *steerageway.*

- **Knot:** A knot is a unit of speed equal to one nautical mile per hour, which is approximately 1.15 miles per hour or 1.85

kilometers per hour. It is commonly used in maritime and aviation contexts for measuring the speed of vessels and aircraft. For example, 7 knots = 8 MPH.

- **Ladder:** Stairs on a boat or ship.
- **Logging header:** A rough trail used to drag harvested logs out of the woods. Headers normally lead to more developed and wider logging roads where logs are loaded onto trucks for transport.
- **Longliner:** A vessel that employs a commercial fishing technique using a long *main line* with baited hooks attached at intervals via short branch lines called *snoods.* A snood is attached to the main line using a clip or swivel, with the hook at the other end.
- **MSP:** Massachusetts State Police.
- **NOAA:** National Oceanic & Atmospheric Administration. A federal agency that forecasts weather, monitors oceanic and atmospheric conditions, charts the seas, and manages marine resources. They broadcast regional weather reports on dedicated radio frequencies non-stop.
- **NMFS:** US Federal National Marine Fisheries Service.
- **Pilothouse:** A deckhouse for a ship's helmsman containing the ship's controls

and navigation equipment. Offers excellent visibility for operation of the vessel.

- **Port** - Left side of the boat facing forward. Also used to signify a change of course, e.g., *steer to port.* Or to signify the relative bearing of a sighting, e.g., *a sighting to port.*

- **Scupper:** An opening cut through the bulwarks of a ship, so that water falling on deck may drain overboard. Also called a scupper hole. There are usually many.

- **Spring line:** A ship's or boat's mooring line led diagonally from the bow or stern of a ship to a point on a wharf (or another vessel) and made fast (secured) to help keep the ship from moving fore and aft while docked or rafted up with another vessel.

- **Starboard**: Right side of the boat facing forward. Also used to signify a change of course, e.g., *steer to starboard.* Or to signify the relative bearing of a sighting, e.g., *a sighting to starboard.*

- **Stern**: the overall back of the boat or ship.

- **Transom**: The vertical or nearly vertical surface on the back of the boat

- **UC**: Undercover operative.

- **Up top**: Upstairs on a boat.

MAP OF EXCLUSIVE
ECONOMIC ZONES

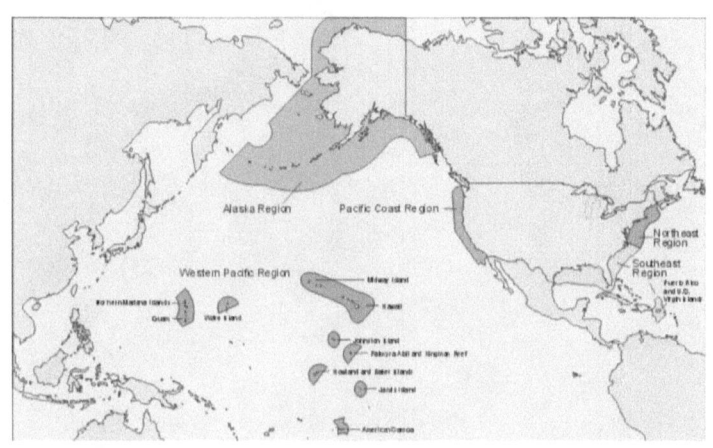

MAP OF WESTERN
MASSACHUSETTS

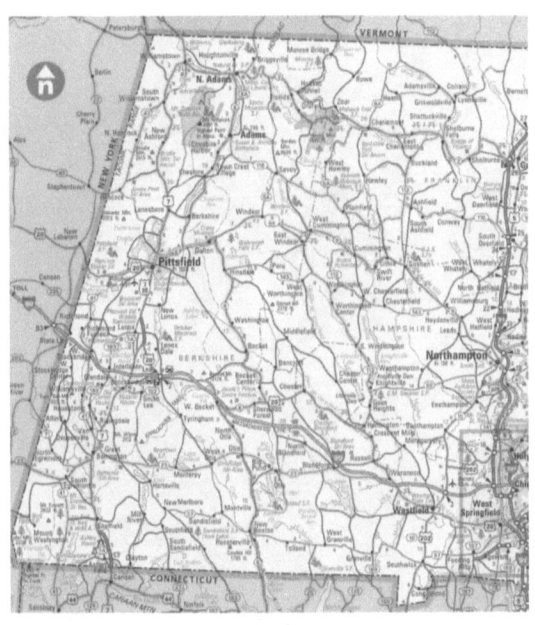

MAP OF THE FLEMISH CAP

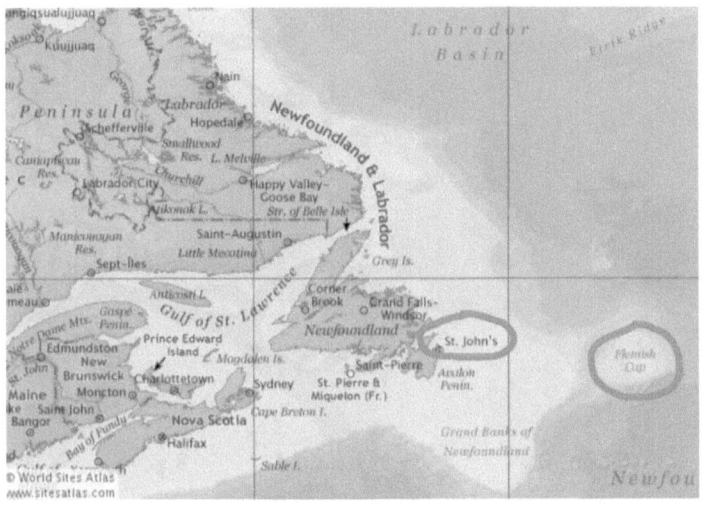

MAP OF GLOUCESTER & NEWBURYPORT

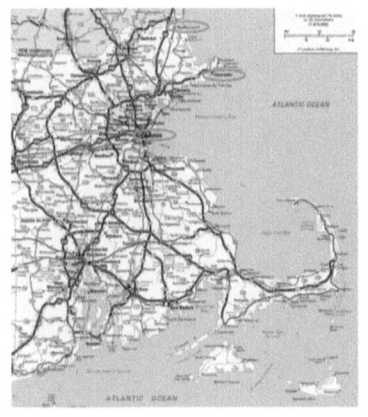

MAP OF TEN POUND ISLAND

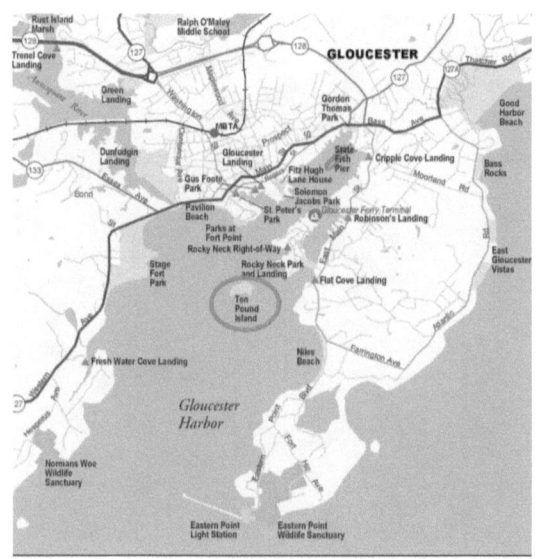

ACKNOWLEDGMENTS

Tom and I would like to acknowledge our amazing nationwide team of pre-publication readers who irritated the heck out of us with brutal but essential critiques on this manuscript prior to publication.

They offered invaluable comments on readability and authenticity in areas outside of Tom's and my areas of expertise.

For that, we are forever grateful, even though it is painful to admit we aren't experts on everything!

- Gene & Tom

OTHER BOOKS BY GK JURRENS

Historical Fiction (Great Depression Era Crime)

- Black Blizzard: A Lyon County Adventure
- Murder in Purgatory: A Lyon County Mystery

Aubrey Greigh Mysteries

- Voodoo Vendetta - Culture That Kills
- Dancing With Death - Who Will Die? Or Disappear?
- Rogue's Gallery - Beyond Evidence

Sam Travis Adventures:

- Lethal Game - Bears Under Siege
- Lethal Trail - No Body Is Safe
- Lethal Bounty - A Dirty Secret

Contemporary Autobiographical Fiction (Drama)

- Dangerous Dreams: Dream Runners: Book 1
- Fractured Dreams: Dream Runners: Book 2

Futuristic Fiction (Paranormal Mystery Thrillers)

- Underground, Mayhem: Book 1
- Mean Streets, Mayhem: Book 2
- Post Earth, Mayhem: Book 3

- A Glimpse of Mayhem: Companion Guide to the Mayhem Trilogy

Non-fiction

- The Poetic Detective: Investigate Rhyme With Reason
- Why Write? Why Publish? Passion? Profit? Both?
- Moving a Boat and Her Crew
- Restoring a Boat and Her Crew

A PEEK AT EXODUS ROAD

AN AUBREY GREIGH MYSTERY
AVAILABLE EARLY 2026

Feeling sneaky?

Are you interested in an *early* sneak preview—an author's brainchild of the yet-to-be-written fourth Aubrey Greigh Mystery, *Exodus Road,* by GK Jurrens?

Brief Story Summary

Shane Greigh, the improbable voice of justice, is the newly adopted nine-year-old son of a best-selling mystery author who is also a part-time Interpol investigator. His new mother is a high-ranking police detective. He must convince his new parents that a human trafficking ring sponsored by a foreign government is populating a not-so-small army of children from other countries.

As the story progresses, these child victims will

become instrumental in a large-scale plot to blackmail public officials with sexual and political extortion. How far has this heinous cancer spread already? And who will drag this insidious plot out of the shadows into the light? Could it be this gifted nine-year-old boy of gypsy heritage who recently immigrated from Budapest, Hungary, by way of Croatia and North-eastern Italy, to America's largest city—Chicago?

The Story's Synopsis

Shane Greigh is a gifted nine-year-old Romani boy thrust into the whirlwind of his new life in the United States. An unusual couple—police detective Chance "Q" McQuillan and best-selling author Aubrey Greigh, who also works as an Interpol investigator—recently adopted Shane.

Upon arriving at his new parents' luxury apartment, Shane uses his extraordinary observational skills to uncover Q's early pregnancy. This is a shocking revelation to both Greigh and Q. Yet adapting to his new surroundings proves challenging. He feels out of place amidst his American peers.

No sooner does Shane start elementary school than his razor-sharp intuition and mature outlook, not to mention his well-rounded wit, distinguish him, but not in a good way. He soon notices subtle but disturbing signs of a sinister plot—suspicious interactions between adults and students, unusual vehicles lurking nearby, and patterns that others dismiss, or don't notice at all. While his adoptive parents chalk up his observations to cultural adjustment anxiety, Shane is undeterred and embarks on a relentless investigation. He meticulously documents every suspicious occurrence.

Armed with a photographic memory and exceptional puzzle-solving skills, Shane encounters dubious acquaintances who reveal fragments of a chilling, large-scale human trafficking operation. A smirk here, an inadvertent whisper there, or a new friend's worries that he's being watched, Shane sees an obvious pattern. Is the boy psychic, neurodivergent, or just hyper-vigilant?

As Shane consumes local news and events with a voracious appetite, he engages in conversations with Greigh and Q about how to wield his gifts without alienating those around him. Social integration remains a struggle, but he forms a tight-knit circle of trusted friends at school who appreciate his abilities and help him gather crucial information. They leverage their own unique and curious skills. Other kids call them *The Freak Squad.*

The stakes rise as Shane uncovers concrete evidence of this trafficking ring—photographs, overheard conversations, and suspicious behaviors. When a fellow student goes missing, Shane can no longer keep his findings under wraps. Shane shows Greigh and Q his collection of evidence. The depth and quality of his work stun them, transforming them from skeptical but compassionate parents into staunch believers in their son's discoveries. They now champion for justice with him.

Together, as an immediate family of sleuths, Greigh and Q leap into action with Shane to investigate his findings. Shane's unique perspective sheds light on a dark underground network. So, they race against time to unveil the full extent of the trafficking operation and the damage it has already caused to both those trafficked, and those extorted.

As clues reveal themselves, their *extended* family from previous books in this series also joins the fray. They include Q's partner, Mac, Shane's new Uncle Rocko, MT, who is one of Rocko's gumshoes, and Shane's biological grandfather, the influential Gaspari Copolla.

Each member contributes their expertise and influence while remaining vigilant to protect Shane from escalating dangers as the criminals become aware of their pursuit. As a result, victims of this ring apply their considerable influence to keep their sins from the pubic eye by killing Shane's revelations, and maybe him.

Tensions further escalate as the investigation reaches a perilous climax. Shane faces increasing threats from shadowy figures surveilling him, his family, and his friends. He worries about them all. Fear grips the boy. But this fear further heightens his abilities in peculiar ways. Greigh and Q grapple with the challenge of keeping the boy safe while allowing him continued involvement in the case at his insistence *and* retaining some semblance of a normal life. That becomes a source of family conflict *and devotion.*

Ultimately, their combined efforts lead to the exposure and dismantling of the multinational trafficking ring, bringing justice to at least some of its victims. But only after crossing swords with powerful politicians and law enforcement officials who have everything to lose if exposed by the Greighs and both their official and unofficial friends.

In the aftermath, Greigh, Q, and Grandpa Gaspari, who is also a storied philanthropist, reveal the truth about Shane's biological parents to him. They tell him of his father's murder, his mother's imprisonment, and their shared gifts for extraordinary observation and deduction. To their surprise, Shane already knows much of his family's history. Of course he does.

The victors celebrate their triumph and newfound understanding of one another. They pave the way for Shane's thrilling journey as a budding young investigator, and perhaps, as another mystery author—like dear new dad.

Embracing both his inherited abilities, his experience from this case, and the accompanying insight not to reveal them to just anyone, Shane plans future investigations with his team of young "irregulars" with zeal.

DISCLAIMERS

This is a work of fiction. Any similarity to actual persons, behaviors, places, or events should be considered coincidental and fictional.

No part of this publication may be stored in a retrieval system, transmitted, or reproduced in any way, including, but not limited to, digital copying and printing without prior agreement and written permission of the publisher, UpLife Press.

Research of this manuscript's period and its theme mandated judicious use of ethnic pejoratives and mild profanity, and are not meant to offend the reader. Quite the contrary, the use of these literary devices is intended to demonstrate the authentic commitment to a higher set of moral standards, and to the strength of each character's faith, or lack thereof.

This entire novel is certified to be *AI-free,* that is, the author—a *certifiable human*—wrote the entire book, *not* artificially intelligent software. The author reserves all rights. No distribution channel has any rights to sub-license, reproduce &/or otherwise use this work in any manner for training artificial intelligence technologies to generate text, video, or audio, including without limitation, technologies that are capable of generating works in the same style or genre as the work *without the authors' specific & express permission to do so.*

ABOUT THE AUTHOR

GK Jurrens writes with undiluted passion. He's published 18 fiction and non-fiction titles to date including 13 action-oriented novels across five series. This book is number 14. He also teaches writing & publishing seminars nationwide.

THIS AUTHOR'S VISION: Create gritty fictional realism based on true stories with social relevance set in the past, present, or future to:

- Protect wildlife & the environment,
- Fight crime & corruption,
- Solve quirky mysteries.

With UpLife Press, GK has independently published:

- Outdoor Environmental Adventures
- Historical Crime Fiction
- Modern Murder Mysteries

- Contemporary Autobiographical Fiction
- Futuristic Paranormal Romantic Mysteries SciFi
- Poetry & Essays
- Writing & Publishing
- Nautical Travelogue & Sailing Yacht Restoration

GK and his wife live and travel in a motorhome. They wander their beloved North America as a source of endless inspiration. They've lived in 42 states in the last decade for a few weeks to a few months at a time.

After studying Liberal Arts and Electronics Engineering Technology, GK earned a Bachelor of Science degree in Business and a Master of Science degree in Management of Technology from the University of Minnesota.

Six years of government service (US Coast Guard Search & Rescue, Marine Law Enforcement) and a successful three-decade career in global high-technology (IBM) preceded more than a decade of voyaging on America's waterways aboard a fifty-one-foot pilothouse motorsailer. GK's backyard included the Florida Keys, and the Eastern Caribbean from the British Virgin Islands to Granada, near the coast of Venezuela.

Brief forays sailing around the Greek Cyclades Islands in the Aegean Sea, as well as the San Juan Islands in the US Pacific Northwest, offered Gene and his wife Kay more unique sailing challenges, *and* inspiration.

With multiple works always in process, GK continues to write with a sense of urgency, and of course, passion. Always. He embeds contemporary social issues in each of his action-oriented stories.

ABOUT TOM KASPRZAK

"LT" spent 32 years as an environmental police officer for the Commonwealth of Massachusetts. Before graduating in 1977 from the Massachusetts State Police academy, Tom earned the coveted "top gun" award for superior marksmanship.

He began his EPO career as a field officer in various assignments involving both inland and marine law enforcement in places like Cape Cod and Boston Harbor. After transferring to the Berkshire Mountains in Western Massachusetts with skills honed from seven years of varied case involvement and courtroom testimony, he forged close relationships with local and state police.

Upon being promoted to lieutenant, he led a region of officers in search and rescue operations involving plane crashes, boating fatalities, narcotics, and the investigation and apprehension of various firearm violators.

Beginning in 1986, LT engaged in or supervised undercover operations focused on endangered wildlife. During that time, he worked with other local, state, and federal agencies on issues ranging from the and environmental crimes to anti-terrorism.

Tom was selected to train in no fewer than three extended tours at the prestigious Federal Law Enforcement Training Center (FLETC) in Glynco, Georgia, where federal agents train.

Those intensive and immersive training tours honed his skills for inter-agency undercover operations, marine operations, and advanced operational readiness. He also trained for and was an Incident Commander in several cases.

During his colorful career, Tom worked with the Massachusetts State Police air wing on helicopter operations, their dive team, apprehension team, marine law enforcement, and environmental police operations.

Tom spent his last seven years assigned to the State Police STOP (apprehension) team headquarters in Chicopee, Massachusetts, along with all the members of the region he supervised.

His undercover assignments brought dozens of individuals to justice who violated state and federal laws. He was also a Deputy National Marine Fisheries agent as well as a U.S Deputy Fish and Wildlife agent at the same time. Tom is also a US Air Force veteran with four-plus years assigned to Security Service, and ultimately, the majority of his enlistment was with the

SR-71 Blackbird spy plane. His security clearance was one of extreme trust by the USAF.

His largest case—Operation Berkshire—closed one of the country's largest illegal commercial wildlife trafficking operations involving twenty-nine individuals, six states and two foreign countries.

The exploits of Tom and his fellow officers from his home state and others led to new exploits in crusading against illegal wildlife commercialization.

National Geographic produced a special called "Wildlife Wars: Bears Under Siege" that featured Tom and his fellow undercover operatives after they closed Operation Berkshire.

Tom taught new recruits at the State Police Academy courses in courtroom procedures, officer ethics and undercover operations. He also delivered endangered species lectures to schools, colleges, municipal police departments, as well as to other state and federal agencies, including US Coast Guard District One in Boston with whom he was specifically trained in LNG (Liquid Natural Gas) tanker escort anti-terrorism protocols in Boston Harbor.

He made a name for himself during dozens of successful missing persons cases, body recovery cases, undercover operations, anti-terrorism and crime scene investigations. Tom and his life partner, Karen, now split their time between Western Massachusetts and Southwestern Florida.

BEFORE YOU GO

Please post a brief review where you purchased this book.

Or email your thoughts to gjurrens@yahoo.com.
Remember, other readers and I *need* to know what you think.
I absolutely read every single review with gratitude. Thank you.
Also, feel free to browse or subscribe at GKJurrens.com for announcements and giveaways.
See you there!
- GK

www.ingramcontent.com/pod-product-compliance
Lightning Source LLC
Chambersburg PA
CBHW030549020726
47494CB00005B/1534